UNINTENDED
CONSEQUENCES

Unintended Consequences

Marti Green

THOMAS & MERCER

Text copyright © 2013 Marti Green
All rights reserved.

Published by Thomas & Mercer, Seattle

www.apub.com

ISBN-13: 9781477818152
ISBN-10: 1477818154

Cover design by Derek Murphy

Book Design by Christopher Fisher

Library of Congress Control Number: 2013917255

Printed in the United States of America

Dedicated to my father, Simon Silverman,
who instilled in me a love of reading,
and to my mother, Ruth Silverman,
who taught me how to write.

I miss you both.

It is Justice, not Laws that cures the society. And Capital Punishment is the only Justice that suits a murderer.

—Saqib Ali

The recent developments of reliable scientific evidentiary methods has made it possible to establish conclusively that a disturbing number of persons who had been sentenced to death were actually innocent.

—John Paul Stevens,
US Supreme Court Justice

Capital punishment, like the rest of the criminal justice system, is a government program, so skepticism is in order.

—George Will

Forty-Two Days

I didn't kill my little girl. The body in the woods—that wasn't my daughter. The words on the page kept ringing in Dani Trumball's ears. *I loved my little girl and only wanted to help her.*

Most of the letters on her desk Dani went through quickly, spotting the scams easily enough and tossing them aside for a quick response from her secretary. "Dear (fill in the blank): We regret that the Help Innocent Prisoners Project is unable to assist you at this time." Others rang true and might warrant some added sentences. "Although we appreciate your circumstances, the many requests for our limited services mean we can only accept a few cases. We wish you the best of luck in finding someone else to help you." Only a few, a very few, were taken on.

This letter—it stayed with her. *I sure hope you can help me because they are going to kill me soon, and maybe I deserve to die, but it's not because I killed my little girl.* Six weeks until his execution. "Impossible," she kept muttering to herself, shaking her head. She pushed her hair away from her face and wiped her forehead with a tissue. It was warm for early April, too early for the air conditioning in the office to be turned on, and she felt limp from the heat. She unbuttoned an extra button on her blouse and then reread George Calhoun's letter. *I kept telling them she wasn't my daughter, but they didn't believe me. I don't know why Sallie—that's my wife—said she was. She must have gone crazy from worry about Angelina. That's our daughter's name. We named her that because she was our little angel.*

The Help Innocent Prisoners Project—HIPP—operated out of a converted warehouse on 14th Street in the East Village. It received letters from inmates throughout the country, and each attorney reviewed some of them. Dani had been going through a stack of folders, each containing an inmate's plea for help, when she came across the letter from Calhoun. She'd already scribbled, "Sorry, no," across the top, put it in her out box, and moved on to other letters. For the third time, she rummaged through her pile of replies and pulled his letter out. After staring at Calhoun's words once more, she started to put it back yet again but wavered. Finally, she stood up and strode out of the office, glancing up at the framed embroidery over the door on her way out. It read, "Everyone on death row claims they are innocent. Once in a while they are." Her mother had sewn it for her after she began working at HIPP. Over time, Dani had witnessed the truth of the saying. The difficulty was in figuring out which ones really were innocent. Sometimes, when she felt most overwhelmed, she wished for a magic ball—perhaps in the form of DNA evidence—that could provide the answer. Without it, the truth was often elusive.

"Busy?" Dani asked as she entered the office of Bruce Kantor, the director of HIPP. She slipped into the plastic chair opposite his desk.

"Always. Too busy. I think I need a vacation."

"Didn't you just have one three years ago?"

"I think it was five, but who's keeping track?" Bruce leaned back in his chair, its fabric as worn as the wood of his desk. His dark brown skin and shaved head glistened with beads of sweat. With his taut body, kept trim with regular ten-mile jogs, he looked like a warrior ready for battle. "So, what's up?"

"Take a look at this letter. I think it's something that might be worth exploring." She handed it to him and sat forward in her chair as he read it silently.

"Six weeks?" he said when he was finished. "You do realize how difficult that is, don't you?"

She did know. Trying to halt an execution in only six weeks was like trying to run a marathon in two hours. "You're right. But I keep putting it down in the 'sorry, no' pile and then pulling it out again."

Bruce looked over the letter again. "I thought you stayed away from child-murder cases."

"I do. I mean, I have. I can't even imagine having to deal with that as a parent."

"So why this case?"

Dani shrugged. "I'm not sure. There's something about it. I mean, if this guy is being honest, his daughter wasn't murdered, but a child's body was found. Who was it? Where's his own daughter?"

"If we take this on, are you willing to head it up?"

It was the question Dani had expected, the one she'd dreaded. She wrote and argued appeals after others had investigated the facts. Cases came to her when the office had already gathered the available evidence. Bruce had tried for years to involve her in cases at the investigation stage, and she'd always resisted. Writing appeals allowed her to leave the office at three and work from home, with a minimal amount of traveling. That way, she was home when Jonah got back from school. Taking on a case from the beginning meant being away from her family, sometimes for weeks at a time.

Suddenly she became aware that she'd twirled the ends of her hair in her fingers, a nervous habit from childhood. The thought of taking the lead had triggered a sense of disquiet.

"I'll think about it, okay?"

"Sure. Just don't take too long. This guy doesn't have the time for that."

Dani sighed. "I know. Tomorrow. I'll let you know tomorrow."

That evening, Dani curled up next to her husband, Doug, on the down-filled couch in front of their living room's marble fireplace, where the last embers were dying. The room had the smoky smell of burning wood. The heat from the day had disappeared with the setting sun, and now the air outside felt raw, with a damp cold that permeated the thinly insulated walls of the old house. The fire brought welcome warmth to the living room. They called this time together the "honeymoon hour," and no matter how busy either of them was, they always set aside an hour to talk about Jonah, about their day, about nothing and everything. If one of them traveled, they spent the hour on the phone. Of course, they were together much more than an hour a day, but when deadlines loomed and pressure built, it was easy to work straight through the night, and after many nights of that, it had begun to take a toll on their marriage. So they had their one hour, no matter what. And it made them feel, after fifteen years of marriage, as if they were still on their honeymoon.

"What makes you think he's innocent?" Doug asked as he stroked the long, dark waves of Dani's hair.

"I don't know that he is. But wouldn't you expect him to just deny that he killed the little girl who was found in the woods? Why would he also insist it wasn't his daughter? And if that's true, if the girl wasn't his daughter, what would have been his motivation for murdering the girl found in the forest?"

"Maybe he's a psycho. Maybe his daughter died, and out of rage he murdered another child."

"But there's no death certificate for his daughter. And if his daughter didn't die, then what happened to her?"

"How about this: He murdered his daughter first, buried her in a secret place, and then started on a spree of murdering little girls."

Dani took a sip of Chianti. It was her second glass and she felt warm and tingly. "You're certainly being ghoulish tonight."

"These are the clients you represent. They're capable of horrible deeds."

"So you think I shouldn't take the case?"

Doug turned Dani's face toward his. His eyes looked black in the darkened room. They were deeply set, framed by bushy eyebrows above and a soft puffiness below. Crow's feet had begun to appear at their edges. It hit her that they were approaching middle age, an epoch they'd kept pushing farther away, as if they could remain young simply by redefining the age of entry.

"You should at least investigate his claims. You won't be comfortable until you've satisfied yourself that he's guilty. Or not guilty."

"But I could be away from home for weeks. That'll be hard on you and Jonah."

"Hmm. Yes, I see your dilemma," Doug said with his most professorial face, a look he'd mastered after years of teaching law. "Despite my ability to manage a horde of law students, I am clearly unqualified for the rigors of meeting the needs of a twelve-year-old, or my own needs, for that matter. Yes, that certainly is a problem."

Dani hit him playfully in the arm and they laughed. The thought struck her, suddenly, how lucky she'd been in marrying Doug. "Two peas in a pod," her mother often said, one of the many clichés she often spouted. It was true and yet not. They weren't the same, Doug being more pragmatic and she, more emotional. But both were fierce advocates for their sense of justice; both shared the same values; both were devoted to family. Dani wanted to believe they'd chosen each other because of those attributes, but she knew it wasn't true. They'd been too young then to realize the people they would become and what would be important in their lives. She knew it was luck that the choice they'd made so many years ago turned out to be so remarkably right.

"We'll manage," Doug said. "Besides, I always have Gracie to cuddle up with at night." Gracie was their cat, fat and affectionate. Usually, she'd have no one but Dani, purring loudly as she nestled herself in the crook of her arm at night. But in Dani's absence, she made do with Doug.

"Well, then ..."

"So, it's settled."

"Yes, I suppose it is." It wasn't her fear of leaving Doug and Jonah that held her back. It was the case. When she handled only the briefs, HIPP had already decided the defendant was innocent. As an investigator, she'd have to make that decision. And to do so, she'd have to relive the brutal murder of a little girl. She wasn't sure she was prepared for that.

When she arrived at HIPP the next morning, Dani saw through Bruce's open office door that he was sitting behind his desk. She hung up her coat and settled into her office, sipping the lukewarm coffee she'd picked up at the corner deli. Behind her functional, brown, laminate desk was a black swivel chair, its thin cushions flattened from years of overuse. Yesterday's stack of folders had been reviewed and now sat on her secretary's desk for follow-up. One folder remained. Inside was a single sheet of paper, the handwritten letter from George Calhoun. She stared at his folder while she finished her coffee and then walked to the office Xerox machine to photocopy a legal brief she'd written at home. With a copy of the document in hand, she marched into Bruce's office and dropped it on top of his already cluttered desk. Bruce had the only window office in HIPP's spartan space. The other attorneys were housed in a row of small boxlike rooms, and the investigators and paralegals sat at desks on the open floor. It was as far removed from a Wall Street firm as a lawyer could get.

"Here's the Brigham brief," Dani said.

Bruce looked up from his computer, startled. "Already? That was fast. It's not due for another week."

"I know. This'll give you more time to go over it." As director of HIPP, Bruce reviewed all the filings that came out of the office. He rarely marked up Dani's work, though, and she'd gotten into the habit of turning in her drafts only a day or two before they were due. "Besides, I've been thinking more about the Calhoun case."

Bruce leaned back in his chair, and with his arms behind his head, fingers entwined, he smiled like a fisherman who's reeled in his catch. "You want HIPP to take his case, don't you?"

Dani took a deep breath. She'd tossed and turned for much of the night as she wrestled with her decision. Finally, she'd given up on sleep, crept downstairs to the kitchen, and after brewing a cup of coffee, begun a list. On the left side were the reasons to reject Calhoun's request; on the right, the reasons to follow up on his letter. She had easily filled the left side. The right column contained only one entry: Find out what happened to Angelina Calhoun. "I do."

"Are you willing to handle it from the start?"

Dani nodded. "I think it's time. Can I pick my team on this?" Considering HIPP's nonprofit status, with underpaid and overworked staff, an impressive roster of credentials was attached to the attorneys, paralegals, and investigators on salary. Even though everyone there was top notch, Dani had her favorites.

"Who've you got in mind?"

She knew just who she wanted. "Tommy and Melanie."

"Should be okay. I'll check their assignments and see if they can free up some time."

Dani walked back to her office and busied herself with paperwork until she could put in a call to State Prison in Indiana, where George Calhoun was incarcerated. She'd already researched the head of State Prison and knew that Jared Coates counted as one of the new breed of prison wardens—smart, tough, and fair.

When she reached the prison, Dani identified herself and asked to be put through to the warden. A few minutes later she heard a deep voice say, "Good morning, Ms. Trumball. How can I help you?"

"Good morning, Warden Coates. I'm a staff attorney with the Help Innocent Prisoners Project in New York City. I'm calling about George Calhoun. I've received a letter from him."

"Yes?"

"I'll be overnighting him a retainer letter, and once it comes back, I'd like to meet with you first. I'm just calling to give you a heads-up, since his scheduled date of execution is only six weeks away. We'll need to move quickly on this."

"George Calhoun contacted you? That's interesting."

"Why?"

"Don't get me wrong. I'm glad he did. It's just that he's seemed resigned to what's coming. Most of the others on death row fight as hard as they can to get out. They go through lawyers like chicken feed. But George stuck with the same lawyer from the beginning. It always seemed like he didn't care what happened."

That surprised Dani. Innocent prisoners, especially those on death row, were usually persistent in their fight for freedom. "Do you think he's guilty?"

"Can't say I don't; can't say I do. The jury spoke and they said he was."

"I'm confused. If that's how you feel, why are you glad George wrote us?"

"As far as I can tell, George has always insisted he's innocent. The way I look at it, if a man keeps saying he didn't do the crime, he should have every chance possible to prove it. That's why I'm glad he contacted you."

"That's refreshing coming from a warden."

Dani heard a soft chuckle on the other end of the line. "I suppose it is. But I sleep better at night knowing something wasn't missed."

Dani got off the phone relieved that she wouldn't get the runaround from the warden. HIPP had worked with enough prisoners in enough prisons for her to know that with one word from the top man, the job could become easier or tortuous. Given the short time they had, an obstructionist warden would make the task truly impossible.

She turned to her computer and logged in to Lexis/Nexis, the online research tool for lawyers. She typed in *The People of Indiana v. George Calhoun* and began reading the earliest appeals court decision, handed down six months after his conviction.

In May 1990, the charred remains of a child were found half-buried in the woods near a gas station a few miles off an isolated stretch of Route 80 between Orland and Howe, Indiana. Through study of the skeleton, the county's forensic anthropologist determined that the child had been a three- or four-year-old Caucasian female. Her fingers and feet had been burned too badly to check databases for matches. Walter Jankiewicz, the gas station owner, recalled seeing a run-down American car, maybe a Chevy, at least six or seven years old, black or dark blue, pull off the road one day several weeks earlier, after the sun had set but before darkness had fully settled. He watched as a medium-built man emerged from the car and struggled with the large package in his arms as he headed into the forest. Twenty minutes later, a truck pulled into the gas station, and after the station owner finished filling the tank, the car parked along the road was gone.

Inevitably, a dead Caucasian girl burned beyond recognition created fodder for the media. But after weeks of constant attention, with talking heads speculating *ad nauseam* about the identity of the victim and the circumstances of her death, the news coverage finally petered out. Two years later, *America's Most Wanted* ran a program around the story and, as always, ended the show with a call for help from viewers. A week later they had received dozens of calls. One of them led to George Calhoun.

"Hey, gorgeous. I hear you want me."

Dani looked up from the computer and saw a grinning Tommy Noorland standing in her doorway. She used to bristle when a male colleague referred to her looks. She thought it a backhanded way of being sexist—you know, a woman mattered only if she were attractive. And if she were, there was no reason to see past that. She'd wanted to matter because she was smart and worked hard, not because she happened to be pretty. As she'd gotten older, she'd mellowed. Now she could appreciate that men like Tommy were natural flirts and that his banter was not demeaning. She knew he respected the hell out of her, so she just smiled and answered, "In your dreams, Tommy."

"Ah, baby, you don't know what you're missing," he said and gave her a wink.

This was Tommy's standard repartee, not just with Dani but with every female in the office. "Did Bruce fill you in on the Calhoun case?" she asked as Tommy settled his large frame into a chair.

"Nope. Just said you had something for me."

Dani told Tommy what she knew about the case. "We're going to have to move fast on this one. Probably early next week, we'll fly out to meet him and then stay on to do interviews. In the meantime, I'd like you to start pulling old news reports about the case. Do you have any buddies that landed in Indiana?"

As a former FBI agent, Tommy knew other retired "Fibbies" all over the country. After leaving the government, many took private jobs that kept them in contact with local authorities, and they were a valuable source of information. "I can't think of anyone offhand, but I'll check around."

After he left, Dani turned back to the information on her screen. One of the callers in response to the television show told police that the four-year-old daughter of her neighbors, George and Sallie Calhoun, had mysteriously disappeared two years earlier. Sylvia Grant had occasionally baby-sat Angelina Calhoun. Although George worked days at a local garage and Sallie, nights at a diner, whenever an extra shift became available, Sallie took it. On those days, Sylvia watched their little girl. One day, after Sylvia had stopped seeing Angelina play in front of her small bungalow-style house, she asked Sallie where she was.

"She's gone," Sallie had said.

"Gone where?" Sylvia asked.

"Just gone."

Sallie never explained what had happened. When Sylvia asked if Angelina had died, Sallie turned and walked away. Sylvia never saw the little girl again. "It just seemed strange to me," she'd told the program director. "And you know, it was about the same time as that little girl's body was found. I suppose it's nothing, but I thought you should know about it."

All the leads were passed on to the FBI. The body had been found in Indiana, and the caller lived in Sharpsburg, Pennsylvania, just outside Pittsburgh, so her tip didn't receive priority treatment. Several months later, they got around to questioning her. Sylvia pointed out the bungalow where George and Sallie still lived, and the feds went next door to question them. They'd arrived at eleven o'clock in the morning; George was at work and Sallie was home alone. The two men told Sallie they were investigating the murder of the young girl found in Indiana two years earlier. When they asked her about her daughter, she looked blankly at them at first and then answered, "That was my baby you found in Indiana. We killed her."

Those words sent George Calhoun to death row and committed Sallie to life in prison. She pled guilty, but George insisted his wife was crazy, and he went to trial. The prosecution offered no forensic evidence to establish that the burned corpse was Angelina Calhoun. After all, there had been no reason to conduct any test to establish parentage: They had a confession from a woman who offered no other explanation for her daughter's absence. George testified at his trial and denied killing his daughter but refused to answer questions about her whereabouts. He simply stared silently at the floor.

Dani looked away from the computer. Of course the jurors found George guilty. How could they have done otherwise? Yet so many years later, he still insisted the dead child hadn't been his daughter. If so, what had happened to Angelina? How could a four-year-old child simply vanish? With lethal injection only a few weeks away, Dani wondered if George Calhoun was finally ready to provide the answer.

After delivery of the afternoon mail, a new stack of folders was placed in Dani's in-box. More letters from inmates were inside, waiting for an attorney's review. Yes or no. Hope or despair. A chance at freedom or continued incarceration. Their answers lay in her hands. Dani hated this part of the job most, sitting in judgment on a person's plea for help. She tried to perform the job objectively, devoid of emotion but focused on the facts, only the facts. The facts of Calhoun's case told her to pass. His wife identified the child as their daughter. Her inquiry should stop right there. Yet it hadn't. His story had triggered an emotional response and she wanted to learn more.

A knock at Dani's door broke her concentration. "Am I interrupting?"

Melanie Quinn stood in the doorway. "Nope. C'mon in."

"Bruce said you have something for me." Melanie sat down and Dani filled her in on their next project. At twenty-seven, Melanie still carried within her the passion of youth and the certainty of her convictions. Dani hoped that didn't change too quickly but knew it would—it must. Doubt was a necessary element of life, one often not appreciated until later in life. Only with doubt could one challenge her assumptions and ensure that her course was proper.

Dani handed Melanie the printout of *People v. George Calhoun*. "We're considering taking his case and time is short. Less than six weeks until his scheduled execution. I'm going to head it up, and I've asked for you and Tommy on my team."

Melanie shook her head. "Just six weeks? We've never turned around a conviction that quickly. Is it even possible?"

"Well, it's not *im*possible. But no question it'll be difficult."

"What do you want me to do first?"

"Research everything you can about the case on Lexis/Nexis. I've over-nighted a retainer letter to George, and when it's returned, we'll fly out there, probably at the beginning of next week. Is your schedule clear for this?"

"I ... I can clear it. Nothing pressing right now."

"What aren't you telling me?"

The hint of a smile passed across Melanie's face and abruptly disappeared as she resumed her professional pose. "It's nothing. Next Tuesday is my one-year anniversary of dating Brad and we were going to celebrate at Per Se. It took forever to get reservations, but Brad will understand. I'm sure he will."

Dani thought back on her courtship with Doug. The one-year anniversary of their first date had been a momentous occasion. It signified that they were a couple, not just a passing fling. Despite

Melanie's casual dismissal of her celebration plans, Dani appreciated how disappointed she was. "Okay. Read up on this case, see what you can find, and report back to me tomorrow."

As Melanie left, Dani wondered whether Brad appreciated what a jewel she was. Certainly, her beauty must have dazzled him. Melanie was stunning. Her thick, shoulder-length, strawberry-blond locks framed a perfectly oval face with thickly lashed eyes the color of an arctic glacier. Her body curved in all the right places, without an extraneous ounce of fat. She was more than her appearance, though. An assistant editor of the *Yale Law Review*, she'd graduated at the top of her class at the age of twenty-two, having skipped two years of school. She could do anything, including clerking for a Supreme Court justice, but she had a fire burning within her that compelled her to right wrongs. Dani felt lucky to have her as part of her team.

Driving to her home in Bronxville, a Westchester suburb a commuter's distance from HIPP's office, Dani's thoughts lingered on George Calhoun. As usual, cars inched north on the FDR Drive in spurts of ten to twenty miles per hour. What should have been a thirty-minute drive home usually took an hour or more. When it snowed, it could take close to two hours. Dani supposed she could take the railroad into the city and then take the subway, but she liked having her car with her in case a problem arose with Jonah and she needed to get home right away.

Before Jonah was born, she and Doug had lived in Brooklyn Heights, in a one-bedroom walk-up on the second floor. It was less expensive than Manhattan and an easy subway ride from the city. She loved living there. At night she and Doug would stroll over to the Promenade and gaze at the Manhattan skyline, the twin towers of the World Trade Center like two fists proclaiming the superiority of the city. She'd moved away before 9/11. After Jonah was born, they'd needed more room and bought a fixer-upper in Bronxville.

Dani passed the United Nations and saw a steady stream of traffic ahead. She slowly wound her way past the Queensboro Bridge, still graceful despite its advancing age, gradually picked up a little speed as she approached the Triboro Bridge, and had a reasonably smooth ride the rest of the trip home. She tuned the radio to a classic rock station. The pounding beats of Bon Jovi in the background didn't stop her from mulling over George's case. Inmates, guilty or not, regularly claimed innocence. It seemed strange, though, that he kept insisting the victim wasn't his daughter. Was he delusional? Had he killed his daughter, thinking she was someone else? Or was his wife delusional, imagining that George had killed Angelina?

She turned into her driveway a little after four o'clock—not bad time, considering the traffic, and early enough to greet Jonah when his school bus pulled up at 4:15. Katie, their housekeeper, was always on hand in case Dani lost the battle with the roads. Katie came in every day at three o'clock, tidied up the house, made dinner for the family, and left at seven. That way Dani knew someone would always be home for Jonah. Even though he was twelve, he needed help.

Jonah had Williams syndrome, a rare genetic disorder that caused mild retardation. But it also gave him the sweetest disposition. Most days a smile graced his face and he was friendly to everyone. Too friendly for today's world, but it was hard wired.

"Hi, Katie," Dani called out as she walked in. "Everything okay?"

"I'm in here," a voice called from the direction of the kitchen.

Before Dani entered the cozy room with its 1940s vintage Wedgwood stove, she recognized the unmistakable fragrance of chocolate chip cookies baking in the oven. "Mmm, smells yummy. Almost ready?"

"Not for you, they aren't," Katie answered with a smile. She knew Dani had been trying to drop ten pounds and acted as her conscience. Dani wished she could take Katie to work with her. The younger people in the office could eat all day and not gain an ounce. They sat at their desks, downing Krispy Kreme doughnuts with their morning coffee and peanut M&Ms for an afternoon pick-me-up, and Dani couldn't resist when they'd offer their extras. So the ten pounds had been an uphill battle.

"You're a sadist, Katie McIntyre."

"True enough, but at least I'm a saint with Jonah."

Dani couldn't argue with that. After returning to work, she had gone through two housekeepers before finding Katie. The first two were disasters, putting her in a state of constant anxiety each morning as she left home knowing she had entrusted Jonah to their care.

Dani and Katie turned their heads turned their heads at the sound of the school bus pulling into the driveway. Dani opened the door for Jonah, and he bounded up the few steps in front of their home and rushed into her arms.

"I had a serendipity day at school today, Mommy."

That was another thing about Williams syndrome kids. Despite their low IQs, they tended to have extensive vocabularies, although their choice of words often just missed the mark.

"What's that palatable aroma? Are there cookies in the oven?"

Katie stuck her head into the foyer and nodded. "You bet. I made them just for you."

As Jonah sat at the kitchen table with a plate of cookies and a glass of milk in front of him, Dani headed upstairs to the home office she shared with Doug. On one of the walls adjacent to the door were two desks, each with a computer sitting on top: his and hers. A bulletin board filled with snapshots of her family hung on the wall over her desk. She settled into her deeply cushioned chair and redirected her thoughts from warm, freshly baked cookies to George Calhoun. Vicious murderer or innocent victim? She had taken his case to find out the truth and prayed he was the latter. If he didn't convince her, she would drop the case. Her rule was hard and fast: She didn't represent child murderers, even if they hadn't received a fair trial.

"Mommy, I feel discombobulated."

Dani opened her eyes and saw Jonah standing over her. His cheeks were flushed and his dark brown eyes looked like pools of muddy water. She turned toward her alarm clock, and the bright red digits read 6:10, almost an hour earlier than her usual wake-up time. Doug slept soundly next to her, the covers of their down quilt pulled up to his chin to guard against the chill from the open window.

Dani preferred a cool room to sleep in; Doug liked it toasty. So the window stayed open, but they'd splurged on the warmest down quilt they could find.

As she sat up, Dani tugged at Jonah's arm to sit him next to her on the bed. She put the back of her hand against his forehead, and it felt warm and sweaty. Definitely a fever. Williams syndrome children were prone to an abundance of medical problems, and Dani strived to resist the immediate panic response to every illness. By and large, she had done well over the years, but behind her calm response a surge of terror often arose, and she needed to remind herself it was probably irrational. At least, she always told herself her fears were absurd as she pushed that sense of dread into the background.

"Come, Jonah, let's go back into your bedroom," she whispered to him. Dani put her arm around his shoulder and led him down the hallway. His bedroom looked like any other twelve-year-old boy's, with posters of baseball heroes and rock stars adorning the walls, clothes hanging over the back of a chair, and stacks of textbooks on his desk. She settled him back into his bed and traipsed to the bathroom for a dose of children's Tylenol and then to the kitchen for a glass of orange juice to wash it down.

With Jonah medicated, she made herself comfortable on the plush carpeted floor in his room, to keep him company. "Try to go back to sleep, sweetie," she said as her own eyes drifted closed.

Deep within the recesses of her head, Dani heard the faint buzzing of an alarm clock down the hall. Her eyes shot open and she realized she had fallen asleep. She looked at Jonah and saw that he too had fallen back asleep. A soft guttural sound came from his slightly opened lips, and a shaft of sunlight peeking through the curtains lighted up beads of perspiration on his forehead. She stood up and felt his neck. Still warm. Quietly, she tiptoed out.

Doug lay in bed, his eyes half-closed. "Where were you?"

"In Jonah's room. He's sick."

Doug's eyes shot open and he raised himself up. "What's wrong?"

"Probably just a cold. He has a fever, though."

"Have you spoken to Dr. Dolman?"

Harvey Dolman, a doctor at Montefiore Hospital, treated Jonah for matters large and small. Dani thought him a godsend, a physician who not only understood Williams syndrome and its far-reaching tentacles but also treated his charges and their families with an inexhaustible supply of patience. The Bronx hospital had opened its Williams syndrome center just a few years ago, and it had simplified their lives immeasurably.

"It's too early to call. I'll wait until nine."

"His service can reach him any time," Doug said as he reached for the phone on the side of the bed.

Dani put her hand over Doug's. "He'll be okay. I'm sure it's nothing serious. We shouldn't disturb Dr. Dolman now."

Doug stared at her a moment. "All right then, if you're sure." He lay back down. "You know he'll want you to stay home with him."

She did know. They were supposed to take turns, but Dani couldn't resist Jonah's pleading for her to stay.

At nine o'clock she called Dr. Dolman and received the reassurance she'd hoped for. Jonah had a cold, an ordinary cold like every child gets from time to time. He felt better after sleeping for a few more hours and awakening to discover he would spend the day at home with his mother. His smile returned, along with his gushing chatter. Dani enjoyed spending time with Jonah. In fact, most adults enjoyed his friendly and cheerful personality. If she hadn't felt pressed by the Calhoun case, she'd have relished a day at home with her son. Instead, she picked up the phone and called her office.

"I'm going to work from home today," she told Melanie. "Let's schedule a conference call for two o'clock and we'll go over what we have. Let Tommy know, okay? Oh, and if the retainer comes in from Calhoun, call me."

An hour later she got a call back from Melanie. "It arrived in the morning mail. George Calhoun's retainer letter. Do you want me to call his trial attorney?"

"He wasn't just his trial attorney," Dani reminded her. "He handled the appeals as well. I'll give him a call from here."

Telling the former attorney he was being replaced always presented a challenge. Sometimes HIPP got lucky, and there was visible relief that he'd be removed from his place as the last link in the chain of events leading up to a person's death. More often there was defensiveness, because the first avenue of review on an appeal was ineffective assistance of counsel. The judicial system afforded everyone the right to counsel. With death cases, the Supreme Court had ruled that it must be effective counsel. Sadly, there were too many instances of overworked, inexperienced, incompetent, or just plain unfit attorneys defending the accused on trial for their lives. Dani had read so many trial transcripts where the defense attorney was admonished for alcohol on her breath or prodded awake when it was his turn for questioning that she wasn't shocked anymore. With George's trial counsel handling his appeals, the issue of ineffective counsel wouldn't have been raised.

Dani looked him up on the Martindale Hubbell website, the bible for lawyer résumés. Robert Wilson was a small-town lawyer with one associate and no partners. Most likely, the current associate hadn't worked there during George's trial. She copied his phone number, but Jonah interrupted her before she could dial it.

"I'm bored," he whined. "Why can't I go to school now? I feel acceptable. I miss my friends. You're too busy to interplay with me."

Despite his pouting lips, Jonah looked cherubic, a characteristic common with Williams syndrome children, whose faces were often described as pixie-like. Dani walked to him and placed the back of her hand on his forehead. It felt cool. She was torn. She wanted to get started with Robert Wilson. The search began with him—the recitation of facts from the man initially charged with defending his client. Did he believe George was innocent? Did he think George was crazy? What had his trial strategy been? The foundation for her attempt to save George's life, if HIPP decided to take his case, would be contained in Wilson's files. But she knew Jonah needed her now. He'd never been good at entertaining himself; the desire for social interaction was too strong. Now that his fever had broken, he'd become restless. A familiar feeling washed over Dani—that she was balancing on a seesaw ten feet in the air, and the slightest movement in the wrong direction would send her tumbling to the unforgiving concrete below.

Reluctantly, Dani turned away from the telephone. "Okay, Jonah, I'll play a game with you, but just for an hour. Then I've got work to do." Jonah's face lit up, and Dani pushed aside the knowledge that she was going to play Monopoly while a man awaited his destiny on death row.

After persuading Jonah to entertain himself with computer games, Dani finally returned to George's case. She picked up the phone in the home office, which had become a tapestry of all the threads that made up their lives. One wall contained the ceiling-to-floor built-in mahogany bookcases they'd promised themselves they'd have once they owned a house. On the opposite wall was another built-in, this one housing a Murphy bed in the center, for rare overnight guests, with large open shelves on either side. The wall opposite the two windows enclosed a twenty-seven-inch television, modest by the standards of the day, along with various knickknacks they'd collected over the years and held on to as memories of their younger days. There was the large conch shell they had found the week they vacationed at the beach in Montauk, when Jonah was a year and a half and just learning to walk. They were so happy when he finally took those awkward baby steps, the kind where he looked like a drunken sailor ready to topple over at any moment. Dani had laughed when he plopped onto the warm sand next to the shell and held it tight to his little body. "Your first shell, Jonah. You can take it home with you."

When she put the shell next to her ear, she could still hear the waves of the ocean crashing against the sand and see the smile on Jonah's face as he carried his prize back to the motel. On another shelf were framed photographs of Jonah at various stages of his life. During the years when Dani had stayed home with him, she dabbled in photography, teaching herself the intricacies of apertures and shutter speed, ambient light and artificial light. She set up a darkroom in the basement and experimented with black-and-white film. Jonah was her subject, her muse, and stored in the recesses of her closet were boxes upon boxes of his image.

Once, Dani had fantasized a family of five children. She was an only child and envied her friends with many brothers and sisters. Their homes were always filled with noise and clutter, unlike the serenity of her own home, but it was a pandemonium that seemed infused with joy. From an early age, she knew she wanted a career, but somehow thought she could combine that with a large family. That changed after Jonah was diagnosed with Williams syndrome. She knew the physical and emotional toll that would go into raising her son. Having more children would inevitably shortchange Jonah or shortchange his sibling, she'd thought at the time. She sometimes wondered whether she'd been right. Looking at Jonah, she rejoiced at his development and knew that the commitment she and Doug had made to him had helped him get to that point. Yet she sometimes missed having a larger family. She'd met many couples with Williams syndrome children who had other children. Not just older siblings, but younger ones as well. They'd managed—even done well. She and Doug had made their decision, though, and it was too late to look back.

Dani shook her head over her procrastination and punched Robert Wilson's number into the phone. After the third ring, a pleasant-sounding female voice answered. "Law office of Robert Wilson. Marion Boland speaking. How may I help you?"

Her formality, especially in a small-town law office, caught Dani by surprise, but she quickly explained that she represented George Calhoun and asked to speak to her boss.

"I've been expecting your call," were the first words she heard when Wilson answered. He had a deep voice, with a gruffness that bespoke annoyance at the interruption of his work.

"Good. I hope that means George told you he'd contacted HIPP."

"Not exactly, but I knew he felt desperate, and when I told him I couldn't do anything more, I figured he'd go fishing for one of you guys." His tone suggested disdain, though Dani didn't know whether it was for Innocence Projects in general or specifically for their mutual client.

"George signed a retainer letter for our services, and with the execution coming up so quickly, I'd like to get a copy of your files as soon as possible," she said. "Of course, I'll fax you the retainer for your records."

"Sure, sure. You go ahead and spin your wheels. I'll have my secretary overnight them. But you're wasting your time."

"Why? Because you believe he's guilty, or because you don't think we'll be able to stop the execution?"

"Oh, he's guilty, all right. No doubt about that. But I meant the legal stuff. I've done all the appeals, even tried twice to get the Supreme Court to hear the case. I've managed to drag it out this long, but there are no more buttons to push. I've wasted plenty of time on him, believe me, and I sure wasn't getting rich off it. Barely covered my expenses. You know how it is."

She did know. Wilson might be right—there might no longer be any basis for appeal—but Dani's gut told her he hadn't pushed himself too hard on this case. If Wilson believed his client was guilty, she suspected, he'd taken whatever money Calhoun had but hadn't work himself into a sweat on his behalf.

"Tell me, Mr. Wilson—"

"Oh, call me Bob. We're informal here."

"Okay, Bob. I've only read the facts from the appellate decisions. I'm still raw on this. What evidence did the prosecution have besides the wife's confession?"

"Besides the confession?" he exploded. "What goddamn else did they need? Neither one ever gave me an explanation for what happened to their daughter. You think a four-year-old just picks herself up and walks away?"

"Is it possible she died in her sleep? Maybe from sudden infant death syndrome? And they panicked, afraid they'd be blamed, and buried her in their yard?"

"Listen, sweetheart, when a jury comes back and hands you a death sentence, you don't clam up because you're afraid you'll be blamed for something you didn't do. You're already blamed for it. It's been over nineteen years and still not one blessed word about where his daughter disappeared to. Just, 'That girl wasn't my daughter,' over and over again. The guy's screwy."

Dani's ears pricked up. "Do you think he's disturbed? Does he ever appear disoriented or delusional to you?"

"He's crazy like a fox—you know, just about this dead girl. On everything else he's as sane as I am." Bob laughed. "Well, who knows how sane I am? I stuck with this crazy case long after I should have."

After she hung up, Dani thought to herself that Wilson was right. He had stuck with the case longer than he should have. A convicted murderer claiming innocence should have had a lawyer who believed in him. She didn't know yet whether she was that lawyer. That decision would have to wait until she got the records and met Calhoun.

Bob Wilson kept his word. The next day piles of boxes were stacked in a corner of HIPP's conference room, all with the return address "Law Firm of Robert Wilson, Esq."

"You take the appeals, I'll take the trial transcript and exhibits," Dani said to Melanie. It would take days to go through everything thoroughly, and they'd both be working well into the night and over the weekend. But Dani could do the work from home, accessible to Jonah, who felt well enough to go back to school. "As you go through the papers, see if you can find anything on these questions: Was an autopsy performed on the murdered child? Did they match the child's DNA to the parents? They found the body in Indiana; the Calhouns lived in Pennsylvania. Did anyone else recognize them along the way?"

"I assume you want me to chart out the issues already appealed and summarize the decisions?" Melanie asked.

"Yes, and also if there were any dissenting opinions, summarize those separately."

"Sure. How quickly do you need it?"

"Yesterday would be good."

"And six more months on the clock would be nice too."

They both felt the pressure of what lay ahead. Sitting on the floor, they each attacked a box, looking for the documents they needed. Dani found the transcripts in the second box she opened. They were the record of everything said during trial: every question, every answer, every comment, even the arguments made at the bench outside the jurors' earshot. Usually, she skimmed through the transcripts first, getting the broad picture quickly, and then started again from the beginning, painstakingly searching for appealable errors. After Melanie collected the appellate briefs and left, Dani settled back into her chair and began her perusal.

The words on the pages became a movie reel in her mind and she became an observer, no longer in her office, but sitting in the courtroom, watching the trial unfold. She visualized the prosecutor as a tall man, his bearing erect, dressed in his finest navy striped suit. She saw him walk to the jury box. "Ladies and gentlemen, you are going to hear about a horrific crime. You are going to see shocking pictures, images that no person should ever be asked to view. But you are here today because someone killed an innocent child, a four-year-old girl.

"Any murder is hateful, and any murder of a child is abominable. But for you to understand the full extent of how monstrous this act of murder was, you will need to see pictures of her burned body, found after she was callously buried in a forest. And when you see those pictures you will understand why the perpetrator must be found guilty and must be punished with death.

"I know how difficult it will be for you to sit through this trial and hear the testimony about this little girl's death, but it will be easy for you to decide who committed this atrocity. It was the defendant, sitting over there in that chair. And the little girl he brutally murdered was his own daughter.

"How will you know it was that man who committed the crime? Because his own wife will tell you what happened. You will hear her say that she watched her husband kill their daughter, set her on fire, and then bury her in the forest. Ladies and gentlemen, when you go back to your room to deliberate after you've heard all the evidence, you will know beyond any doubt whatsoever that George Calhoun deserves to die."

Dani skimmed through Bob Wilson's opening statement. He made some valid points about the lack of forensic evidence, but in the movie running through her mind, she saw the jurors' eyes glaze over.

She read quickly through the testimony in the prosecutor's case. The most damning evidence was Mrs. Calhoun's confession. As Dani read the transcript, she envisioned the jurors listening with rapt attention as Sallie said, "My husband beat our daughter unconscious. He poured gasoline over her body and set her afire. I watched him do it and I did nothing. I didn't stop him. He wrapped her body in a blanket and we drove to Indiana. I was with him in the car. He pulled off the road when we came to a forest. I stayed in the car while he carried our daughter into the woods. He came back without her and we drove away."

"Why did George do this to your daughter?" the prosecutor asked.

"She had the devil inside her. George said we had to do this to get the devil out."

Bob Wilson limited his cross of Sallie to attacking her credibility. "Mrs. Calhoun, during the two years between your husband supposedly doing this to your daughter and the police knocking on your door, did you ever notify the authorities?"

"No."

"Did you ever tell any friend or relative what your husband had done?"

"No."

"And isn't it a fact that you've been given a sentence of life imprisonment instead of facing the death penalty in exchange for your testimony?"

"They just told me to tell the truth and that's what I did."

After reading Sallie's testimony, Dani needed a break. Her whole body felt dirty, as if even considering taking on George's case had blackened her. She poured a cup of coffee and headed to Bruce's office.

"Have a moment?" she asked as she walked in and made herself comfortable in the chair opposite his desk. It was just as threadbare as the one in her office.

Bruce looked up and smiled. "Do I have a choice?"

"I'm not feeling so good about this case."

"Okay. Don't take it then."

Just like Bruce. Always pushing his staff to make decisions. Most of the time she liked that. Today she wasn't so sure. "I'm not finished reviewing the transcript, but already it gives me the willies."

Bruce fixed his eyes on hers. "You shouldn't take the case if you think the guy is guilty, no matter how many mistakes were made at trial. But if those mistakes got in the way of the truth, he deserves to be heard. Your personal feelings about the nature of the crime are irrelevant. Only the truth matters. And it's your job to find the truth. So, have you read enough to know what the truth is?"

"No, I haven't even gotten to the defendant's case."

"Well, then two things might happen. The defendant's attorney could have done a bang-up job and convinced you doubt existed about his guilt or left you certain after hearing both sides he was guilty, or—"

She didn't let him finish. "Or he did a lousy job and I need to conduct my own investigation, right?"

"You got it, girl."

She thanked Bruce and went back to her office to finish reading the transcript. After Sallie's testimony, the prosecutor entered into evidence photographs of the burned and battered body of the murdered child, despite objections about their inflammatory nature. Side by side with one gruesome photo was one of Angelina Calhoun, a pretty toddler with blond hair framing her face. The contrast was designed to enrage the jury, as it no doubt did.

The prosecution then ended its case, and the judge sent the jurors home for the day, leaving them with the sickening images of the corpse to linger in their thoughts overnight.

Wilson began his defense the next day with George Calhoun's testimony. Once again, Dani's mind turned the words on the page into a movie of the trial. She saw George take the stand, saw him swear to tell the truth. Wilson took him through the preliminary testimony: where he lived, where he worked, how far he'd gone in school—meaningless questions to get him comfortable with testifying. Then, "Mr. Calhoun, did you murder your daughter?"

"No sir, I did not. I loved my Angelina more than anything else in the world. I would never hurt her."

"Then how did that little girl get in that grave?"

"I don't know. She's not my daughter."

"Your wife says she is."

"My wife's not thinking right."

"No further questions," Wilson said as he turned and walked back to the defense table.

The prosecutor easily discredited George on the stand.

"Where is your daughter?" he asked.

"I don't know."

"Did you ever report her missing?"

"No."

"Did you ever tell anyone she was missing?"

"No."

"Did you make any effort to find her?"

"No."

"Is your daughter alive?"

The transcript noted silence by the defendant.

"I'll ask you again: Is your daughter alive?"

More silence until the judge said, "Mr. Calhoun, you must answer the question."

"I don't know."

"Mr. Calhoun, are you asking us to believe that your four-year-old daughter whom you love more than anything in the world simply disappeared, and you did nothing about it? And you don't even know if she's dead or alive?"

"That's what I'm saying," he answered, assuring his conviction by a jury of his peers.

The first reading confirmed Dani's suspicion about Bob Wilson. His lackluster defense during the trial bespoke an attorney who foresaw an inevitable guilty verdict and expended little effort to alter that outcome. Over and over he failed to attack the prosecutor's witnesses, despite glaring holes in their evidence, or raise objections to improper questions. But even more noteworthy was the absence of any real defense. Aside from a handful of character witnesses, the only testimony refuting the charge was Calhoun's. Although George had sworn he hadn't murdered his daughter and that the child found in the woods was not his own, the defense presented no forensic evidence to back up his claim. How could that be? The files contained photographs of the murdered girl, her features burned beyond recognition. Surely, given George's insistence that the dead child wasn't his daughter, DNA testing would have been ordered, if not by the prosecution, then by defense counsel. Dani stopped herself. Seventeen years ago, DNA testing was not routinely done.

Bob Wilson should have done more to discredit Sallie's confession. His cross-examination of her was shockingly inadequate. Perhaps he thought she was a more sympathetic witness than her husband and that he would do more damage than good if he questioned her aggressively. He was wrong. Her testimony sealed George's fate. If Wilson had cross-examined her more thoroughly, he might have been able to show inconsistencies in her story, create doubt in the jurors' minds. Sallie mentioned the devil in her testimony for the prosecution. Were she and George devoutly religious? Had they ever confided to their pastor their concerns about their daughter? Dani didn't know the answers because Wilson hadn't asked those questions. Letting the jury hear Sallie's testimony without his having made any effort to contradict her seemed a colossal error by Calhoun's attorney.

Dani's brief review of the transcripts and exhibits suggested a number of avenues for appeal. Many had no doubt been raised as the case wound its way up through the court of appeals, the state supreme court, and petitions for certiorari to the United States Supreme Court. Calhoun's case had made it to the highest court twice, a not uncommon journey for death-row inmates. She would have to wait until Melanie completed her review of the appellate briefs and decisions to see what arguments were still available. Dani still didn't know whether she believed that George Calhoun was guilty or innocent, but she did know this: They needed to take a trip to Indiana State Prison.

Dani called the travel agent used by HIPP and booked three seats on a Monday flight to Indianapolis. After hanging up, she glanced at the clock. It was almost four, past the time she liked to leave for home. And it was Friday to boot, the worst day for early traffic. She briefly considered calling Doug at his office to suggest he stay in the city and meet her for dinner. With Jonah so recently sick, though, she didn't want to be far away in the evening. Even though Katie could handle any emergency, there was no substitute for the comfort of a mother's touch.

She walked out of her office into the large common room and saw Tommy still seated at his desk. Tommy had left the Bureau after ten years because his wife couldn't take the strain of his undercover stints, which had often kept him away from home—and their five children—for months at a time. He had a swarthy complexion, a full head of wavy black hair, greased down a bit too much for Dani's taste, and a thick mustache. No doubt he had once been handsome, but now his body, although still trim, had softened, and his years in the field showed in the lines of his face. He still had a razor-sharp mind, though, and he could uncover truths—and lies—like no other investigator in the office.

"Tommy, would you check into whether any other girls between ages three and five were reported missing around that time?"

"Sure."

"And can you give me a hand?"

"I can give you both hands, baby. Just tell me where and when."

"Give it a break, Tommy. I'm not in the mood for this now. I've got a bitch of a ride home and a weekend of work to look forward to."

"Ouch. Okay, no jokes. What do you need?"

"Would you help me carry the cartons in my office down to my car?" The one perk of her job was a free parking spot in the outdoor parking lot two blocks from HIPP's office. Monthly parking spots, when you could get them—there were waiting lists for most—went for four hundred dollars a month in the East Village. Tony, the owner of the lot, was a former exoneree freed through the efforts of HIPP. He provided HIPP with four spots, gratis. When first offered, Bruce turned them down, but Tony was so adamant about doing something for HIPP that Bruce ultimately relented. He understood that Tony's gesture provided him with a measure of self-esteem that had been all but obliterated during his twelve years in prison.

Tommy looked at the stack of boxes. "You got it, boss."

Out on the street, the sky was still bright, with the fragrance of sprouting buds lingering in the air. Although the temperature hovered around sixty degrees, the still air made it feel warmer. Dani loved spring. It carried the hope of warm, lazy days ahead; summer vacation with Jonah; and sunlight that seemed to last forever. But this summer would be different. By the beginning of summer, she knew, George Calhoun's fate would be determined. He would be a free man, released after seventeen years in prison for a crime he didn't commit, or—rightly or wrongly—dead from a lethal injection.

Traffic crawled, as Dani had expected, and she didn't arrive home until after six o'clock. She was exhausted, barely able to muster the effort to eat dinner. After Jonah fell asleep, she decided to give herself a break for the evening. Her mind was too fried for the tedious scrutiny of the transcript that awaited her. Instead, she settled down in front of the fire, Doug's arms wrapped securely around her.

"Do you ever regret giving up the US Attorney's Office?" she asked. Like Dani, Doug had started his law career as an assistant US attorney in the Southern District of New York.

It would have been easy for Doug to respond with a quick no, but he was too thoughtful to toss off an answer. "Most of the time, no. Teaching has so many rewards, and by and large the students keep me entertained. But sometimes I miss the energy of the agency, the stimulation of getting close to nailing our target, knowing I have the power to stop bad things from happening."

Power. There were many reasons an attorney joined the US Attorney's Office, and one was for the feeling of power. For Doug, that had been a strong draw, one that fueled his interest in law from the outset. There was an adrenaline rush in putting together an investigation, preparing for trial, and securing a conviction, but under all that was an awareness of one's power. Doug had luxuriated in that knowledge yet gave it up without complaint to spend more time with Jonah.

"I've been thinking about Sara recently," Dani said.

"You haven't spoken to her in a while."

"I've been so busy. But I've been thinking lately how so much of my life now is tied to her, or at least to things about her."

Dani didn't grow up expecting to be a lawyer. She wanted to be a psychologist. During her undergraduate days at Brown University, she volunteered for several social action groups. One of them was Fast Friends. Looking back, that choice seemed prophetic, but at the time, it was fueled by a selfish desire to enhance her graduate-school opportunities.

Fast Friends paired volunteers with developmentally disabled "friends." At the college chapters, volunteer students committed to meeting with their friends at least twice a month, with more regular contact by phone and, nowadays, e-mail. But inevitably it became much more than that. Most of the volunteers were close to their friends, and the benefits of the relationships flowed both ways.

Dani's friend was Sara Klemson. An unusually pretty, mildly retarded eighteen-year-old, Sara had always found it difficult to make friends. Her overly effusive personality was off-putting to her non-disabled peers, and she had gradually become more withdrawn. She and Dani had hit it off immediately and saw each other regularly. Fast Friends held numerous social activities for the volunteers and their friends, but gradually Dani began to invite Sara to some regular campus social events. One was a fraternity party during her sophomore year.

She didn't know how it had happened. She swore she hadn't been drunk; she never liked the feeling of being out of control. But somehow she'd lost sight of Sara and didn't realize it until it was too late. She found her sobbing in a bedroom, her clothes torn, blood on the sheets. Sara had been raped. Eventually, two of the fraternity brothers were arrested and tried. With her inappropriate smiling and slow speech, Sara didn't make a very good witness, and the boys' expensive attorneys had little difficulty getting a "not guilty" verdict. It was then that Dani decided she'd have more impact as a prosecutor than as a psychologist.

"You would have ended up as an attorney even without Sara," Doug said as he stroked her cheek. "You're so naturally suited for it."

The flames from the fireplace cast a soft glow in the darkened living room. The images in the photographs on the mantle were barely visible, but Dani could see her favorite: seven-year-old Jonah, flanked by his parents, blowing out the candles on his birthday cake, a look of pure joy on his face.

Decorators would have considered their living room a nightmare. No unifying style, no coordination of fabrics and color, just a hodgepodge of pieces they'd picked up over the years. Dani called it "comfy style." Their cushioned burgundy couch, deep enough for her and Doug to lie entwined in each other's arms. Two armchairs, on their third set of slipcovers. A water-marked, maple coffee table Dani had picked up at a garage sale. An oval, braided rug in front of the fireplace in a rainbow of colors, frayed at the edges.

The sounds of early cicadas outside the window mixed with the crackling of the burning wood and imbued her with a sense of deep contentment. Their lives had turned out differently from what they'd planned, but they were happy. They were a family.

Thirty-Five Days

As the announcement came of Flight 84's imminent boarding, Dani glanced nervously down the expansive corridor, hoping to see Tommy. Melanie sat next to her, their carry-on bags at their sides. "Damn, he'd better get here soon," Dani said.

LaGuardia Airport was crowded with business travelers, laptops by their sides and cell phones at their ears. Dani didn't travel often, usually for just a few days to argue an appeal now and then, and she still needed to suppress a sense of dread when the airplane taxied down the runway and began to rise seamlessly into the atmosphere.

"There he is," Melanie said as she tapped Dani's arm and pointed to a man running toward their gate.

"Well, he certainly played it close." Dani barely contained her annoyance. Every moment counted with an execution so near, and she couldn't have members of her team treating responsibilities casually. Showing up late was not an option.

"Sorry," Tommy said as he reached their seats. "I got a call from a pal at the Bureau just as I was ready to leave. He had some info for me on missing girls."

Now Dani felt embarrassed to have judged Tommy so quickly. She should have known better. "What'd he say?"

Before Tommy could answer, a crackled voice announced over the loudspeaker, "Those passengers seated in rows 30 and higher may begin boarding now." A mass of bodies rose from their seats and headed to the gate, far more than the few invited to board first. A line quickly formed just behind the gate, giving minimal clearance for those ready to hand over their boarding passes. Despite having assigned seats, it seemed everyone wanted to be first on the airplane.

"I have it written down. It's in here," Tommy said as he patted his briefcase. "I'll fill you in on the plane."

The plane was only half full, and they spread out. With his notebook open on his lap, Tommy leaned across the aisle to speak to the women. "There are five cases of girls between the ages of three and five reported missing during the two years prior to the body being found in Indiana. In two of them, the parents were divorced, the mother had custody, and the father disappeared at the same time as the child. It's presumed those children are alive and with the father somewhere. Two other children were recovered."

"What about the fifth?" Dani asked.

"A three-and-a-half-year-old girl—her name is Stacy Conklin—is still officially missing. Now here's the interesting thing: Stacy was reported missing two months before the little girl's body was found in the woods."

"Where was she reported missing from?"

"Another interesting point. She lived in Hammond, Illinois, just over the Indiana border and right near Route 80. It's maybe four hours from where the body was found."

Dani shook her head. "If Stacy was reported missing so close to the discovery of the body in the woods, why didn't the police suspect it could be her?"

"They did. Well, not immediately, but eventually. Remember, this crime happened over nineteen years ago. They didn't have the computer database we have now. And it was another state. But soon enough they matched the age and gender to Stacy Conklin and they brought in her parents."

"And?"

"And the parents said it wasn't their daughter. Her face was too badly burned to identify, but supposedly they could tell by the shape of her body. Too skinny for their daughter, too small. The police checked the parents out anyway and cleared both. Loving and devoted, never hit their child, pillars of the community, yadda yadda yadda."

"Is it possible? Could it be true that George Calhoun's daughter is still alive?" Dani tried to stop herself from getting caught up in the excitement of her client's possible innocence. It was a double-edged sword if he wasn't guilty. Proving innocence meant she'd helped a man or a woman escape from an unfair death. Failing to exonerate an innocent person and then watching that person's execution was torturous. She always attended when she lost an appeal. Her clients needed to have one person witness their death who knew the truth.

Tommy gave her a warning glance. "You think every client is innocent. Toughen up, Dani. Most of them aren't; you know that. And this guy is probably guilty too. We haven't even met with him yet and you're already on a crusade."

Most of the staff at HIPP opposed the death penalty. Tommy was one of the few who believed heinous criminals should face a heinous end. Despite those feelings, he was the best investigator in the office. Tommy believed in truth as strongly as he believed in retribution, and he worked doggedly to uncover whether the person facing the death penalty deserved to die. Dani long ago gave up trying to sway Tommy to her view that no person deserved to die at the hand of the government. She was just grateful that he used his incredible detecting skills to sniff out the facts.

Some people accomplished a lot of work on airplanes, but Dani wasn't among them. Concentrating while thirty thousand feet in the air with nothing but clouds and sky between her and the ground wasn't in her makeup. She could fly—she just felt an undercurrent of uneasiness during the flight. She closed her eyes and let her mind wander.

Like most states, Indiana executed death-row inmates by lethal injection. It hadn't always been that way. First, prisoners had been executed by hanging, a salute to the days of the Wild West. Then the state moved to the electric chair, pulling back from the concept of punishment as righteous revenge and embracing the notion of humane treatment. After all, the Constitution banned cruel and unusual punishment, and strapping a murderer into an antiquated wooden chair and zapping him with twenty-three hundred volts of electricity supposedly killed the convict more quickly. It was done in three rounds: eight seconds, then twenty-two seconds, then eight seconds again. And if that didn't do the job, another three rounds followed. Dani had once counted off twenty-two seconds and then imagined electricity shooting through her body during that interminable wait; she shuddered every time she thought about it. Still, it was quicker than hanging and easier to implement. With hanging, unless the length of rope and the weight of the prisoner were calculated precisely, multiple attempts were needed to get the job done.

By 1980, electrocution had replaced hanging as the most popular form of execution. Problems still existed, though. It turned out that sometimes parts of the prisoner's body ignited. Blasts of blue and orange flames bursting from a man's head, filling the room with smoke, made for uncomfortable viewing. Continuing the quest to be more humane—at least for the viewing public—most states retired electric chairs in favor of lethal injection. Indiana made the switch in 1995.

When first convicted, Calhoun would have been executed in an electric chair. Now, if HIPP didn't succeed, the state would mix up a potion of three chemicals: a barbiturate to put him to sleep, a muscle relaxant to paralyze his diaphragm and lungs, and potassium chloride to stop his heart. Sometimes, though, the barbiturate didn't put the prisoner to sleep. And so he remained conscious when the drugs stopped his breathing and his heart, causing unimaginable pain.

Dani hadn't even met George Calhoun and yet she already thought he could be innocent. No, if she were honest with herself, she had to admit she wanted to believe in his innocence. She was on her way to meet a man who was convicted of the most unspeakable of crimes: a parent murdering his own child. She didn't want to meet that man. She wanted to meet a father who loved his daughter, who, as his letter said, would never have harmed her. So, yes, she allowed herself to believe he could be innocent. He wouldn't be the first of her clients to be convicted for an act he hadn't committed. She had worked long enough at HIPP to learn that the judicial process was flawed, that many innocent men and women were convicted of crimes they hadn't committed. But she kept coming back to his failure to explain his daughter's disappearance. It seemed to shout "guilty." And she couldn't help wondering if he were guilty of something—maybe murder, maybe something else. But what?

The crystal-blue skies of New York were nowhere to be seen when the plane landed at Indianapolis International Airport. The drenching rain that kept the plane circling for almost an hour before landing had stopped, but deep puddles permeated the roadways. They piled into their rented car, airport map in hand, and made their way downtown to the Indianapolis Women's Prison. If Sallie had been convicted later, it's likely she'd have been sent to the newer women's prison in Rockville. Most of the women incarcerated now in Indianapolis had special needs: some elderly, some mentally ill, some even pregnant. Sallie didn't seem to fit into those categories, but Dani could be wrong. Maybe she was mentally ill. She'd get a better sense when she met her.

"Ladies, what say we stop for lunch first?" Tommy always had food on his mind, but he had a point. They didn't know how long they'd be at the prison.

"I'm up for that," both women answered in unison.

They parked near the prison and began walking. Almost immediately, Tommy spotted a coffee shop just a block from the parking garage. They strolled over, checked the menu in the front window and peeked inside. It looked clean and homey, so they went in. The tufted benches in their booth were faded and cracked, with strands of cotton wadding sticking out from the red vinyl fabric. The waitress, a pretty young woman with rouged cheeks and dirty blonde hair pulled back in a ponytail, came over to the table to take their order.

Flying always revved up Dani's appetite. She didn't know why. Doug was the opposite. On family vacations, she and Jonah would fight over Doug's airplane snack. "I'll have a hamburger, rare, no mayonnaise, just ketchup on the roll."

"You want fries with that?"

She hesitated. Fries were diet killers.

"It's only a dollar more and they're real good here. Everybody says so," the waitress said with an inviting smile.

Dani shrugged. It was hard enough to eat well at home. On the road it was impossible. "Sure, add the fries."

"And anything to drink?" she asked like Lucifer drawing her into the inferno. She knew she should just have water, especially after flying, but she'd already blown the diet with a hamburger and fries.

"Do you have milkshakes?" Dani asked, dropping her voice so Tommy and Melanie wouldn't hear.

"Sure do," the waitress said loudly enough for the next table to hear. "Chocolate, vanilla, and strawberry, but chocolate's definitely the best."

"Make it a chocolate shake," Dani mumbled.

She leaned back and let her thoughts wander, drifting away from Tommy and Melanie's conversation. Each city she traveled to when she argued an appeal seemed both different and the same as New York City. No place was like Manhattan, of course. No place had the mass humanity on its city streets. No place had the crowded skyscrapers or bustling energy or unending streams of neon lights. She supposed people living in Chicago or Los Angeles or maybe even Houston or Atlanta might argue with that. But they were wrong. Manhattan was unique. Yet despite its uniqueness, every city, large or small, shared common characteristics. Every city had paved roads heading to its center; every city had its office buildings and restaurants, gas stations and pharmacies, doctors' offices and schools; every city had its residents trudging off to work to earn a living. Some worked to support themselves—Dani guessed that was the case with their waitress. Maybe she was a college student, working part-time to pay her tuition. Or maybe she'd forgone college and worked to pay her rent and have a little fun on the weekends. Or perhaps she didn't work to support only herself. Maybe, like the woman Dani would meet within a few hours, she worked to support her child. What would make a woman, a woman like this young waitress with her cheery smile and warm eyes, stand by and watch her child being murdered? Horribly murdered—burned beyond recognition and tossed away like a chewed-over turkey bone. And then say nothing for two years?

Sallie Calhoun had been a young waitress once, working nights so she could be home with her baby during the daytime. Neighbors described her as a devoted mother. They never heard her yell at Angelina, never even heard her raise her voice. They never saw her plopped in front of the television while Angelina ran about on her own. No, she showered attention on her daughter, hugging her and covering her with kisses every chance she got. What had happened to that adoring mother who now sat in a cell at Indiana State Women's Prison?

Dani didn't know if she'd find any answers to this riddle when she sat down with Sallie, but all thoughts of the interview disappeared as the waitress delivered their lunch. The hamburger was blood rare, just as Dani liked it. She managed to finish every last french fry and her milkshake—which tasted as good as promised—before it was time to leave. It took them just five minutes to walk to the prison gate. The building dated back to 1873, when it became the first correctional facility in the nation to incarcerate only women and the first maximum-security prison for female prisoners.

They each showed their identification at the prison gate and were marshaled into the waiting area.

"What do you think she's going to tell us?" Melanie asked. "Does she realize how close the execution date is?"

"I don't know. I don't know if they've been communicating with each other since the trial. I mean, her testimony got him the death sentence. I would certainly understand if he wanted nothing to do with her after that."

"Still, they were married a good number of years. And had a child together. Doesn't that mean something?"

Dani suppressed a smile. Despite her intelligence and top legal skills, Melanie's naiveté sometimes surprised Dani. Melanie had grown up in a loving, intact family and didn't yet appreciate how hurtful married couples could get with each other. Maybe Sallie and George continued to write each other from their respective prisons. Maybe they even used their hoarded telephone calls to see how each fared. It was just as likely, though, that the poison that led to the death of their daughter had destroyed their marriage as well. Dani didn't expect Sallie to be of much help to them, but she held out hope anyway.

After a half-hour wait, they were ushered into a windowless five-by-seven interview room. The walls were barren and the floor showed scuff marks. Sallie sat at the bare table and a female guard stood positioned outside the door. Dani looked her over before making introductions. She was a slight woman, severely underweight, with prominent neck bones and pencil-thin arms. The dark circles under her eyes looked painted on. Her chestnut-brown hair hung in limp strands framing an oval face. Her eyes focused on the table, and she made no acknowledgment of their presence.

"Sallie, my name is Dani Trumball, and these are my associates, Melanie Quinn and Tom Noorland. We're with the Help Innocent Prisoners Project in New York City. We're trying to help your husband."

Sallie's gaze lingered on the wooden table and she remained silent.

"Do you know where George is now?" Dani asked.

Sallie lifted her head. "He's in hell." The words spit out of her mouth like a hot ball shot from a cannon, and then, as if spent from the energy it took to speak, her head dropped down to the table again.

"Sallie, would you look at me, please?"

Slowly, she lifted her eyes and stared at Dani's face.

"Sallie, George is in prison, just like you. Do you know why he's there?"

Her voice was quiet now. She spoke barely above a whisper. "Because of Angelina."

"Yes, that's right. Because of Angelina. Do you know what he did to Angelina?"

"I know. I saw it."

"Would you tell me, please?"

Sallie shook her head. Tears began to roll down her cheeks. Nineteen years had passed, but Dani could see that it remained as fresh as yesterday to her. A struggle took place within Dani. Should she back off? She didn't want to frighten Sallie into withdrawal. Although her responses had been terse, at least she was talking to them. Dani knew Sallie held the key to George's fate, but she didn't know how to turn it. Should she go more slowly, try to gain her trust first? Or just forge ahead? That's what she wanted to do—jump right in and pull the answers from Sallie's mouth, force the truth from her locked-up mind. But she sensed she'd lose any chance at answers if she pushed too hard.

"How are you being treated here, Sallie? Is there anything we can do for you?"

"They leave me alone, the other women. They don't bother me."

"Is that the way you want it?"

No answer.

"How do you keep busy?"

No answer.

"Do you have a job here?"

"In the kitchen—that's what I do. I clean up the dishes."

"You worked in a restaurant before—before you came here, right?"

"I shouldn't of worked. A mother should be home with her baby. If I'd been home with Angelina, I could of taken care of her. It's his fault. He made me go to work."

"Do you mean George?" Dani asked. She was just trying to make conversation now.

Sallie nodded.

Dani understood her conflict. Doug had pushed her to go back to work when Jonah was seven. "Did George do something to Angelina while you were at work? Did he abuse her?"

Sallie shook her head. At the risk of the guard's barging into the room and pulling them apart, Dani took Sallie's hands in hers. Physical contact was frowned on, but this woman seated across from her seemed to be in desperate need of someone to care about her.

"I know how hard it is for you to talk about Angelina, but it's very important for us to know what happened. Can you tell me? Can you tell us what happened to Angelina?"

"She's gone."

"Gone where?"

"I don't know."

The answer Dani had hoped to find, the reason she had taken on the case, seemed just as elusive now as it had yesterday in New York. If the dead child found in the Indiana woods was not George and Sallie's daughter, what had happened to her? "You testified at George's trial that he beat Angelina, that he killed her and disposed of her body. Is that what happened?"

For the first time, Sallie displayed agitation. "Didn't I say what I was supposed to say? Didn't I do it right? Am I going to be hanged too?" she asked with a plaintive wail.

Dani squeezed Sallie's hand. "No one's going to hurt you. Did someone tell you to say those things? It's okay to talk about it."

Sallie buried her face in her hands and her body heaved with deep sobs. It took only a few minutes for her cries to subside, but it felt much longer.

When she calmed down, Dani asked again. "Please, Sallie, tell me what happened."

"George made me do it."

"Made you do what, Sallie?"

Sallie didn't answer. She wrapped her arms around her body and began swaying back and forth.

"Did George make you hurt Angelina?"

A nod.

"How, Sallie? How did you hurt her?"

"I didn't stop him."

"Stop him from doing what? What did you watch George do?"

Sallie continued swaying. Her lips were clenched shut, as if she were fighting to keep the words locked inside her.

Dani put her hand on Sallie's arm, a gesture she hoped would comfort Sallie. "Did George kill your daughter?" she asked quietly.

Sallie stopped her swaying and stared into space. Then, as she slowly rose from her chair, she said, "We both killed our daughter. That's what happened. We killed our daughter." She turned and walked to the door that led to the prison cells and knocked. One last time she turned to face Dani. Her eyes were dry and her mouth set. "I don't want to talk about it anymore. Do you understand? I can't talk about it. George is in hell, and I'm in hell, and we both belong there."

With that, the guard opened the door and Sallie, their best hope, walked away.

The Holiday Inn was like every other Holiday Inn Dani had stayed in: clean and simple. No luxury towels or perfumed bath soaps or terry-cloth bathrobe in the closet. Before Jonah had arrived, she and Doug stayed in hotels with all the extra touches. Travel was their reward for hard work fifty weeks of the year. Those days were gone. Now, on the rare occasions when they traveled, they headed to kid-friendly destinations: Disney World, Lake George in upstate New York, or Montauk Point at the tip of Long Island. They'd gone camping a few times with Jonah, as well. But no luxury hotels anymore.

Dani took the elevator to the lobby and headed to the hotel bar. She spotted Tommy and Melanie and slid into a seat at their table. They hadn't discussed the interview with Sallie since leaving the prison. Dani usually preferred to let an interview rumble around in her head and settle into place before discussing it.

"What are you guys drinking?"

"Apple martini," Melanie said. Tommy just held up his glass. He always drank scotch and water.

"Any good?" she asked Melanie.

"Decent."

Dani followed her lead and ordered the same. "So, is she crazy or sane?"

"Calhoun's lawyer never pushed for a psych evaluation of her," Melanie said.

"And there's been no need to do one since. I spoke to the assistant warden. She's a decent prisoner. Keeps to herself most of the time. She does her work, doesn't cause any trouble, so she pretty much flies under the radar."

"She seemed pretty emphatic this afternoon that they both killed their daughter," Tommy said.

"That's not what she said in her testimony. There she said she stood by and watched George kill Angelina," Melanie said.

Heading up this investigation was new turf for Dani. Before, the facts had been handed to her and she stirred them up into a legal argument. For it to be a winning argument, though, she had to analyze the facts, something she excelled at. Her analysis of the facts so far didn't add up. "You're right, Melanie. When they questioned her at her home, she said, 'We killed her.' Her story changed when she testified at George's trial. Now she's back to her original statement: 'We killed her.' But she said something else today that throws everything in her testimony into question. Remember when she asked if she'd said what she was supposed to say? If she'd done it right?"

Tommy shook his head. "Let's go over it again. The police knocked on her door, asked questions, and she fingers herself and her husband. I assume they took her down to the station, she went over the details, and she realizes she's in big trouble. She figures they'll go easier on her if she was just a watcher, so her story changes. Then they ask her to do it again for the trial. Don't you think that's what she was referring to, doing it right at the trial?"

"It could be that. Or maybe she was told to say something different."

Melanie looked puzzled. "Why would the prosecutor have her change her story? Her immediate confession was enough to convict George. How would it help them if she'd only been a bystander?"

"I don't know. But if the police or the prosecutor asked her to change her story, there must be a reason. Maybe her version didn't match the details of the crime, so they fed her a story. It certainly wouldn't be the first time that happened."

They sipped their drinks silently for a moment. Before flying to Indianapolis, Dani had held on to a slim hope that they'd know after interviewing Sallie whether her version of the events was real or a delusion. Instead, the truth seemed even more distant.

The clouds had drifted away and Dani rummaged through her pocketbook for her sunglasses. They headed north on Interstate 65 to Michigan City, less than three hours away. Melanie drove while Tommy continued to track down leads with his cell phone and Dani studied the file. They hadn't advanced any further in their understanding of the case since finishing dinner last night. Today they'd meet first with Warden Coates and then with their client. They traveled in silence, all of them aware of the limited time and the stakes at hand.

As they drove, the realization struck Dani that never before had she met with a death-row inmate in a case where the decision for HIPP to represent him resided with her. She must decide whether she believed in his innocence. She must decide whether he got one more chance to try to escape the sentence he'd lived with for seventeen years. The heaviness of this responsibility weighed on her, and she wondered if she'd made the right choice in her career path. As an associate editor of the *Harvard Law Review*, graduating with honors, she could have gone anywhere. She'd been handed offers on silver platters, from obscenely well-paying positions with white-glove Wall Street firms to federal judicial clerkships with some of the brightest legal minds on the bench. She'd chosen the US Attorney's Office. Assistant US attorney for the Southern District of New York. That's where she met Doug. Those were heady days while they lasted, but then Jonah came along. They could have turned him over to day care and kept going in the fast lane, but really, they couldn't. Not after his diagnosis. Jonah deserved his chance in life, whatever that might be, and they both wanted to make sure he got it. Dani dropped out of law for about seven years, and Doug accepted an associate-professor position at

Columbia Law School. And four years ago she'd signed on with HIPP. Now that Doug taught criminal law, specializing in death-penalty law, she guessed you could say she practiced and he preached. A bad lecture didn't condemn a prisoner to a lethal injection, but she didn't have it so easy. If she couldn't sort through the facts and figure out what really happened, her client would die. And that scared her.

The state's case relied on two witnesses. If Sallie's confession could be discredited, there was still the gas station owner's identification of George and his car. Although eyewitness testimony often made jurors comfortable with returning a guilty verdict, it was notoriously unreliable. Dani leafed through the trial transcript again, looking for errors to form the basis for appeal. She knew she'd find them. Ineffective assistance of counsel would top the list. Bob Wilson could have been asleep at trial and he'd have done a better job. And because he represented George on his appeals, he certainly hadn't raised his own inadequacy as a reason to overturn the jury verdict. Until four or five years ago, they wouldn't have been able to attack the verdict and sentence on grounds of ineffective counsel. Unless raised in the first appeal, that defense was gone. Thankfully, the Supreme Court had recognized that when the trial lawyer handled the direct appeal, he wouldn't claim he'd been ineffective.

Dani turned toward the backseat and saw Tommy, lost in his laptop. "Hey, can you add to your to-do list a checkup of George's lawyer? Let's see if there's any dirt on him." Tommy nodded without looking up from his screen.

They spent the rest of the trip in silence.

"Thank you for meeting with us, Warden Coates." They were all seated in front of the warden's immaculate mahogany desk in a room large enough to house the entire HIPP staff. Bars covered the three large windows overlooking the prison yard, but sheer white curtains draped over them softened the effect. A uniformed man stood guard in the corner, silent, although his very presence shouted loudly that they were in a prison facility. The warden looked younger than most, perhaps pushing forty, with dark-brown hair free of graying wisps. His handshake had been strong enough to hurt the beginning arthritis in Dani's fingers. "So," Dani continued, "as you know, we're looking into an appeal for George Calhoun. You were very helpful when we spoke on the phone last week, but I wonder if there's anything else you can tell us about Mr. Calhoun?"

"Such as?"

"Well, you mentioned that he's always maintained his innocence. How does that come up here?"

"You have to understand, prisoners on death row are kept separate from the rest of the men. Except for about thirty minutes each day, they're in their cells alone. They don't even get much chance to talk to each other."

"I'm confused," Dani said.

"Well, I'm getting to that. See, everyone needs to talk, whether it's to the chaplain or often to the guards. Otherwise they'd go crazy. Lots of convicts boast about their misdeeds. Others blather on and on about being railroaded. George never says much one way or the other. But he's gotten close to one of the guards. George doesn't talk much about his daughter, but after every visit with his lawyer, he'd storm back to his cell shaking his head and complaining to the guard about his lawyer not believing him. And then he'd say he'd never hurt a hair on his precious daughter's head, never had and never would. You can take that for what it's worth, which isn't much in a prison. But like I told you before, when it comes to killing a man, I like to be sure we got the right person."

Dani didn't know if a warden with a conscience was hard to find or typical nowadays, but whatever the case, Warden Coates had an open mind. "Has George ever had a psych consult here?"

"Nope. No need to."

"So, no evidence of delusional thinking?"

"Seems lucid every encounter I've had with him. In fact, most of the men facing death here seem like coiled snakes, ready to attack. It's not a stretch to picture them murdering someone. Not so with George. He's always been calm, almost serene. Whatever he's done, he's at peace with it."

"As far as you know, has he ever told anyone what happened to his daughter?"

"Other than those times he's upset about his lawyer, he never talks about her."

There it was again—the one piece of the puzzle that didn't seem to fit anywhere. George had been steadfast that the child found in the woods was not his daughter. Yet with a lethal injection awaiting him in little more than a month, he still hadn't offered any explanation for Angelina's disappearance. No matter how powerful a legal argument she could make that he hadn't received a fair trial, she hoped, for a whole litany of reasons, it would come down to that one question: What happened to Angelina Calhoun? They weren't going to get that answer today. The warden had informed them when they arrived that George, fighting off a bout of pneumonia, had been removed to the medical wing. It could be a few days before they'd be able to meet with him. Dani figured they'd use that time to meet with Bob Wilson and try to track down the couple whose daughter disappeared around the same time. She couldn't shake her concern, though. George had reached out to HIPP, so she guessed he wanted to be saved. But did he want it enough to give them answers?

"I miss you."

"Isn't Gracie a good enough substitute for me?"

Doug laughed, and the sound of it rushed through Dani's body, briefly lightening the feeling of apprehension that had filled her these past few days. "Not even close."

"How's Jonah doing?" She felt torn. She wanted Doug to answer that her son missed her terribly, that his world had fallen apart without her. But she knew it was better for Jonah that he didn't.

"Katie is spoiling him rotten, so he's quite happy. By the way, the camp application came in the mail today."

It was an application for music camp. Camp Adagio, in the Green Mountains of Vermont, served children with Williams syndrome. Jonah had played piano since the age of three. It had begun with the typical toddler's toy keyboard. Instead of plunking random keys, he quickly began to mimic melodies he heard on the radio. By five, he'd graduated to a professional keyboard, and a year later they bought a used upright for him. Two years ago, he'd begun composing piano concertos.

Williams syndrome children often had a great passion for music. Some expressed it through singing; others, through playing musical instruments; and still others, through composing music. Many were considered musical prodigies, and most had such an acute perception of sound that they could hear tiny deviations in pitch.

"Are we really sure he's ready to be away for a whole month?"

"Dani, we've gone over this a hundred times. He's ready. It'll be good for him."

"He's growing up so fast. I know he'll always need us, but going away for a month makes it feel like he'll need us less."

"And isn't that a good thing?"

"Yes—of course."

"How're the interviews going?" Doug was a master of redirection when she felt sorry for herself.

"Unproductive so far. And we hit a roadblock today. George is sick and we can't see him until his fever breaks. Hopefully, that won't be more than a day or two, but it does set us back."

"So what happens in the meantime?"

"I planned to wait until after we see George to meet with his trial counsel, but I think I'll take a ride over there tomorrow."

"Well, good luck with that. And hurry up home. Even if Jonah doesn't need you, I still do."

No, she thought as she hung up. Doug might want her, but right now it was George who needed her.

Tommy searched through the mini-bar in his hotel room for a shot of scotch. With none in sight, he settled for a Coors, twisted off the cap, and sank into the cushioned vinyl chair in front of his desk. Dani worried him. Before even talking to George, she'd already thought him innocent. And that was bad. Most of the men on death row were guilty and deserved to die. Although he understood that it was important to make sure a mistake hadn't been made, you needed to investigate with a clean slate. At this stage, the presumption of innocence was crap. As far as he was concerned, presume guilt and search for any evidence otherwise. This was Dani's first investigation, and her inexperience showed. At least to him. She was smart, all right. When the evidence showed that an inmate was innocent, no one did a better job of marshaling the facts into a top-notch brief. And he'd watched her argue cases before appellate courts—even the Supreme Court. Damn, she was persuasive, looking like a fox but sounding like a tiger.

Sallie may have mixed up her story along the way, but it always came back to the same culprit: George. Maybe she'd taken part; maybe not. That didn't matter. It was George who was being readied for execution,

George who was their client. And so far it looked like the jury had gotten it right. Still, he needed to check out every lead, no matter how far fetched. He picked up the phone and dialed.

"Hammond Police Department. How can I direct your call?"

"Is Detective Hank Cannon in?" Tommy waited several minutes before he heard a loud raspy voice answer.

"Cannon here."

"Detective Cannon, my name is Tom Noorland. Jimmy Velasquez said you could help me."

"How do you know Jimmy?"

"We worked together at the Bureau back in the '90s. I'm retired now, working with the Help Innocent Prisoners Project in New York."

"Got to be pretty slow work for you. I don't know many innocent prisoners."

Tommy laughed. "I'm with you there. But this one's got a needle waiting for him in five weeks. We just want to make sure he deserves it."

"Didn't a jury already decide that?"

"C'mon, detective. You know sometimes they slip up. Most of the time it's letting a bad guy off. Once in a while it's the other way around. Nothing's perfect."

"What do you need from me?"

"You investigated a missing-child case back in '90. Name of Conklin, Stacy Conklin. Do you remember that?"

Tommy could hear a sigh at the other end of the line, then silence. He took another swig of Coors and waited. When the voice at the other end next spoke, it was more subdued.

"You know how some cases just stick with you? You work them and work them, and no matter how hard you look, you just get nowhere? That's Stacy Conklin. It's buried in the department as an unsolved case, but it's not buried in my head. I wish it was. I got just two years left till retirement, and I sure don't want to spend my days wondering about what happened to her."

"Were there any leads? Any witnesses still around?"

"No. She disappeared from her bed in the middle of the night. The parents were asleep, and when they woke up, she was gone. No fingerprints, no sign of forced entry, but it was summer and the bedroom windows were open. We got a list of people who'd been around their house, but nothing panned out."

"And the parents themselves—they checked out?"

"Well, they were pretty hysterical when it happened. Anyone seeing them could tell it had hit them hard. They weren't putting on a show, if you know what I mean. When that body turned up right next door, in Indiana, we took the parents in for an ID. Seeing that burned body of a little girl near killed them. The mother couldn't even look at her. I stood right next to them. Thankfully, it wasn't their daughter."

"How could they be sure, with the body so badly burned?"

"Different size, different weight. And some hair was still left. It wasn't the same shade as their daughter's."

There was no reason to think the Hammond police force hadn't done its job right, especially considering Detective Cannon's zeal for closure on the case before he retired. Tommy decided to press further anyway. "Was any forensic testing done to confirm she wasn't their daughter?"

"Like DNA?"

"Yeah, like DNA. Anyone compare the victim's DNA to the Conklins'?"

"You gotta to remember, this was back in '90. DNA testing wasn't routine then."

Tommy didn't want to risk alienating Cannon. He'd need his help if this were a thread worth pursuing. "Okay, I keep forgetting that."

"Why are you asking about Stacy, anyway? Do you have some information about her?"

"Nope. Just checking all loose ends for a guy on death row. By the way, do you know where the parents are living now?"

"Sure. Same house they were in when Stacy was taken. I tell you, I wouldn't have stayed there. I still keep in touch with them. Nice couple. They never got over their daughter, though. Never had any more kids."

Tommy thanked the detective for his help. Nothing for nothing, he thought to himself as he hung up.

A loud knock at the door awakened her. "Housekeeping," Dani heard someone say. She'd done it again—forgotten to put up the "Do Not Disturb" sign. The clock on the nightstand read 8:15. She tumbled out of bed, opened the door to the hallway and asked the woman on the other side to come back later.

She'd needed to be awakened anyway. Melanie and Tommy were meeting her in the lobby at nine for the hotel's continental breakfast. She quickly showered, got dressed, and headed downstairs. They were already waiting for her at a small table. She grabbed a muffin and a cup of coffee and joined them.

"Hear from the warden yet?" Melanie asked.

"Yeah, I just spoke to him. Calhoun's still in the infirmary but getting better. We'll probably get to see him tomorrow."

"I reached Detective Cannon last night," Tommy said.

"And?" Dani and Melanie said in unison.

Tommy filled them in on his conversation with Cannon.

"Is there any way we can get a DNA sample from the Conklins?" Melanie asked.

"Hold your horses," Tommy said. "Just because they have a daughter who disappeared around the same time as Angelina doesn't mean the child buried in that grave is theirs."

"But all the other children who disappeared then are accounted for."

"Only the children whose disappearances were reported. That doesn't give the full picture. Say a set of parents murdered their kid during that time frame. They obviously wouldn't have reported it to the authorities and so she wouldn't be in the FBI database. Even if the dead child isn't Angelina—and that's a big if—it could be anyone."

"Still," Dani said, "it would be helpful if we could figure out how to get a DNA sample from the Conklins. Even if it's just to rule them out."

"Don't forget the victim," Tommy said. "Who knows whether there's anything in the evidence kit that we could get a DNA sample from. Or if they even still have the evidence kit. Without the child's DNA, we've got nothing to match it with."

"Isn't it standard to hold on to that evidence?" Melanie asked.

"Maybe not in 1990."

"We're getting ahead of ourselves, guys," Dani said. "We know from George's lawyer's file that no DNA testing was done on the victim or the Calhouns. That may be because they had a confession from Sallie or because DNA just wasn't part of their arsenal back then. But if there's an evidence kit that contains something with the child's DNA, we need to find out fast. We could run it against George's DNA and see if it's a match. Tommy, can you call the police station in LaGrange, see what they still have?"

"I'll get on that."

Dani took a bite of her muffin and washed it down with a swig of coffee. "And also, Tommy, do you think the detective in Hammond would introduce you to the Conklins?"

"My guess is he would. If there's any possibility the child in the woods was Stacy and not Angelina, he'd want to know."

"Okay. Work with him on that."

"What are you thinking? That the Conklins may have been responsible for their daughter's death?"

"Frankly, it doesn't matter to us if they are or aren't. If we can show that the child isn't Angelina Calhoun, then we get a new trial for George, if not outright dismissal. But if it is Stacy, her parents' insistence that the victim wasn't their daughter certainly raises suspicion."

Melanie shook her head. "If I were looking at a burned corpse, I'd want to believe it wasn't my child. I'd want to protect myself from imagining the pain my daughter experienced."

Dani looked around the breakfast room. Groups of families were sitting at tables, some chatting quietly, others visibly irritated by their children's whining demands. *How would it feel if that whining child were taken from you, never to be seen again? God, the agonizing recriminations you'd put yourself through: Was it my carelessness? Could I have done more to protect my child?* She could understand a parent viewing a body in the sterile room of the medical examiner and proclaiming, "No! That can't be my child! I won't permit it to be my child!" Melanie was right; self-protection created a very strong armor.

"Tommy, I think you should drive over to Hammond and have a chat with the detective."

"Consider it done."

With the day clear for her, Dani decided to visit Bob Wilson. She drove toward LaGrange in another rental car, this time a subcompact, the least expensive. Tommy took the original rental to Hammond, Illinois, in the opposite direction.

She hated driving in strange cities with no satellite radio, only unfamiliar stations. She hated country music, which inevitably was the only music she could find on the dial outside New York. But she also hated driving without music; the silence unnerved her.

Meeting the attorney who had handled the trial of a death-row inmate usually made for an uncomfortable situation. Most were defensive. Some started out cooperatively, but when the investigating attorney dug in deeper, they retreated into familiar justifications for the jury verdict. The worst was the one Dani had gotten from Wilson: His client was guilty.

She pulled up to Wilson's address and found just what she'd expected: a storefront on a back street, with a peeling sign out front and worn furniture inside. Small-town defense attorneys usually weren't well paid for their efforts. After introducing herself, his secretary pointed her toward an office down the hall. "Go on back, dear. He's expecting you. Just knock on the door."

Dani entered and they exchanged pleasantries. Wilson appeared to be in his late fifties or early sixties. He had on a light-gray suit, although his jacket was draped over a hanger on the back of his office door. Despite the deep crease lines in his face, he carried the reminder of someone who'd been attractive in his youth. His office was no different from the reception area, perhaps even more shopworn. A large walnut desk was littered with files, and a nearby wastebasket overflowed. Other than a diploma from Indiana University School of Law, the white walls were bare. Dani got down to business. "Bob, is there anything about this case I should be aware of that's not in the files?"

"No," he answered quickly. "It's all there."

"So, no one attempted to identify the child in the woods, other than by Sallie's confession?"

"Well, they couldn't do a run for finger- or footprints. The body was too badly burned."

"And no DNA?"

"Keep in mind defense attorneys didn't usually do DNA testing back then. And what'd be the point? Sallie said it was her daughter."

"But George insisted it wasn't."

Wilson leaned back in his chair and looked her over. "Sweetie, you big-city, ivy-towered lawyers think money grows on trees," he said with a smirk. "It costs big bucks for DNA testing, especially back then. When you do criminal-defense work, you get a sixth sense. You know when a client is hustling you and you know when they're laying it all out. George was no innocent—I knew that right away. No point in throwing money away chasing dead ends. Sallie said that was their daughter, and no matter what any testing showed, the jury damn sure would believe her."

Dani felt her anger rise. She wanted to throttle Wilson's neck and shout, *You were representing a man facing death. How dare you decide to give up on him? How dare you take his case if you weren't going to do everything within your power to find the truth? How dare you practice criminal law, you worthless excuse for an attorney?* Instead, she asked calmly, "Did you believe Sallie told the truth?"

"Well, I admit, she was harder to read. She couldn't manage a sentence without bawling. But I had no reason to disbelieve her."

"How about her mental processes? Did you try to have a psych evaluation done on her?"

"I keep telling you, these things cost money. I didn't receive a whole lot of money for representing him, and he didn't qualify for pauper status, so the court wasn't giving away money for all these tests you think should have been done."

"Tell me, then, if you were so convinced of George's guilt, why didn't you encourage him to take a plea?"

Wilson got up from his chair and looked out the window. After a moment, he turned back to Dani. The belligerence was gone from his voice when he answered. "I'd have got down on my knees and begged him to take a plea if that would've done any good. The D.A. offered life, no parole; took death off the table. But George wouldn't hear of it. He sounded like a broken record, saying he didn't kill that girl. Seemed to me that he had a death wish, the way he insisted on going to trial."

Dani hesitated to come across as too condemnatory of Wilson—he had too much knowledge of the case for her to dismiss his value. But she had hard questions about his handling of the case. "I was surprised you put George on the stand, especially since you thought he was guilty. Did you think he was going to offer the jurors an explanation for his missing daughter?"

Wilson shook his head. "I knew he'd be a disaster. Didn't matter how many times I told him he was putting the noose around his own neck if he took the stand. He just kept insisting he had to tell the jury he wasn't a murderer. Finally I gave in. I figured he was going down anyway. Might as well let him have his say."

Dani wondered what it felt like to represent a man facing death when you believed he was guilty. She practiced in a rarefied world—HIPP represented a last-ditch hope for condemned men and women. If HIPP lawyers didn't believe in their clients' innocence, they walked away. Dani had never faced arguing on behalf of someone whose innocence she doubted. Defense attorneys were a different breed. Some were true idealists who viewed themselves as crusaders upholding the sacred tenet that everyone had a right to counsel; others started out as prosecutors and used the skills they learned to open a practice defending accused criminals. And a few—a very few, she hoped—just wanted to get through the day earning a buck. Wilson struck her as one of those.

"Isn't it surprising for a guilty man to risk trial when his life is on the line?"

"Not in my experience. Some of these criminals are so deluded, they convince themselves they didn't do the crime, even when they're caught red-handed."

Dani flashed back to a three-year-old Jonah, standing on a chair, his hand holding a cookie he'd just retrieved from the kitchen cabinet. "Jonah no take cookie," he'd said when confronted by his mother, a look of total innocence on his face. Dani appreciated that Wilson's assessment of some criminals was true. She switched to another line of questions. "You didn't cross-examine Sallie for very long. How come?"

"I could see the jurors were believing her. A lot more than they were going to believe George. No sense in giving her more time to get their sympathy."

"But still, you could have tried to impeach her. The state didn't have any forensic evidence tying George to the victim, only Sallie's testimony."

"You forget the gas station attendant."

"His testimony was questionable at best. And you did a good job showing that to the jury."

Wilson chuckled. "Look, don't waste your time trying to butter me up. It's no secret you'll argue ineffective counsel. My feelings won't be hurt. I doubt it'll get George a new trial, but you go ahead and try."

Whether HIPP would even take the case was still to be decided. Even if Dani believed George's claim of innocence, she would have to evaluate her chance of succeeding. Wilson was right—getting a new trial this close to a scheduled execution would be tough.

They talked some more, going over details of the trial and the appeals. Dani thanked Wilson for his help and gathered her notes to leave. On her way out the door, she turned back to him. "And you're certain neither George nor Sallie ever explained what happened to their daughter, to Angelina?"

Wilson closed his eyes and rubbed them with balled-up fists. When he opened his eyes, they looked tired, worn out by years of eking out a living representing society's outcasts. "Not once before trial. Not even during the appeals. Only later, much later, about five or six years ago—I think maybe when I worked on his last grab to the Supreme Court— George wrote me. Made up some cockeyed story about his daughter being sick and then rambled on about no one helping her. It was bunk—a desperate grab at reversing his fate. I threw the letter away."

The shock on Dani's face must have been apparent. "You didn't follow up on his letter?"

"What for? Some prisoner probably helped him come up with the story. You wouldn't believe how creative they get in there. Liars, all of them. There was no point in wasting my time anymore."

"But what if it was true?"

"Then he would have told me when it mattered."

Wilson may not have been a bad attorney. He was certainly not a stupid attorney. Dani didn't really know him, but she guessed he wasn't even a lazy attorney. Plenty of all three types were defending clients in courts all over the United States. Wilson's problem was not being paid enough by a client he believed was guilty—a toxic combination for a defendant facing the death penalty.

T ommy kept the speedometer at just under fifteen miles over the speed limit. He knew from experience it was the safety zone, the gap between the speed posted as the maximum and the point at which he might be ticketed if he had the bad luck to pass a traffic cop. He arrived at the Hammond police station in just under two hours, and Hank Cannon was waiting for him.

"I don't know that there's much more I can tell you," Cannon said. "I pretty much covered it on the phone yesterday."

"Well, I don't expect to come away with anything more by coming here. But our interview with Calhoun has been pushed back a day, and I never had the patience to sit on my ass, so I figured if nothing else, I'll get to meet Jimmy's friend."

A big smile broke out on Cannon's face as he swung his arm over Tommy's shoulder. "Yeah, I bet we could share some pretty wild stories about Jimmy. C'mon into my office."

Tommy followed Cannon down the hallway. The once-stark white paint on the walls was now a dingy gray and peeling at the corners. The industrial carpet underfoot was well worn.

The mixture of voices, ringing telephones, and keyboard typing created a familiar hum, and a wave of nostalgia for his FBI days washed over Tommy.

Cannon brought him into a large open space filled with desks and a row of three rooms at the far end. "This here's my office," Cannon said as he pointed to one of the twenty or so desks in the room. "Take a load off your feet." Cannon dropped himself into the chair behind his desk and waited for Tommy to get comfortable in the plastic chair beside it.

"So, what's this visit really about? I could jaw all day about Jimmy, and I'm sure we'd yuk it up, but I don't believe you drove out here just for the heck of it."

"Nah, you're right. I just got to thinking maybe you wouldn't mind taking me to meet Stacy's parents."

Cannon stared silently at Tommy for a moment. "You thinking I got too close to them and overlooked some key evidence?"

"No, nothing like that. It's just, sometimes a fresh pair of eyes can't hurt. I don't expect it's their daughter they found in Indiana back in '90. But if it was, wouldn't they want to know?"

"And just how do you think meeting the Conklins will help you find out whether it was Stacy buried in those woods?"

"Look, I'm trying to be straight with you. I'm kind of hoping the Conklins held on to something of Stacy's. Maybe a comb or hairbrush. Maybe her favorite doll might have some of her stray hairs. Then we could compare it to any DNA left in the evidence kit over in LaGrange."

"LaGrange?"

"Yeah, that's the precinct that grabbed the case of the kid found in the woods, over by Orland."

"So they have DNA from the kid?"

Tommy shifted his eyes downward. "I haven't talked to them, but I'm figuring they've got to. I mean, don't they always in a murder case?"

"Maybe you guys at the Bureau routinely kept DNA evidence back in '90, but us local guys, it wasn't necessarily on our radar. Don't you think you should check with LaGrange before we go bothering the Conklins?"

Tommy gave Cannon his warmest smile. "You know, I'm here now. It's a beautiful day outside. This'll give us an excuse to get out of the office. Besides, maybe the Conklins will be encouraged to know someone else is trying to find out what happened to Stacy."

Cannon eyed Tommy quizzically. "You sure you're not trying to pin this rap on the Conklins? 'Cause if you are, I'll tell you right now you're off in left field. No way, no how."

"Relax. I'm not thinking they did this. I'm not even saying our guy didn't do it. All I know is, Calhoun insists the girl in the woods wasn't his daughter. I haven't even met him yet. When I do, maybe I'll come away thinking he's full of crap and he's going to get exactly what he deserves. Frankly, that's what I expect will happen. But in the meantime, I just want to be thorough. If there's even a small chance that Calhoun is telling the truth and the girl in the woods wasn't his daughter, she has to be somebody else. Maybe that somebody is Stacy Conklin. If I were her parents, I'd want the person responsible for putting her there to rot in hell for it. And the one thing I'm sure of is that George Calhoun didn't murder Stacy Conklin."

"The Conklins eyeballed that little girl's body. It wasn't Stacy."

"From what I've read, the burns were pretty extensive. They could've been wrong. I mean, if it were my daughter, I'd want to believe it wasn't her."

Cannon shrugged. "I think this is a wild goose chase, but I don't have anything pressing today. Let's give it a go."

Thirty minutes later, Tommy shook the hand of Mickey Conklin. The man's grip was as strong as he looked. A bodybuilder, Tommy thought to himself as he eyed the muscles bulging against Mickey's tight-fitted cotton sweater. Janine Conklin stood by his side, her arms crossed in front of her slim body.

"Thanks for seeing us," Cannon said after introductions were made. "I promise we won't take up much of your time. How've you folks been doing? It's been a while since we last talked."

Janine stood impassively at the front door, in contrast with Mickey, who rocked back and forth on the balls of his feet. "We're good, good. Right, Janine?" Mickey said, the words tumbling quickly from his mouth as he eyed Tommy.

"Would it be all right if we came in for a bit?" Cannon asked.

"Sure, of course; pardon my manners, Hank. It's just that we weren't expecting you," Janine said and stepped aside for the two men to enter her home.

"Please, make yourself comfortable," Janine continued as she motioned toward the couch. "Can I get you something to drink? There's a fresh pot of coffee made."

"Love some, Janine. Thanks. The usual way," Cannon said.

Tommy shook his head. "None for me."

As Janine left the living room, Tommy turned to Mickey. "Detective Cannon has told me about your daughter's disappearance. My sympathies to you and your wife."

Mickey nodded silently.

"Would you mind showing me the room she was taken from?"

"What business is it of yours?" Mickey asked.

"Sorry, I'm getting ahead of myself. I represent a man who's about to get the needle for murdering his daughter. When the body was discovered, there'd been some thought it might have been Stacy, and you were brought in for a possible ID. You said it wasn't her. I'm just doubling back to make sure that's the case."

Tommy saw Mickey's back stiffen. "Don't you think I'd know my own daughter?"

"I think that any father would want to believe it wasn't his daughter who'd been murdered and set on fire," Tommy said, his voice soft. "And I think the mind can trick us into seeing what we want to see."

"I know what I saw. I know it wasn't Stacy."

"What do you want from us?" Janine stood in the doorway, a cup of coffee in each hand. "Haven't we been through enough?"

"I don't want to cause you any suffering, Mrs. Conklin. I just thought maybe something remained in Stacy's room that had a strand of her hair. That way we could know for sure that it wasn't her."

A gurgled sob came from Janine's throat as she turned and retreated into the kitchen.

Mickey stood up. "Look, there's nothing left in Stacy's room. It's our office now. We threw away anything of hers years ago. I think you'd better leave now."

Tommy and Cannon stood and walked to the front door. "I know this is unpleasant. But if it is Stacy, wouldn't you want her killer found? Wouldn't you want him put away?"

"No," Mickey said. "I just want our nightmare to be over."

It had been three days since Dani flew to Indiana and she already missed home. How could Jonah possibly handle being away from his family for four weeks when she'd been away from him and Doug only a few days and yet even now felt the tugging of an addict going through withdrawal? She'd forgotten about the teenage urge for independence that she'd felt herself when she became a mother, the one left at home to worry about the dangers lurking in the shadows. As a child, she'd thought she was indestructible. No harm could befall her, no illness could overtake her, no risk was too great. How sad that everyone learned, as they grew up, that they were as vulnerable as the neighbor hit by a car or the grandparent who succumbed to a lingering illness or the friend's parent who underwent chemotherapy for breast cancer and then died anyway. There were times when she longed for that dreamy ignorance, that certitude that she would live forever, that nothing could sabotage her happiness. No wonder she wished to protect Jonah from growing up too fast and learning that nothing was certain. A chance happening, be it illness, accident, a careless decision, or an extra chromosome, could change one's life forever.

Despite her longing for home, Dani felt tingly with excitement—today they'd sit down with George Calhoun for the first time. She didn't know what to expect. There was nothing ambiguous in Bob Wilson's assessment of George. Yet something was missing, something unexplained that only George could answer. Whether he would provide the answer was still unknown.

She met Melanie and Tommy for breakfast in the hotel lobby. Again she poured herself a cup of coffee, picked out a plump blueberry muffin, and settled into the plastic chair at a table in the corner.

Dani finished describing her conversation with Bob Wilson and then turned to Tommy. "Did you speak to the police in LaGrange?"

"Yeah. I got one of the detectives originally on the case, back in '90."

"And?"

"And nothing. The evidence kit was pretty bare. There wasn't anything in it that contained DNA."

That surprised Dani. Despite the relative newness of DNA as an evidentiary tool at the time, she thought something would have been retained—a strand of hair, fingernail scrapings, a blood sample. "How'd it go with Cannon?"

"With my usual charm, I convinced Cannon to take me on a visit to the parents," Tommy said. "I hoped they might have kept something of their daughter's. You know, like maybe they still had her hairbrush. No luck. They cleaned everything out and turned her room into an office."

"Did you get to talk to the parents?"

Tommy nodded and took a bite of his bagel. "The dad insisted it wasn't Stacy. Maybe too insistent. Or maybe I'm just reading something from nothing."

With anyone else, it would be easy to dismiss Tommy's musing. But years of working undercover for the FBI had honed his already sharp instincts to razor-blade precision. If Tommy had questions about Mickey Conklin, Dani took it seriously. Whether they pursued that strand would depend on the outcome of their meeting with George.

***

As an appellate attorney, Dani had appeared in courthouses through-out the country but rarely ventured inside a maximum-security prison. Indiana State Prison, built during the Civil War to sequester prisoners of war, was considered one of the most dangerous prisons in the country. It had the appearance of a massive fortress, with im-posing walls and multiple checkpoints. At the first checkpoint, Dani, Melanie, and Tommy were frisked and their bags hand-checked before they were allowed to move to the next gate. One gate closed behind them before the next opened, and they passed through five gates before they were led to a small interview room. After a short wait, a guard brought in George Calhoun, his hands shackled behind him.

He looked different from what Dani had expected. She'd imagined George would resemble his wife: slightly built, with brown mousy hair and deeply recessed eyes. Instead, he was short but burly, with a muscled chest and forearms. His hair, a sandy-brown color, had probably been blond as a child. Unlike his wife with her receding posture, George seemed like a bull waiting to be released into the arena.

Dani didn't need to proceed slowly with him. She could see he wanted to tell his story. As soon as introductions were finished, Dani began with the question that had been unanswered for nineteen years. "George, tell me what happened to Angelina."

He tapped his foot on the floor. He didn't speak for a long time, and when he did he asked Dani, "Do you have any children?"

"I do. I have a son."

"Is there anything you wouldn't do for him?"

"I wouldn't kill for him," she answered quickly.

George nodded his head slowly. "That's fair." He leaned forward on the table. All motion had stopped. "There wasn't anything I wouldn't do for Angelina." The words were spit off his tongue like an accusation seeking its target.

Dani asked again. "What happened to your daughter?"

George sat up straight, his shoulders pulled back. "We did what we had to do. To help our little girl. So she'd have a chance."

"I don't understand."

"I expect most people wouldn't."

For a moment, Dani feared that they'd leave the prison as confused as they had been on leaving Sallie. If that happened, her decision would be clear: HIPP would decline to take his case. "George, please, I want to understand. I want to try and help you. The only way I can is if you tell me about Angelina."

George slumped in his chair, the belligerence sucked out of him like the air from a punctured tire. When he started to speak, in a voice soft but with firm resolve, he said, "We wanted a baby so bad. We tried and tried for so long."

"And then Angelina was born?"

"Yes, ma'am. But not before we'd been married a real long time. Sallie and me, we were just out of high school when we married. It wasn't like we had to, like some of our friends. We were just madly in love with each other. College wasn't something we'd planned on, so it just seemed to make sense to tie the knot. I mean, why wait? I'd been working on cars since I could hold a wrench in my hands. Every garage in town offered me a job. Sallie never was much of a student. She couldn't even type straight. But we hadn't figured on her working much anyway. Just a few years till we could save up some money for a down payment on a house, and then we'd try for a baby. Well, a few years turned into almost fifteen before Sallie got pregnant. We'd just about given up trying at that point." George stopped speaking and stared into space.

"You must have been thrilled when Angelina was born," Dani said, prompting him to continue.

"It was nothing short of a miracle—that's what we thought. I broke down and sobbed when I saw her the first time. I held that precious little girl in my arms and just wouldn't let go. I tell you, I'd never seen anything so beautiful." George stared at the table. Dani could see his hands, still handcuffed behind his back, squeezed tightly together. "It wasn't a miracle, we learned soon enough. Miracles are supposed to last, aren't they?"

Dani shrugged.

"Sallie, she'd been waitressing before the baby came. When we brought Angelina home, she up and quit that job, swore she'd never take another while she had our baby to care for."

Sallie had told Dani she'd worked after Angelina was born. Something had changed her mind. "Why did Sallie go back to work?"

"We had bills that needed to be paid. Doctor bills. Hospital bills. See, our precious Angelina got sick. Unless you have a sick child, you can't know how it feels. To watch your baby all weak and crying and you helpless to stop it."

Although life with Jonah had made Dani all too aware of that feeling of despair, she didn't want to interrupt George. Melanie took notes so nothing would distract Dani as she listened to him.

George looked up at Dani and she saw his eyes burn with a searing intensity. "Before it happened, before she got sick, we were never so happy. Every day I'd come home from work and Sallie would say to me, 'Look what Angelina did today,' and I'd see my baby roll herself over, and later sit up all by herself, and Sallie would have a great big grin on her face. When Angelina took her first step and didn't fall down, well, it was as if she'd walked on the moon or something, it seemed so incredible."

"And then she got sick?"

George nodded. "The doctor said she had to have chemotherapy. I knew how bad that was. My uncle, he had cancer in his lungs, from smoking too many cigarettes, I suppose. He got awfully sick from the chemotherapy and then he up and died anyway. But Angelina's doctor, he was hopeful."

"George, let's step back. Why did Angelina need chemotherapy?"

"She got leukemia."

Dani glanced at Melanie and saw she'd stopped taking notes. She suspected George's revelation had shaken Melanie as much as her. "I'm sorry, George. I'm truly sorry." Dani waited a moment. "When was she diagnosed with it?"

"Just after her second birthday. We had a little party for her, just us celebrating, but we had balloons all over the house and a big chocolate cake that Sallie baked. Couldn't have been more than a week later Sallie called me at work. And she's crying on the phone that Angelina is sick, she has a fever, a really high fever, like one hundred and four degrees. Now, our little girl, she'd been sick a lot, always getting colds and sniffles, but we didn't have health insurance. I'm just a mechanic, you know. So every time the baby got sick, we'd treat her at home, and she'd always get better. But she never had a fever that high before, and it scared Sallie, so we took her to the emergency room. The doctor, he said Angelina had an ear infection, and he gave Sallie medicine for the baby. But she didn't get better when she should have."

"Do you remember the doctor's name?"

George remained quiet for a moment. "I can't seem to bring it to mind. Everything else is so clear from that time, everything he said and all. I can picture what he looked like, but his name—it's just gone."

"Did you bring Angelina back to the doctor?"

"Yes, ma'am. About four or five days later I took a few hours off from work and we took Angelina back to that same doctor, and now he looked her all over, you know, more careful, and he saw these red spots on her skin. And he asked us a bunch a questions. 'Does she get tired easy? How's her appetite? Do you ever see her limp?' Things like that. And now we're getting scared, but the doctor said we shouldn't worry. He said he had to do some tests. Tests cost money, but it didn't matter, because nothing was more important to us than Angelina. Nothing. So the doctor took some blood from her arm and she kept screaming while Sallie held her, but we were thinking all this time, 'Please, God, don't let anything be wrong with our baby.' We said that over and over and just tried to close our ears to her screaming.

"Well, it didn't matter how much we prayed, because when we went back to the doctor, he said to us, 'Your daughter has leukemia.'" George stopped, took a deep breath, and dropped his head to his chest. They all waited silently for him to continue. When he looked up, his eyes were liquid pools of anguish. "Do you know what it feels like to be told your baby might die? Your precious baby that you waited fifteen years for and then comes to you as a gift from God?"

Dani did know what that felt like. When Jonah's doctor had told them that their child had a heart defect, that their five-year-old son needed surgery, that surgery always had risks, her own heart had stopped. It felt as if the walls of the room closed in on her, trapping her in a tiny space with no light or air. No parent should ever be faced with a child's life-threatening illness. No parent should ever be faced with the death of a child. It turned the natural order of the universe on its head.

She didn't tell George how deeply she empathized with his plight. Instead, she murmured, "I'm so sorry."

"We had no money and no insurance, so we signed some agreement to pay for the treatment over time. They put that stuff in her body—it was supposed to cure her—but I tell you, it was near impossible to watch what it did to our baby. She threw up day and night. Her poor little body could barely take it. By the second month, her beautiful blond hair fell out, and her mouth was full of sores. She cried all the time and there wasn't anything we could do for her."

"How long was she on the chemo?"

"Six months. And when it was all done, the doctor said she was fine. In remission, he called it. Her hair came back along with her smile, and everything seemed good again. But there were bills we owed. Big bills for her treatment, you know. I told Sallie she had to go back to work. She didn't want to. Leaving our baby with someone else—well, it just broke our hearts. There wasn't any choice, though. Sallie tried awfully hard to find a job with health insurance, but the only work she'd ever done was waitressing. She ended up taking a night job at the diner. That way she took care of Angelina during the day and I stayed home with her at night. We were so happy that next year." George stopped and smiled. "You see, God had given us back our little girl."

Once again Dani asked the question still unanswered. "I understand. Angelina was very sick and you both were very frightened. She got better, though. So what happened to her?"

George shook his head. "We just thought she was better. But the leukemia—it came back. Along about the time she was nearing her fourth birthday, Angelina started falling down a lot. We thought it was just growing pains—you know, they grow so fast, they're falling all over themselves. We weren't worried when we took her back to the doctor. That was stupid of us. It was like we got too cocky and had to get our comeuppance. The leukemia—it'd gone to her brain. The doctor said she had to start with that chemotherapy again. Radiation too. And a bone-marrow transplant—that's what she really needed. But we had to find some that matched. Sallie and I, we were both tested, but ours wasn't right for Angelina. We were still paying back the doctor for the first round, and now there'd be hospital bills too. The doctor said we shouldn't worry about him but that we had to come up with money for the hospital. He said they'd need proof we could pay before they'd treat her."

"Did you get the money for her treatment?"

"No, ma'am. We tried everything. We even went to the Medicaid office, but they said we earned too much money. Too much money! Can you believe that? We didn't have one extra cent in our pockets." George shook his head. "I asked you before if there was anything you wouldn't do for your child. Well, there's nothing I wouldn't of done for Angelina. She would die if she didn't get treatment. The doctor didn't come out and say that, but it was clear in his voice."

"Did Angelina die?" Dani asked softly.

"I don't know," George answered, his voice flat.

They were all puzzled, and for a moment Dani was at a loss for words. Finally, she once again asked the question she had begun with. "What happened to Angelina?"

"You have to understand. We were desperate. No hospital would treat her. I went to the library and read up on her illness. I read how bad it was when the cancer went to the brain. I read that the Mayo Clinic was the best, that their doctors were saving kids like mine. But they would want money too. So we drove, all of us, we drove to Minnesota. And we took all her medical records and all her tests and we blacked out all the names—Angelina's, the doctor, the hospital, even the laboratory—so no one could bring her back to us. We put it all in a pouch and tied it around her waist. And we put a letter in the pouch, not with our names or anything, not even Angelina's name, and we said in the letter that we were leaving our daughter with them, that they needed to fix her, make her better. We knew that if she didn't have parents, it wouldn't matter that she didn't have insurance. If she was all alone, they'd have to help her. Medicaid would pay for her because she'd have no income. We thought, they'll put her in a foster home, and then maybe if she got better, someone would adopt her. And we left her there, in the hospital, and told her we loved her, would always love her, but she had to wait there until someone came to help her. We told her no matter what, don't tell anyone your name. And then we walked away. We never saw her again."

Dani's head spun. How could a parent leave a child, only four years old, alone in a hospital? How agonizing it had to have been for George and Sallie, faced with a Hobson's choice of watching their child certainly die without treatment or abandoning their beloved daughter.

Could the story be true? Or was this a last-ditch effort to avoid a lethal injection? Watching the anguish on George's face made Dani believe his nightmare was real. But after seventeen years in prison, it was the first time he'd offered this explanation for his daughter's disappearance. "Why haven't you told anyone this before?" she asked. "You were on trial for murdering Angelina. You knew you were facing the death penalty. How could you not tell your lawyer? Or explain to the jury what you told us today?"

"Tell them what? That we left our daughter—sick and alone—and just walked away? My Sallie sure had a hard time accepting why we had to do that. I didn't expect any folks not in our shoes to understand. Especially if our baby had died there. And if she was getting treatment and doing okay? Well, then I was afraid if I told them where she was, they'd stop treating her. I couldn't take a chance on that. No matter what it meant for me. When I thought it was safe, when my telling couldn't harm her, I tried telling my lawyer. If she lived, she'd have been 18 then. They couldn't return her to us if she still needed treatment. My lawyer, he sure didn't believe me, but I guess I can't blame him."

"Couldn't you have pushed him, gotten him to pay attention?" Dani said.

George shook his head. "It wouldn't have mattered."

Dani realized he was right. By then, Wilson's mind had been closed to the possibility of his client's innocence.

"After the jury came back and they sent me here, I'd fall asleep every night thinking that my Angelina didn't die, that she was taken in by a nice family that loved her and had means to keep her healthy. How could I take her away from that? I told you I'd do anything for my child. And I meant it. I was willing to die so my little angel had a chance to live."

"And now? Why are you telling us now?"

"Because I need to know before I do. Before I die, I mean. I need to know if my baby is alive."

Impossible! That was the thought that kept running through her mind. From the beginning it had been impossible. What had possessed her to accept this case? No DNA remained in the police kit from the child in the woods. Why would it? The science had been so new that it was rarely used back then. She should have known the police wouldn't keep a strand of hair, a fingernail, anything that might have been used to show it wasn't Angelina Calhoun who had been found in the woods. If George had been honest with them, how would Dani ever be able to prove it? *Impossible!* It was too late to back out. The case was inside her now. She'd never be able to walk away without attempting to confirm what was true and what was a lie.

They walked in silence back to their hotel. A week ago, Dani had fervently hoped she'd get answers from Sallie or George. She'd imagined all sorts of explanations for Angelina's disappearance, all sorts of excuses for George's silence. But not this. They entered the hotel lobby and headed to the dining room. Dani and Melanie ordered coffee, and Tommy ordered a scotch.

"He's telling the truth, I'm convinced of it," Dani said to the others after the waitress left.

Tommy looked at her skeptically. "I hate to burst your bubble, Dani, but he's been incarcerated seventeen years now. If he didn't know how to spin a yarn before being sent inside, he certainly learned the ropes over the years. It's a work of art among the inmates. They take bets on who'll come up with the biggest lie and carry it off."

"That man was too broken up to be lying," Melanie said. "I agree with Dani. Maybe he did an awful thing abandoning his daughter, but I'll bet anything that body they found in Orland wasn't Angelina."

Was it a despicable act to leave his child, sick and alone, in a hospital? Abandoning Jonah, leaving him behind, scared and unable to comprehend the loss of his parents, seemed inconceivable. No matter what, Dani would want to be by his side, to soothe him, to reassure him, even if her words were hollow. She'd keep fighting the system that withheld treatment from him, fight with every fiber of her being. But she recognized that the tools she had in her arsenal were more powerful than those available to George and Sallie. She was educated, trained to be an advocate. If the first answer was no, she had the know-how to keep fighting until the answer was yes, to keep going up the ladder of command until she reached the person able to look beyond standard procedure. She wasn't saying that, in the end, she would have been able to obtain medical treatment, only that fighting for it would have provided a semblance of hope, eased the feeling of powerlessness that must have overwhelmed George and Sallie.

Tommy leaned back in his chair, his arms folded across his chest. "It's a good thing you gals have me along. One of us has got to be tethered to reality. Face it—there's absolutely no evidence to support his fairy tale. I guarantee we won't find doctors' records or hospital records. And let's not forget Sallie. Don't you think she would have thought to mention that they had a dying daughter? Not a word!"

"There's no evidence because no one looked for medical records." Dani's body was flushed from the anger she felt. Whether it was Tommy's dismissiveness that had raised her ire or a system that would turn away a deathly ill child, she didn't know. She only knew she wanted to throttle someone. "Why would they, if neither George nor Sallie talked about it? And as for Sallie, she could be so consumed with guilt that to her it feels like they did kill their daughter, that leaving her alone and sick was like a death."

"Or," said Tommy, "maybe she truly was sick and they couldn't handle it, so they killed her."

Now Dani knew: She wanted to throttle Tommy. She forced herself to calm down. There were still unanswered questions and she'd chosen Tommy for her team because he was the best at ferreting out answers. "Either way, we have to check out George's story. You'll need to stay behind and follow up with the doctor and hospital. Hopefully, they still have records from back then."

Melanie was quiet. Dani could see her struggle with herself. She wanted to believe George, but Tommy had shaken her confidence in her own judgment. Her battle was one Dani had observed before, not only in young women but in older, more experienced women as well. No matter how smart or accomplished women were, they'd been raised to defer to men. It was true that women's liberation had changed the world; women now could do any job and be taken seriously. Yes, they'd come a long way. For Dani's mother, smart as she was, becoming a lawyer was something she'd considered to be beyond her reach. Melanie's mother, on the other hand, had no doubt encouraged her daughter to pursue any career she fancied. When Dani stood in court arguing an appeal, the justices took her very seriously. Still, old stereotypes ran deep, and Dani knew too many women, smart women, who caved in when challenged by men.

Thank goodness Bruce, her boss, wasn't one of those men in power who, subconsciously or otherwise, viewed women as lesser mortals. Perhaps it stemmed from the professional path he'd chosen: helping the indigent. Power was secondary in this environment, and anyone willing to help was eagerly embraced and equally valued. It was different in the Justice Department, where power was the reward for hard work and long hours and went to those whose commitment was not suspect by virtue of one's gender. Dani guessed that was the case at the FBI as well, where Tommy had learned his investigative skills. If so, it was inevitable that Tommy had adopted some of the Bureau's beliefs. She knew he thought she was too soft. Sometimes she wondered herself.

The flight back to New York was uneventful. When the plane landed, Dani headed back to HIPP. Before she had removed her jacket, Bruce popped into her office.

"How was your first field trip?"

Daily phone calls had kept him abreast of her findings. Now he fished for her reaction to being out front, cutting through the tangle of information to discern the truth, and making the decision to take on a client. Fear and excitement alternated within her. "Unsettling. Tell me, when you've interviewed prospective clients, how do you know when they're handing you a line?"

Bruce chuckled, the easy laugh of someone who'd faced the question untold times. "Starting to doubt your initial impression?"

During most of the flight back from Indiana, Dani had wrestled with the question, weighing Tommy's impression against her own and trying to dissect George's story from every angle. "No, I still think the girl in the woods isn't George's daughter. But we may never know for sure. There's no DNA sample in the police kit, and who knows if we'll find any hospital records?"

"Well, without DNA, you can never be certain. You just have to trust your instincts. If the evidence trail that led to conviction is flawed, then there's good reason to think the verdict may be flawed."

"You know, Tommy disagrees with me."

"That's good. It helps to have someone take the other side. It'll push you harder to find the truth."

"Sure, but …"

Bruce raised one eyebrow, a trick she'd never been able to master herself.

"He thinks I'm just being a softy. I am a softy—I know that about myself. And watching George tell his story was heart wrenching. That's not why I believe him, though. At least I don't think it is. It's just—the look in his eyes, the heartache from wondering what happened to his daughter—it seemed real to me."

Bruce looked at the calendar on the wall. "You don't have the luxury of waiting until Tommy finishes investigating to decide whether we take on George's case. Execution is less than five weeks away. If you believe he's innocent, then you have to keep going. Do we have a basis for appeal?"

"Sure. His case could have been handled by a high schooler for all the work put into it. It screeches 'ineffective counsel.'"

"It's your case, Dani, and your call. What do you want to do?"

"I want to believe him. I want Tommy to find evidence that makes it right to believe him."

"And if Tommy can't find that evidence?"

"My gut says he's innocent."

"Then go with what your gut tells you."

As Bruce left her office, Dani knew it wasn't as simple as he'd suggested. Once, before she began working at HIPP, her instincts led her to believe in the truth of a defendant's confession. Over time she'd learned that even something so clear should be questioned. Sallie had confessed. George had given them a reason to doubt her. In the end, trusting her gut only meant making hard decisions.

Most people Dani met assumed she was not a big supporter of the death penalty. Why would she work for HIPP otherwise? And they were right, of course. She'd learned from experience that mistakes were made too often. She hadn't always been an opponent of the death penalty, though. She staunchly supported it when she started her career as an assistant US attorney, prosecuting defendants who were the scum of the planet. It was easy to lack sympathy for people who preyed on the weakness of others. Remove them from the future gene pool, so they didn't continue to pollute the Earth, she rationalized. The gratitude of the victim's family when she secured a conviction, the relief that washed over their faces when the jury imposed a sentence of death, reinforced her belief in the justness of that penalty.

Until Darryl Coneston. Darryl was the nephew of Jenny Slenku. From Dani's toddler years, Jenny had cared for her while her parents worked. She greeted Dani with fresh-baked cookies when she returned from school, got dinner ready before her parents arrived from their respective jobs, and kept their house tidy. She had immigrated with her parents and her older sister before the beginning of World War II, from Bucovina, in the northern region of Romania, where she was called "Jenica." Although she'd been in this country for over thirty years before becoming Dani's caregiver, she still carried the vestiges of her Romanian accent. Jenny's cheer and exuberance spilled over onto anyone around her. She doted on Dani, filling her with Romanian delicacies like *covrigi* and *gogosi* and, on special occasions, *cozonac*, a rich fruit bread that was a traditional Christmas treat in her homeland. She thought Dani could do no wrong, and Dani adored her. By the time Dani entered high school, it was no longer necessary to have an adult waiting for her at home, but Jenny had become a part of Dani's family and it would have been inconceivable to let her go.

Dani remembered vividly returning from band practice one bright autumn day in her junior year, still tingling from the attentions paid to her by the dashing trumpet player, his smile as dazzling as the pure, sharp notes of his instrument. She walked into the kitchen and found Jenny sobbing at the kitchen table. Her short, round body and mass of tightly wound, graying curls shook like the contents of a blender turned up high. Throwing her arms around her vibrating body, Dani asked, "What's wrong, Jenny. What happened?"

Jenny could barely speak through her anguish, but over the next hour Dani pieced together the cause of her despair. Jenny's only nephew, her sister's son, had been arrested and charged with the brutal rape and murder of a teenage girl. The enormity of the event would have been enough to send Jenny over the edge, but what had rendered her dumbstruck was this: He had confessed to the crime. Dani comforted Jenny as best she could, but inside she seethed with righteous satisfaction that he would not escape punishment for such a heinous act.

Over the next several weeks, Dani often overheard her parents discuss his plight with Jenny. It was a mistake, a miscarriage of justice, a travesty. Darryl was a good boy, studious, always considerate of others. A friend of the victim had mistakenly identified him as the person last seen with her.

"Why did he confess?" Dani heard her parents ask.

"They beat him—they made him," Jenny answered, her shoulders sagging, her once cheerful smile lost. "They wouldn't let him call his mother; they wouldn't let him eat or drink or go to the bathroom. They told him if he didn't confess, he'd get sentenced to die. He's just a boy. What did he know?" With the smug certainty of a teenager, Dani knew he must be guilty, knew that an eyewitness couldn't be wrong, knew that an innocent person wouldn't confess.

Jenny finally stopped working for her family when Dani began law school. She was in her sixties by then, ready to stay home with her husband and tend to her grandchildren. She had never truly recovered from her nephew's incarceration. At Dani's law-school graduation, which she attended as a valued member of their family, she took Dani aside. "You're a lawyer now, you can help Darryl. Please, show them he's innocent, that he didn't do such a horrible thing."

"But he confessed," Dani reminded her.

"No, no, they made him; he told me so. Help him. You're the only one I can ask."

The years in law school hadn't changed Dani's view of the criminal justice system. She believed eyewitnesses were reliable. She knew innocent people didn't confess, no matter how seriously they were mistreated. But Jenny was family. Dani promised she'd see what she could do. Being a new lawyer, first studying for the bar exam and then caught up in the energy of a new job; falling in love with the man who would become her husband; struggling with the demands of motherhood—it was easy to forget a promise amid all that. Once in a while, Jenny would call and ask, "Anything yet? Did you find anything?"

"No, I've been looking, but nothing yet," Dani would answer with only the mildest twinge of guilt about her deception.

And then Jenny became ill, riddled with cancer that spread from her breast to her lymph glands and then her brain. Dani had left the US Attorney's Office by then, devoting her full attention to Jonah. When she visited Jenny in the hospital and Jenny clutched Dani's hand in hers, looked at her with her rheumy eyes and whispered, "Please, before it's too late, help him," Dani knew she couldn't avoid it any longer.

Darryl had been sentenced to life in a Florida state penitentiary. True to the cops' promise, he'd avoided a death sentence through his confession. By then, Dani's parents had retired to Florida, and she planned a trip with Jonah to visit them and arranged to meet with Darryl while she was there. As a result of that meeting, she began to question her previous assumptions.

Darryl had been nineteen when the police picked him up for questioning about the rape and murder of Janice Priestly, a sixteen-year-old high school student working part time at a local Burger King. It was one of the many fast-food restaurants frequented by students at a nearby college, where Darryl earned straight A's and edited the college literary magazine. He readily admitted to having been at Burger King that night, along with his friend Lance, planning the next steps for a shared research project. He hadn't noticed any of the employees and left shortly after eight. But according to Janice's friend and coworker Rona McAfee, Darryl had been flirting with Janice, and when she finished her shift at eight, both Darryl and Lance followed her out the door.

When brought in for questioning, Darryl assumed that it must have been a mistake and saw no need to have a lawyer present. After all, he hadn't done anything wrong. Twenty hours later, Darryl understood that his innocence was irrelevant. During his interrogation, he had been beaten in the head, the chest, and the legs, never on the face, and always with a phone book held against his body so as not to leave evidence of the brutality. They threw a chair at him and repeatedly slammed his head on the table. When the abuse failed to produce a confession, the police told him Lance had confessed and would soon implicate Darryl. They told him he'd receive the death penalty unless he too confessed. They showed him photographs of death row. They held a hypodermic needle to his arm and said, "This is how we'll kill you."

At that moment, Darryl knew his only two choices were life in prison or death. He chose the former. The police had lied about Lance; he hadn't confessed, nor had he implicated Darryl. But to escape the death penalty, Darryl had agreed to testify against his friend. They were both sentenced to life in prison.

Twelve years later, the governor of Florida received a letter from a convict on death row in Georgia, saying two innocent men were in prison for the rape and murder of Janice Priestly, a crime for which the letter-writer took sole responsibility. Instead of interviewing the convict, Florida police interviewed Darryl in prison. Fearful that asserting his innocence would harm his chance for parole, Darryl reaffirmed to the police that he had committed the crime.

Now he sat before Dani, looked her straight in the eye, and said, "I've never hurt anyone in my life." She believed him. When Darryl had been convicted, DNA testing was in its infancy. By the time she'd met him, it was proven technology. Over the next few months, Dani tracked down evidence files from his trial and discovered that biological specimens from the victim still existed. She filed a motion for DNA testing. The state objected. After a hearing, she prevailed. Testing was conducted and it showed conclusively that neither Darryl nor Lance had raped Janice.

Jenny died two days after Dani told her of the DNA results, comforted by the confirmation all these years later of her nephew's innocence and reassured that an injustice would soon be rectified.

Dani expected that his story would have a happy ending. She filed a joint petition with the state of Florida to set aside the convictions of Darryl and Lance on the grounds of actual innocence. After fifteen years in prison, both would become free men. Before that happened, though, an inmate viciously beat Darryl, and he suffered irreversible brain damage. He needed the constant care of a group home. Although freed from prison, his future, which once held so much promise, was gone forever.

When Jonah got older and Dani wanted to return to work, she sought out HIPP. Her view of the world had changed because of Darryl Coneston, and working at HIPP became her atonement for her earlier blindness and arrogance.

Hunched over a small table at a Dunkin Donuts shop, Tommy brought the paper cup filled with hot coffee to his lips. Still too hot. He drank his coffee black, no cream, no sugar. Coffee should be hot, steaming hot, but damn, this coffee in his hand would scald his tongue and leave him with an annoying burn on the roof of his mouth that would pester him the rest of the day. Better to wait and let it cool off. No need to rush. A wild goose chase—that's what he was on. Still, it was his job to follow the trail, no matter how far fetched. He had to admit he'd been wrong before. Not often. Hardly ever, in fact. Dani seemed so sure this guy was innocent, but Tommy knew she was a marshmallow inside. Maybe outside, too. It took the kind of experience Tommy had to harden up and realize how perps lied so convincingly. He'd seen that plenty at the Bureau.

He tried his coffee again. "Mmm," he said out loud. "Just right." He broke off a piece of his cinnamon Danish, dunked it into the coffee, and then took a long sip of the rich brown liquid. His favorite breakfast: not eggs or bacon or pancakes, just a good cup of java and a Danish. Maybe sometimes a splurge with a bagel and cream cheese. He believed in keeping fit. Working out regularly at the gym and eating healthy—well, maybe the Danish wasn't so good, but surely better than bacon—were part of his regular routine. Traveling broke that routine and put him out of sorts. When he'd miss more than two days at the gym, he thought it must be what withdrawal felt like. He'd done his share of traveling with the Bureau. Now he preferred settling in at home.

Tommy finished his breakfast and opened up a road map of Indiana. He had a straight ride east on Route 80, then Route 76, to Sharpsburg, Pennsylvania, the Calhouns' hometown. A six-hour drive if he didn't hit any traffic. In his leather briefcase, his initials stamped on the front in gold—a gift from his wife when he'd taken the job with HIPP—were signed releases from Calhoun. With any luck, they'd be enough to get the hospital officials and the doctors to open their records to him. If there were any records left. After all, if Calhoun told the truth, the records would be almost twenty years old. Had there even been computers then? Tommy didn't remember, it was so long ago.

After paying the bill, he sauntered to his rental car and began his drive. An unbroken expanse of prairie lay ahead. During the summer, cornfields might line the roadway, he thought, but now the brown land was flat and dry. With nothing to distract him, he reached over to his briefcase on the passenger seat and pulled out a CD and popped it into the slot on the dashboard. When riding in a car, alone like this, he liked to listen to books on tape and always brought one along with him on forays into the field. Mysteries were his favorite—Dennis Lehane, George Pelecanos, Robert Parker, pretty much anything by P. D. James.

Fiddling with audio controls while driving at seventy miles an hour was an art that Tommy had mastered long ago. Soon he heard a British-accented voice reading the words of John LeCarre's newest fiction. Tommy adjusted the volume and settled in for the ride. Books were better than music, he figured. Music was a diversion; books were an absorption, displacing all other thoughts except the story unfolding. That's what he wanted right now—to push aside all thoughts of George Calhoun and his date with the executioner.

***

Meadowbrook Hospital looked like most other community hospitals: a faded brick façade four stories high surrounded by acres of parking spots filled with cars. Tommy drove around for five minutes before he caught a blue Toyota pulling out and managed to beat out a Mercedes for the empty space. He figured he'd start with the hospital before trying to track down the doctor whom George claimed had treated his daughter. Even if he found the doctor—and without a name, he gave it a slim chance—it was so long ago that maybe the doctor wasn't even practicing anymore. Maybe he wasn't even alive. Hospitals kept records, though. If he could get a look at them, they could tell him whether George had been truthful about his daughter. At least the part about her being sick. The rest of his story seemed too cockeyed to believe. He couldn't imagine walking away from one of his kids. Not for any reason. And especially not if the kid was sick. That's when a kid needed you the most.

Tommy walked through the parking lot to the main entrance. As he stepped through the revolving door, the odor of ammonia mixed with decay hit him. He walked to the information desk and smiled at the elderly woman sitting behind it. "Hello, dear. Can you tell me where I can find the guy in charge of this hospital? I'm not sure what his title might be. Maybe 'executive director'?"

The woman knit her brow and seemed momentarily lost. "Oh, my. I've never been asked that question before. Usually I'm asked for directions to a patient's room or the cafeteria or even the restrooms." She smiled shyly. "I'm just a volunteer, you see. Two afternoons a week. It helps the time go by."

Tommy pointed to the phone on her desk. "Maybe you could call somebody and ask."

"How silly of me. Of course. I'll do just that."

Twenty minutes later, Tommy sat on a chair in the office of Ronald Cornwall, director of operations for Meadowbrook Hospital. The administrator held in his hands the medical records release signed by George Calhoun.

"Mr. Noorland, I've already explained to you that we have procedures here. This release will be sent to our records department and they'll do a search. If we have anything, we'll send it to you. The process usually takes several weeks."

"And I keep explaining to you that our client doesn't have several weeks," Tommy answered, barely able to control his frustration with this bureaucrat.

Cornwall shook his head. "Even if I wanted to circumvent our procedure, you've said these records are from twenty years ago. We didn't computerize everything then. It'll take that amount of time for our records clerk to search through our archives—and that's assuming I push this ahead of other record requests that are pending."

Tommy leaned back in the chair and folded his arms. "Well, we've got to figure something out, 'cause I'm sure you don't want an innocent man to die just because your people are too busy to look through a shitload of papers."

Cornwall's face blanched. "Surely it can't come down to our records."

"It just may."

"But—but—he's been in jail, you said, for seventeen years. How could it be that you're now first asking for our records? You can't just lay this on me—you must know you're being unfair." Cornwall's voice had risen in pitch and his widened eyes practically pleaded with Tommy to lift the burden he'd placed on him.

Although skeptical of finding documents that would jibe with Calhoun's story, Tommy conducted all his investigations as if he believed his clients. He was a trained investigator, comfortable with himself only when he knew he'd been thorough. Shortcuts weren't an option for him. He didn't plan on walking away from the hospital empty-handed.

"Listen, I can help your guys look through the boxes."

Cornwall shook his head. "No, that'd violate privacy laws."

"Fuck privacy laws."

Cornwall's shoulders drooped. "I'd like to help you—really I would. But I'm not a miracle worker. Doctors make miracles, not hospital administrators."

"I'm not looking for a miracle, just information. Seems pretty simple to me."

The two men stared stonily at each other, like gunslingers waiting to see who'd draw first. Cornwall suddenly sat up erect in his seat. "Wait a minute. Maybe we can go about this a different way. You said she was treated here in 1989 or '90. Maybe the treating doctor is still on staff here." Cornwall opened a drawer in his desk, took out a sheet of paper, and looked it over. "I think we may be in luck." He picked up the phone on his desk and punched in four numbers. "Is Dr. Samson available?" Minutes went by before he spoke again. "Gary, I'm glad you're here. Were you on staff in '89? Good. By any chance, do you remember treating a little girl back then for leukemia—her name was Angelina Calhoun, about three or four years old?" Cornwall nodded and smiled. "I'm going to send someone up to see you, if you have a moment now. His name is Thomas Noorland. He's an investigator and has a signed release from the girl's father." He hung up and turned to Tommy. "You're in luck. Dr. Samson is the head of our pediatric oncology unit now, but back then he was a staff physician. He remembers the Calhouns. I'll have someone bring you up to his office and he'll tell you what he knows about their daughter's condition back then."

Tommy had to admit his surprise. He'd expected the hospital to be a dead end, certain that Calhoun had fabricated the story of his daughter's illness. Now it seemed that at least one part of his tale was true. As for the rest, Tommy remained skeptical.

Cornwall buzzed his secretary on the intercom. "Vicky, is Billy around? Good. Send him in here, please."

Moments later a middle-aged man in workman's clothes entered Cornwall's office.

"You need me, Mr. Cornwall?"

The man's slow speech and shuffling gait suggested some degree of developmental disability. "Yes, Billy. I'd like you to take this man up to see Dr. Samson. His office is in Room 521. You remember how to get there, right?"

Billy nodded.

Tommy thanked Cornwall before leaving the director's office, and followed Billy as he wound his way around the corridors to the elevator.

"How long have you been working here, Billy?" Tommy asked, just to make conversation.

Billy stopped to think about the question. "A long time."

"You like it here?"

He nodded. "I like the children. I like making them laugh."

They took the elevator to the fifth floor and made their way through another labyrinth of corridors to Room 521. "Here's Dr. Samson's office," Billy said before leaving. "He's a real nice man."

The door was open, so Tommy knocked once to announce his arrival and stepped inside. A thin man, who looked to be in his early fifties, with sprouts of gray hair at his temples and wire-rimmed glasses over his eyes, sat behind a desk. The small office contained only a metal desk at the far end, two chairs in front of it, and file cabinets along a side wall.

"You must be Mr. Noorland," the doctor said as he looked up from his papers.

"Please, call me Tommy."

"How can I help you?" he asked, his voice quiet, almost sad.

It must be the worst specialty for a doctor, Tommy thought. Having to deal with children with cancer. The tragedies he saw every day had to take a toll, and the doctor's hunched back and expressionless eyes seemed to confirm Tommy's expectations.

"I understand you treated Angelina Calhoun," Tommy said as he sat down and slid a signed medical release over to Dr. Samson. "It was way back in '89, maybe '90. I was hoping you might remember something about her condition and, well, how she did."

"I remember Angelina very well. I treated her for leukemia." Tommy thought he detected moisture in the corner of the doctor's left eye. "Every child I treat here is special to me, the ones I save and the ones I lose," he continued, his voice barely audible. "But some get to me deep inside." He paused and shook his head. "Angelina was such a beautiful child, always smiling, always brave. All of the staff here were so taken by her. They talked about taking up a collection to help pay for her treatment, but it never would have been enough. I waived my fee, but the hospital wouldn't. I lobbied hard for that, but they're a business and you know how it is with businesses, always looking at the bottom line. Her parents were hard-working folks, but they didn't have health insurance. It's different now. The times have changed. Now, with the Cover All Kids program in Pennsylvania, they'd have been able to get health insurance for her, if not for free then for a very low cost. But back then …" He stopped speaking and stared out the window.

After a few moments, Tommy asked, "What happened to her? Did she die?"

Samson turned back to Tommy. "I've often wondered that myself. I assume she did. I never heard from her parents after the hospital turned her down for treatment, so I couldn't tell you with certainty. But even with treatment …" He shook his head. "Her prognosis wasn't good."

"I don't suppose you still have her medical records."

Dr. Samson shrugged. "I'm sure I do, somewhere. I've moved the older files to my garage."

"Do you think you could take a look for Angelina's?"

The doctor nodded. "If I find them, I assume you'd like a copy?"

"You've read my mind." Tommy stood up to leave. "Thanks, Doc. You've been very helpful."

"Wait a moment. You can't go off without explaining why you're asking me these questions. Do you know something about Angelina Calhoun? Is she alive?"

Tommy sat back down. "That's the million-dollar question, Doc. Her father is facing execution in five weeks for murdering her."

"My God! That's impossible. He was devoted to that child. Both her parents were."

"Yeah, well, he says he didn't kill Angelina. Claims he and his wife drove her to the Mayo Clinic and then left her there with all her medical records, hoping they'd treat her for the cancer."

"I suppose that's possible. She would have been turned over to Child Protective Services. If they couldn't find her parents and knew of her medical condition, the state would have paid for her treatment. But— leaving a sick four-year-old alone in another state and just walking away? I can't imagine the Calhouns doing that."

Tommy chuckled softly. "You know, Doc, I couldn't imagine it either. I thought he had to have made up this nutty story. And maybe he has. But he told the truth about Angelina being sick and him not being able to pay for her care. And I'll be damned, but I'm starting to believe the crazy son of a bitch."

As he made his way through the hospital corridors and out to the street, the doctor's words kept running through Tommy's head. He'd been so certain Dani had sent him off on a fool's errand. Now, for the first time, he entertained the idea that George Calhoun might be telling the truth. There were still many unanswered questions, but foremost was the one that would be hardest to answer: Who was the little girl found buried in the woods nineteen years ago?

Tommy walked toward the sea of vehicles in the parking lot. *Now, where's my damn car?* When driving his own car, he always found it easily: his dark-blue pearl Lincoln Navigator stood out tall and proud above the other, mostly small, gas-saving vehicles. He felt entitled to a big car; five children and a wife took up a lot of room. Now, though, he had a rental car, a silver-gray Hyundai that looked like every other car in the lot. And how the hell could he be expected to remember the license-plate number? He walked in the direction from which he remembered coming and took out the remote, pressing the emergency button. A piercing sound came from his left, and as he turned in that direction, he saw flashing headlights. "There you are," he muttered to himself as he strode over to it. He reached for the door before noticing a white paper flapping under the windshield wiper. Expecting to see a flyer for some business, Tommy pulled it out and began to crumple it into a ball. But out of the corner of his eye, he caught sight of the red ink scrawled on the page, unfolded the sheet, and read: "IF YOU WANT TO STAY ALIVE, DON'T STICK YOUR NOSE WHERE IT DOESN'T BELONG. THIS IS YOUR ONLY WARNING."

He opened his briefcase, pulled out a plastic evidence bag and, holding the tip of the paper with a tissue, carefully slipped the note inside and sealed the bag. He scanned the parking lot but didn't see anything unusual, just rows of empty cars. He looked out to the street, and again nothing caught his attention. As he turned back around, he glanced toward the hospital entrance and caught sight of Billy leaning against a tree, a cigarette dangling from his lips, staring right at him. Tommy considered confronting him with the note but thought better of it. *He may be a man, but he has the mind of a kid.* He got into his car, but before starting it, he took out his cell phone and dialed Dani.

"What's your pleasure? Good news first or bad?" he asked when she answered the phone.

"Take your pick. No, good news. I need to hear something positive."

"I found the doctor who treated Angelina Calhoun. He confirms she had leukemia and her folks couldn't afford the treatment. He says he doesn't know what happened to her after he sent them away." Tommy filled her in on the rest of his conversation with Dr. Samson.

"That's great news," Dani said. Tommy could hear the excitement in her voice. "Does he have records for us? I'll need them for our appeal."

"Well, it'll take some time to find the hospital records. If they exist at all, after so many years, they'd be in deep storage. The head administrator here promised me they'd put the search on a priority status, but it could still take weeks. And then no guarantee they'll be found. The doc has his own records, though, stashed in his garage, but again, no guarantee Angelina's are there."

"If that's the bad news, I can deal with it. We'll get an affidavit from the doctor."

"No," Tommy said. "The bad news is that somebody wants us to back off."

"What do you mean?"

"I mean—" he looked around to make sure no one was nearby—"I mean someone is following me. And he or she isn't happy about my being here."

*H*e watched as the investigator retrieved the note from the car's windshield, saw his eyes widen as he read the words. He knew it wouldn't scare him off, but still, it had made him feel better writing it. Made him feel in control. He knew the man was trouble. The words he spoke didn't matter. It was about the child's death. That's why he had come. He knew that from the detective, his friend now, always forthcoming when he called asking about new developments in the child's death.

The investigator scanned the parking lot before taking a briefcase from his car. He took something from the case and then the note disappeared. The man got into his car and just sat there. Had he made a mistake leaving the note? He'd always been careful, meticulous in covering his tracks. Could his fingerprints be lifted from the note? He hadn't worn gloves, but so what? Even if the investigator took the note to the police, even if they found fingerprints, it wouldn't lead back to him. His fingerprints weren't in any file.

The parking lights of the investigator's car were turned on, and the car was slowly backed out of its spot. He waited until the investigator's car turned toward the exit before sliding into his Honda Civic. He started the motor and, keeping his distance, followed him. He stayed two cars behind, careful to avoid detection. When the investigator turned onto Highway 28, the man thought he might be headed to the airport. He dropped back behind another car; it was easier to see up ahead on the highway. Besides, he knew the exit for the airport. He could move closer to the investigator's car when he approached the exit.

He'd been right. The investigator drove straight to the car-rental return at the airport and then boarded the shuttle bus. The man stayed behind the bus and watched for the investigator's terminal. United Airlines. They flew all over the world. The investigator could be going anyplace, but the man supposed he was returning to New York because he knew that's where he'd come from.

There was nothing more for him to do. He didn't even know why he'd followed him to the airport. The investigator's showing up at the hospital had told him everything.

Dani felt both elated and confused. The missing piece was now in place, evidence that Angelina Calhoun had been gravely ill. That was the information she'd needed to confirm her belief in George's innocence. She knew Tommy might still say that it got them only so far, that it was a leap from knowing she'd been sick to believing George and Sallie had abandoned her at a distant hospital. And sure, maybe they were both crazy and killed their daughter because of her illness. Listening to George tell his story, seeing the heartache written on his face almost twenty years later, Dani believed him. He didn't seem crazy to her. Just sad. Overwhelmingly sad.

But the note left on Tommy's car? She didn't understand why anyone would try to stop their helping George. She'd have to think about it. Later, though. Now, she knew, she had her work cut out for her, trying to get a court to hear HIPP's appeal.

She walked to Bruce's and Melanie's offices and filled them in on the news. "I'm going to do the brief," she said to Melanie. "I need you to work on the record on appeal."

Melanie looked at her soberly. "Do you really think it's possible? That Angelina is alive?"

For a moment, Dani let her fantasies run wild and pictured Angelina Calhoun, now a grown woman, accompanying them to the Supreme Court and smiling beatifically as she told the nine justices, "Of course I'm alive, thanks to the enormous sacrifice of my parents. It's horrible what they've had to endure. If only I'd known, I'd have come forward sooner." The picture in her head faded and she answered Melanie, "Probably not. The doctor said her condition was grave. Even with the best care—I just don't know. But if we can find someone who remembers a child with leukemia abandoned at the hospital, that would be a home run. And even though it's twenty years later, it's not something they'd likely forget."

They finished their conversation and Dani settled in to work. She glanced at the clock on the wall and saw that it was five o'clock. Damn. She hadn't called Katie to let her know she'd be late, and Jonah no doubt wondered where she was. At least Dani liked to think he wondered. More likely, he'd lost himself in his own world of music, playing the piano as he composed new sonatas, preparing himself for his summer at music camp. Although he hadn't received official word on his application, the camp director had assured Dani there would be room for him.

She called Doug. "Want to stay in the city for dinner tonight?" she asked when she reached him at the law school.

"Sure. What's the occasion?" Doug knew she usually preferred eating at home during the week.

"I thought it'd be nice for a change. Besides, I'm still here at the office. With this god-awful rain, traffic will be a mess now."

"Well, I have about an hour's worth of work left. Let's meet at Cuccina's at 6:30, okay?"

"Perfect. I'll see you then."

Dani hung up and called Katie to let her know about the changed plans.

"No problem, Dani. You deserve a night out. And don't hurry home. Whenever you get back is fine with me."

Yes, she acknowledged to herself once again, Katie was a godsend.

***

Despite its being early on a Thursday evening, well before the hour fashionable New Yorkers dined, every table at Cuccina's was full. The smell of garlic permeated the air, and the walls vibrated with the sound of conversation mixed with the bustle of the wait staff. They had to strain to hear each other at times, but the outstanding food, the reasonable prices, and the location convenient to Columbia Law School kept them coming back. When Dani and Doug found themselves staying late at work, they usually ended up at Cuccina's.

Dani's second glass of wine had gone straight to her head, and she felt somewhat woozy. She sat back in her chair and only half-listened to Doug's ramblings about a trip they could take while Jonah was at summer camp. With the lines on Doug's face blurred by her hazy vision, he still looked youthful and, with or without the lines, handsome. She'd met Doug on her first day of work at the US Attorney's Office. She had been staring dumbly at a photocopy machine, trying to figure out its various buttons, when Doug walked by, coffee cup in hand. He smiled at her and Dani could see the dimples in his cheeks widen, the green flecks in his eyes sparkle, and she was instantly smitten. After that, she made up excuses to seek him out until he finally invited her to a friend's party. They'd been together ever since.

"So, what do you think?" Doug asked, bringing her back to the present.

"Um, I'm not sure."

"You didn't hear anything I said, did you?"

She shook her head. "It's the wine. You know how I get."

"It's okay. You've had a hard couple of days. I asked what you thought about sailing through the Greek islands this summer."

Instantly, Dani's mind pictured billowing white sails surrounded by azure waters. She sat at the bow of the boat, her hair swirling around her face, her legs hanging over the side. "Sounds dreamy, but neither of us knows how to sail."

"No problem. We hire a captain and we serve as his crew. He'll show us what we need to do."

"Can we afford it?"

"I've already checked out a few places. I think we can handle it. What do you think?"

Dani hesitated. She knew how Doug would respond but said it anyway. "We'd be so far from Jonah. It's his first time away from us. What if he gets homesick? What if he gets hurt? How would the camp even reach us on a boat?"

Doug put down his fork and reached for Dani's hand. "You worry too much. It's the twenty-first century. We can get calls on the boat. Besides, your parents will be around to take him for the few days it might take us to get back if an emergency comes up."

Dani pulled her hand away. "Maybe you worry too little. We're both lawyers, remember. We're trained to think of all the things that can go wrong and cover every contingency."

"Just consider it, okay?"

"I will, I promise."

Doug looked at her silently for a moment. "Is there something troubling you tonight? You've seemed far away even before you had any wine."

Dani told him about the note Tommy found on his car. "I keep running it through my head and trying to figure out who would want us to stop our work. I can only think of two possibilities: Either someone knows George killed his daughter and wants to make sure he doesn't escape punishment, or someone knows George didn't kill his daughter and is afraid we'll find out."

"Have you notified the police about the note?"

"Tommy called in the local police in Pennsylvania. They're checking to see if they can get a fingerprint match from the note."

"Now *this* is something you should worry about. Not that you should stop what you're doing. Just be careful."

"So, what do you think? Why would someone try to stop us?"

Doug pondered a moment. "I think you should make a list of everyone who knows you're investigating Calhoun's case."

Dani reached for her pocketbook and pulled out a small notepad and a pen. "Let's see. Well, of course, everyone at HIPP, but they can't count."

"Probably not, but for this exercise write down everyone's name."

She began writing on the notepad. "The wardens at both prisons know, George's attorney and his secretary, the detective in Illinois—I think his name is Cannon. Those are the people who know we may try to stop the execution. But they could have told anyone. And those people could have told others." She put her pen down. "This is pointless. There's no way I can figure out everyone who might know that we represent Calhoun."

"Okay. Let's try this. Who would be harmed most if Calhoun is exonerated?"

Dani thought for a moment and picked up her pen again. "The person who actually murdered the girl found in the woods."

"Then that's your answer."

She grimaced. "It's not an answer. I have no idea who killed the girl if it wasn't George."

They retreated into silence as the waiter brought over coffee. As he walked away, it hit her. "We have to find out the identity of that little girl. Then we might know who's threatening us."

"I think you're right."

Dani scribbled a reminder in her notepad: Exhume body of dead girl.

The next morning Bruce, Melanie, Tommy, and Dani gathered in HIPP's conference room.

"Okay, what's the strategy?" Bruce asked.

"I think we need to attack it on two fronts," Dani said. "First, we go to the superior court in LaGrange—that's the closest court to where the body is buried—and try to get an order of exhumation."

"Hasn't Calhoun exhausted his state court appeals?"

"He has. I wouldn't fashion the request for exhumation as an appeal, though. Before now, no one has questioned the identity of the girl found in the woods. They convicted George of killing that girl. The appeals have all been based on an assumption that it was Angelina. If we get an order of exhumation and it turns out to be someone else, then going back into state court with that information might be too late, or maybe not—I'm not certain. But that's not where we'd go. That brings me to the second front. He hasn't exhausted his habeas corpus appeals, so we can go into federal court and try to show that the conviction or sentence violated his constitutional rights."

"What's your timing?"

"Ideally, I'd go first with the state case, get an order exhuming the body, then be able to bring those results to the federal case. But we don't have time for that so we may have to file the second case before we get a ruling on the first."

Bruce turned to Tommy. "How about your investigation? Are you finished with that?"

"I'm going to try to see if Calhoun's story about the Mayo Clinic holds water. I've already got a few calls in and I'm waiting for callbacks."

"Okay," Bruce said. "Sounds good. You need anything from me, just let me know."

Dani sighed. "A miracle. That's what I need."

Sunny Bergman still wasn't used to the crowded streets of New York City. Really, after living in Manhattan for almost two years, she should have adjusted to the teeming humanity. Yet she felt a jolt each time she left her apartment. The confined walls of the elevator, the perpetually smog-filled air, even the smell of the streets triggered a yearning to be back in Byron, the small town where she'd grown up. An ideal childhood, she thought, with the coziness that came with knowing just about every person in town. A trip to the supermarket always included chats with friends she'd run into or parents of her friends or even just the smiling workers behind the cash register. And a city was only twenty minutes east, with all the stores and restaurants anyone could want.

Manhattan was so different. No one smiled at her or barely even nodded in response to her cheery attempts at chatter. Once in a while someone would smile at Rachel, but even the most coldhearted person couldn't resist such a beautiful child. Sunny's own heart fluttered each time she looked at her daughter. She hadn't planned on having a child so early. They had agreed she would work until Eric finished his medical training and then she would go to nursing school. Taking turns—that's what marriage was about. One day she'd go back to school, but not yet. She couldn't bear the thought of leaving Rachel with a stranger.

Stepping onto the sidewalk from the vestibule of her apartment building, the bright sunshine momentarily blinded Sunshine. Sunshine—that was her real name. She'd heard the story of her name numerous times from her parents. How they'd waited so long to have a child and how when they first set eyes on her, the hospital room brightened, as if drenched in sunlight. Holding Rachel's small hand, she led her toward the park, an oasis of green in this city of concrete and brick.

"Mommy, can we see the aminals today?" Rachel asked in her dainty voice, so melodic in its tones that it sounded like a song.

"It's 'animals,' not 'aminals,'" Sunny said. "And not today. It's too far away. After the park, we're going to meet Daddy for lunch."

"But I wanna see the aminals."

"It'll be fun to see Daddy for lunch."

Sunny understood Rachel's silence. Residents worked long hours and Eric rarely got home before Rachel went to sleep. Ironic—it was Eric who loved children so much that he chose pediatrics as his specialty; Eric who'd brought her to Manhattan, so far from the family and friends she loved; Eric who left her alone all day in this city of strangers. He'd left her alone again yesterday with his sudden visit back to his hometown in Pennsylvania. He'd gotten a call the evening before from his sister. Carol was in trouble again, he'd said. Her marriage was shaky, and she wanted to drink. Two years of sobriety were about to go down the drain. He needed to go back and straighten her out. "We'll go with you," Sunny had offered, desperate to spend more time with Eric.

"No, Rachel will be a distraction. Besides, I'll be back home tonight. It's just for the day."

He returned late that evening, withdrawn, unwilling to join in her effort at conversation. He went to sleep early and left for the hospital before she and Rachel had awakened that morning. He'd told Sunny many times that he had to work harder than the other residents to prove himself. He was much older than the rest—he'd been almost thirty-two when he began medical school. "I was the black sheep of the family," he'd told her when they first met. "The wild one who didn't want to settle down to any serious work. Now I have to make up for it."

Sunny took Rachel's hand in hers. They walked past the few brownstones interspersed between new apartment buildings and stopped to admire the first buds on the forsythia in their carefully tended gardens. Sunny kept her face turned away from the bags of garbage, heaped layers deep, that lined the curb. The trucks had not yet arrived to pick up the trash. Another change from the neat plastic or metal cans that sat at the end of the driveways in her childhood suburban home. The acrid odor couldn't be good for Rachel. She always worried about disease when the pungent smell entered her nostrils.

Sunny held her daughter's hand tighter as she crossed the road to escape the offending litter. Prewar brick buildings lined the street. Most were six or seven stories high, with an occasional restaurant or store on the street level. Her own apartment building was one of the highest in the neighborhood, at twelve stories. But neighborhoods in Manhattan were strange. Just one or two blocks away, their character changed completely. So unlike the sameness of Byron, its streets lined with simple ranches and the occasional two-story, the lawns carefully manicured, the backyards fenced because even in the Midwest one had to be careful the toddlers didn't run out into the streets, though the drivers were always cautious.

"Look, Rachel, Billy's at the park." They were just steps from the entrance to the playground. When Rachel saw her friend, she dropped her mother's hand and ran to him, plopping herself next to him in the sandlot. Sunny strolled over to Billy's mother, Ellen, and sat next to her on the bench.

"I didn't expect to see you today," Ellen said as she smiled at Sunny. "Didn't you say you were meeting Eric for lunch?"

"We are, but it's so lovely out that I left a few chores for later so we could get some fresh air first."

"I know how you feel. I couldn't wait to get outside today. It almost feels like spring."

"Well, it is spring."

"Yeah, the calendar says it's spring, but in New York, spring is about five days in May. Before then it's cool and rainy, and after it's hot and steamy. We don't get too many gorgeous days like this."

Her eyes closed, Sunny bent her head back and let the sun stream over her face. On a day like this, sitting among the greenery of the park, it almost felt like being back home. She could hear peals of laughter coming from her daughter, and the sound brought a smile to her face. Yes, having Rachel made everything worthwhile.

"Have you heard about MaryLou?" Ellen asked. "She walked in on Stephen in bed with a young floozy. She was supposed to be at the theater, but she must have eaten something rotten at lunch because she felt so sick, she left during intermission."

Ellen was a notorious gossipmonger, a neighborhood busybody who thrived on scandal and could prattle nonstop. The drone of her voice melded into a sonorous hum as soothing as the white noise of an air conditioner. Sunny knew she didn't need to respond. A few grunts here and there would suffice.

"Stephen just looked at her and said, 'You're home early.' Can you imagine that? He didn't even try to hide the girl or make some lame apology. Well, you know the rumor's always been that MaryLou had her own flings on the side, so maybe she got what she deserved. I heard she bedded the boy who delivers her groceries from Gristedes. He brings me my groceries too, and he's adorable, but my God, he can't be more than eighteen!"

Sunny opened her eyes and looked for Rachel. Her daughter was still happily ensconced in the sand with her little friend. As she glanced toward the entrance to the park, she saw Ralph approach with his daughter, Brianna. The brief flutter of her heart unnerved her, but she caught herself. In the past, she'd felt foolish around Ralph, stammering her responses to his polite conversation. But she was better now, able to smile and be composed without betraying the nervousness she always felt in his presence.

"Morning, ladies," he said as he approached their park bench. "Have room for me?" Brianna ran off to join the other children as Ralph squeezed onto the end of the wooden seat. "Hard to stay indoors and paint on a day like this."

"When's your show?" Ellen asked.

"Opening is two weeks from tomorrow. But I'm set for the show, I've just got to pack up the canvases and get them to the gallery. There's some new stuff I'm experimenting with now. That's what's keeping me busy. Never too busy for an hour in the park, though, when a spring day is beckoning."

Sunny smiled, but she could feel that flutter in her heart again, the annoying ba-dum, ba-dum that began every time she saw Ralph.

"I hope you'll both come to the opening. With your husbands, of course."

"Why spoil it with my husband?" Ellen said with a coy smile.

All the women flirted with Ralph. He was tall and muscled, and his angular face and wavy black hair set off his cerulean eyes. The day's growth of stubble he usually sported on his chin added to his rakish good looks. With his wife's income as an investment banker, Ralph could stay home in their loft apartment and pursue his artistic talent. Caring for Brianna when nursery school wasn't in session was part of their marital bargain. An attractive man in a gaggle of play-ground moms—it was inevitable that he'd become the object of their fantasies.

"Well, your husband can keep you company while my wife is drag-ging me around to meet and greet."

"There you go, bringing up your wife again."

"Yes, I suppose that is an annoying habit of mine."

"Well, I'll overlook it this time, but really, what's the point of having a man in our midst if he's just going to talk about his wife?" Ellen said with a fake pout.

"I'll work on that," Ralph said with mock seriousness.

Sunny envied the casual joking of her friends. She didn't consider herself to be shy, yet something in her didn't allow for playfulness. A piece missing from her, she thought, when she bothered to think about herself. She looked at her watch, a digital chronometer she'd bought for timing her runs but wore all the time, preferring it over the gold Rado watch Eric had given her when Rachel was born. The gold watch was beautiful, with its round face surrounded by tiny diamonds, and she wore it on the few occasions when they got dressed up. She'd never owned anything so beautiful. She never really felt comfortable wearing it, though; it didn't fit her sense of herself. But she'd had that feeling about a lot of things over the course of her life.

She stood up and called over to Rachel. "It's time to go meet Daddy. Say goodbye to your friends." She turned to Ralph and Ellen and said goodbye. As she walked away, she wondered if their conversation would change with just the two of them. She wondered whether, if she had been left alone with Ralph, she'd gather up the gumption to flirt with him. It wasn't as if she didn't love Eric; certainly she did. But with his long hours at the hospital, leaving her alone with her thoughts, she sometimes let her mind wander.

Silly of me, she thought, as she took Rachel's hand and headed to the hospital to meet her husband for lunch.

The next evening, Sunny fussed over the floral arrangement. She'd picked out each flower that afternoon at the florist shop two blocks from her apartment. There were bunches of flowers already made up into bouquets, wrapped in cellophane, and ready to be placed in a glass vase. Sunny liked arranging the flowers herself, though, deciding which ones worked well with each other, how a gardenia looked different when placed next to fern or rubbing up against a daffodil. The flowers were beautiful this time of year. No matter how she arranged them, it would brighten the dark foyer. It had to be exact, though, an elegant display sitting atop their antique foyer table. It seemed as if she'd searched every antique shop in the East Village before venturing north to Gramercy Park, looking for the right table for their entryway. And then, almost magically, at a neighbor's tag sale, she'd stumbled across a slim dark mahogany table, built in the early 1900s by a Chinese artisan. How lucky she was! It was just what she fancied, just the style that Eric's mother would admire. The flowers had to be positioned just right to complement the luscious wood grain of the table. That's what she wanted Eric's parents to see first when they entered her apartment—perfection.

It wasn't the first time Eric's parents had visited from the home they'd retired to in Florida. They had visited once before, shortly after she and Eric moved to New York City and Eric had started his residency. They had hardly any furniture then. The painted white walls were peeling at the edges and the wood floors were bare. They weren't expected to have turned it into a home yet. Now, though, Mrs. Bergman's practiced eye would certainly take in the results of Sunny's attempts at decoration.

"It's fine," Eric called in from the living room, a note of annoyance in his voice. He'd been short with her ever since he'd returned from his visit to his sister. Whenever she tried to change his mood, he'd brush her off. "Stop fiddling with the flowers. Mom's not going to care whether the rose is in front or back."

"You're wrong. She notices everything." Phyllis Bergman was a perfectionist. Her home could have been featured in *Architectural Digest*. Although she'd furnished it with a decorator, Sunny knew Phyllis could have done it on her own. She had impeccable taste.

"You don't have anything to prove to Mom. She already adores you."

"She adores Rachel. She tolerates me."

"You're being ridiculous."

That was the problem with Eric. He assumed everyone loved the things he loved. If he loved Manhattan, Sunny must love Manhattan. If he loved sushi, everyone must. And since he loved Sunny, so must his parents. Sunny thought Eric's father liked her well enough, but his mother was another story. No matter how hard she tried, Sunny could detect the scent of disapproval from her mother-in-law. In her heart, Sunny knew Mrs. Bergman thought she'd trapped Eric, thought this woman from a working-class home had latched on to the handsome medical student from a wealthy family and purposely became pregnant.

The truth was so different. Yes, Sunny had become pregnant unexpectedly. And yes, she and Eric had married sooner than they'd planned. But Eric had implored her to keep the baby. She wanted to end her pregnancy and had gone so far as to make an appointment at the clinic. Over and over Eric begged her to cancel the appointment. They'd argue, she'd cry, they'd argue all over again. For weeks, it felt like an unending cycle of tears and infuriation. Eventually she relented. Eric was too forceful to resist.

It had been so hard to give up nursing school. Since childhood Sunny had dreamed of becoming a nurse. She loved Rachel— certainly she did—yet she looked forward to the time she could return to school. There had been no question that Eric would continue his studies. After all, medicine was more important than nursing. A husband's career was more important than a wife's. She had agreed with him when he laid out their future: He'd finish medical school, then his residency, and then settle into a practice. She could return to school later. By then, Rachel would be in kindergarten, maybe even first grade. It made sense to postpone her dream for the family, Sunny often told herself.

"Listen," Eric called to Sunny, "don't mention to Mom and Dad that I visited Carol. I don't want them worrying that she's relapsing again."

"Sure." He hadn't wanted Sunny to say anything to Carol, either, if she spoke to her. Carol felt too ashamed of her weakness, he'd said. It would be humiliating if Sunny mentioned it. "Maybe she'd like to know I'm rooting for her, that she can lean on me too," Sunny had said.

But Eric was adamant. "No!" he'd barked at her. "Just trust me. I know her better than you." And so Sunny kept quiet.

"So, are you getting enough sleep?" Robert Bergman asked his son as Sunny cleared the dinner dishes from the table.

"Sure, Dad, it's not a problem."

"Because I heard how they make you residents work day and night and then the next day again."

"It's not like that anymore. Hospitals changed that a long time ago. I get enough sleep. Don't worry about it."

"I still don't understand why you didn't pick surgery," Mrs. Bergman chimed in. "I mean, you waited so long to settle down that you might as well go into the field that pays the most. You don't have as much time to save your money as those younger residents."

Sunny could follow the conversation in the dining room as she stacked the dishes in the sink. Their apartment was small—the dining room was a tiny alcove next to the kitchen—so from just a few feet away, she could discern the disapproval in the tone of the question, and she peeked in to see Eric's reaction. His voice remained even, but Sunny saw that his body carried the same tension he'd displayed since his visit to his sister. "I picked pediatrics because I wanted to work with children. You know that, Mom. We've had this discussion before."

"I know, I know, but surgery's where the money is. That's nothing to sneeze at. With money, you could live someplace nice, buy some decent furniture. It's no shame to make money. Although, I suppose I should be grateful that you're in medicine. For a while, I thought you'd end up in jail."

"Phyllis, that's enough! Eric's a fine boy. You're exaggerating his youthful indiscretions."

Sunny busied herself in the kitchen, making coffee and preparing the dessert. She didn't want to be part of their conversation, afraid that if she were, she'd blurt out something she'd regret.

Eric's father cleared his throat. "Your mother has a point, son. You remember my friend Dan Edelman, don't you? His son became a pediatric cardiologist. He's still working with children but doing something special, not just ordinary, you know what I mean? And he schedules his surgeries. No phone calls waking him in the middle of the night."

Sunny glanced back into the dining room and could see Eric's body stiffen, his mouth set in a rigid grin. "Sure, Dad, I know what you mean. A pediatrician doesn't give you enough bragging rights with your friends."

"No, no," came a chorus from both his parents.

Eric's mother reached over and patted his hand. "Whatever you do, we're proud of you. You've always been too sensitive to our advice. We're just trying to be helpful."

"Coffee's ready," Sunny chimed in from the kitchen.

All heads turned toward her voice. As Sunny walked into the room with a platter of homemade gingersnap cookies, they smiled at her and then at each other, the picture of a happy family.

Twenty-One Days

The LaGrange County Courthouse stood on a tree-lined street in the center of town. The ornate three-story building with a cylindrical steeple in the center reminded Dani of movies depicting small-town America in the '40s and '50s. It seemed as far removed from the clamor of Manhattan as a place could be. She'd been standing outside courtroom 215 for a half hour, waiting for George's case to be called.

The hearing on her motion for a court order to exhume the body alleged to be Angelina Calhoun's was the first case on the morning docket. She and Melanie had arrived in LaGrange the night before. Although just a local superior court, far removed from the majesty and formality of the United States Supreme Court, Melanie had peppered her with questions last night, as if she would be arguing before that austere body. And although this lower court was usually not the final arbiter of justice, the right to exhume the dead child's body might make the difference between life and death for George Calhoun.

Dani had argued motions or appeals dozens of times, maybe hundreds, yet each time she stood before a judge or a panel of judges, she needed to remind herself to calm down. She usually did settle her nerves once she actually started speaking. Even interruptions from the bench didn't rattle her train of thought. But at the beginning, as she'd rise from her seat, she'd feel the dampness of her hands and the quickening of her heartbeat.

At five minutes before 10, she and Melanie headed into the courtroom. Their motion papers had been submitted, and the LaGrange County prosecuting attorney had filed his objections. Almost immediately after Dani sat at the table in front of the court reserved for defendants' counsel, a middle-aged man wearing a brown tweed suit that seemed much too warm for the balmy spring day approached her.

"Ms. Trumball, I presume," he said as he held out his hand. "I'm Ted Landry."

"That's me," she answered as she shook his hand. "And this is my associate, Melanie Quinn."

"I must say I was surprised to get your papers. It's a bit late in the game, don't you think?"

Dani shrugged. "Well, I certainly wish we had more time on the clock. But as long as the clock is still ticking, there's still time to uncover the truth."

"Or," he said with a smile, "to throw monkey wrenches in the path of the truth."

He turned as the bailiff entered the courtroom. They knew the judge would be close behind him. "Well, good luck to you, Ms. Trumball. May the truth win out." He headed back to the prosecutor's table just before Judge Edwards entered the courtroom.

"All rise," intoned the bailiff, and everyone in the courtroom did as instructed. "You may be seated," he said after Judge Edwards had settled himself in his leather swivel chair behind the raised bench.

"*People against George Calhoun*," he called.

Dani answered, "Ms. Trumball for the defendant."

"Mr. Landry for the state."

Judge Edwards looked over at her table. "You have a motion before me, Ms. Trumball. I've read the papers, yours and the state's. Is there anything else you'd like to add?"

She stood up. "Yes, Your Honor."

"Well, now, before you get started, let me tell you what I'm thinking. I've read the cases you've put in your brief, but I have to say this just looks like a Hail Mary to me. Your client's been in prison over seventeen years and he's first asking to do DNA testing on the child's body?"

"Your Honor, I agree this appears to be late in the game, but my client notified his prior attorney at least five years ago of the reasons for exhuming the body claimed to be his daughter, and that attorney failed to follow through. It was a clear dereliction of his duty to defend his client diligently."

"Well, then, it seems to me you have a basis for attorney misconduct, but that's not the motion before me."

"I'll be filing an application for a writ of habeas corpus with the district court, but with execution scheduled for only three weeks away, you can appreciate the urgency of finding out just who's buried in that grave. If it's not Angelina Calhoun, then—well, the implications are obvious."

Landry stood up. "Your Honor, if I may. There are so many holes in this motion, it's leaking water all over the floor. And the mess can be mopped up with a single word: *laches*."

It was the argument Dani expected. It was based on the concept that fairness dictated that people shouldn't be allowed to procrastinate in asserting their rights. She had prepared for that claim. "Your Honor. Laches only applies when an adverse party has been prejudiced. The state can hardly claim that they've been hurt by the delay. They have no vested interest in seeing an innocent man put to death."

Landry quickly responded. "The state certainly does have an interest in finality. The Supreme Court has recognized that interest. The defendant had ample opportunity to ask that this body be exhumed and the child's DNA tested. Seventeen years of opportunity. This motion is nothing but a delaying tactic while they attempt to convince the federal courts to undo his conviction. An attempt I'm sure will be as unsuccessful as his previous appeals."

Dani started to speak, but Judge Edwards held up his hand. "Ms. Trumball, I'm sure your motion is well-meaning, but I have to agree with the state here. Your client should have spoken up at his trial."

"But Your Honor—"

"I know what you're going to say. I told you I read your papers. He was afraid his daughter wouldn't get the medical care she needed if he spoke up. Frankly, I find that story to be highly incredible. Motion denied," he said and called the next case.

Although disappointed, Dani was neither surprised nor discouraged. She'd already prepared an appeal in anticipation of this ruling. She just needed Judge Edwards's written order to append to her papers and she'd be ready to file.

"Do you believe that guy?" Melanie fumed as they walked out of the courtroom. "He barely let you say a word. It didn't matter what you were going to say—he'd already made up his mind."

"I knew it was a long shot with this judge. He has a reputation for being tough on crime. He's up for election next year and probably doesn't want to be known as the man who helped George Calhoun get out of prison."

"But the only way his ruling would get George out of prison is if it turns out the body isn't his daughter. How could setting an innocent man free hurt the judge?"

They didn't teach young lawyers about courtroom politics. Melanie still held the notion that justice was the guiding principle for all officers of the court. She needed to toughen up and come to terms with the real world. "Look, it's all about winning for everyone. The prosecuting attorney wants to win a conviction. She'll convince herself that weak evidence shouldn't stand in the way of removing criminals from the street. Maybe she'll hold back something that might help the defense even though she knows she shouldn't. Maybe she'll coach a witness whose memory isn't the best with what to say. The defense counsel convinces himself that the Constitution requires due process for even the lowest scum, and the Supreme Court has said that includes the right to adequate counsel. So he'll use just as many backhanded tactics to win an acquittal and assuage his conscience by believing he's upholding the Constitution. The judge wants to win reelection, so she'll choose to play it safe. Don't get me wrong. There are great judges, prosecutors, and defense attorneys committed to performing their roles with integrity and passion. But you have to realize there are too many of the other kind as well."

"Okay. So assume this judge wants to play it safe. I still don't see how ordering exhumation is risky."

"Let's say he ordered the exhumation, and the DNA test comes back proving she's Angelina Calhoun. Now the press is all over him for allowing this horrible murderer another chance, for delaying the justice they've all been waiting for. Edwards is a coward. He doesn't want to risk looking like he favors defendants. He knows we'll appeal, and if he's right in denying the order, it proves how smart he is. And if he's overturned, well, then, townsfolk can feel comfortable that he's a tough judge."

Melanie shook her head. Dani knew how she felt: disgusted. She had experienced it many times, both as a prosecutor in the US Attorney's Office and working at HIPP. Law school didn't prepare hopeful attorneys for the vagaries of judicial decision. The study of law was devoid of politics, of pettiness, of bad judges and incompetent attorneys. There was a purity to the study of law that Dani loved. Over the years, she'd come to terms with the messiness in the real-life practice of law.

They headed to Judge Edwards's office. A young woman sat at a desk outside his chambers. Dani handed her a business card. "Good morning. We just came from Judge Edwards's courtroom on the *People v. George Calhoun* case. I'd like to make sure we get a copy of the judge's decision as quickly as possible."

The young woman looked at the card. "I'm sure everyone wants the decision as soon as possible. It usually takes about a week, sometimes longer, depending on his calendar."

Secretaries were the gatekeepers. If this one weren't on Dani's side, she could delay typing up a decision out of spite. "I appreciate how busy everyone is. But my client is facing execution in three weeks. For a crime we don't believe he committed."

The young woman stared at her and sighed. "All right. I'll see what I can do."

"You are an angel of mercy," Dani said and thanked her.

"What now?" Melanie asked as they left the clerk's office.

"Now we pray Tommy comes up with something."

It seemed as if the rain would never stop. Six days in a row of nonstop showers made Sunny feel as if she were lost at sea, with nothing but water wherever she looked and no hope of rescue. Six days of putting together puzzles with Rachel, six days of reading *Goodnight Moon* over and over, six days of watching *Dora the Explorer* on the television. She thought she would lose her mind. Eric didn't understand. He'd come home exhausted in the evening and think Sunny's life was a breeze, taking care of a three-year-old her only responsibility. He didn't even demand dinner when he came home: Takeout from the Chinese restaurant or pizza parlor worked as well as a home-cooked meal. Nor did he mind when she hadn't tidied the apartment, Rachel's toys strewn all over the living-room floor and the laundry still waiting to be folded.

Stuck inside the apartment day after day made her feel trapped. Eric promised they'd move away from New York when he finished his residency. Sunny hoped it would be closer to her mother. She loathed being so far from her. She wondered whether Rachel would remember her life in New York City—the noise, the smell, the crowds. She recalled so little of her own childhood. Her first real memory was from when she was six and entering first grade. When she attempted to conjure up earlier events, she'd felt a strange uneasiness, so she'd stopped trying.

"Mommy, I'm bored."

Even her sweet-natured angel had turned whiny after six days of being cooped up.

"I know, Rachel. I think tomorrow the sun will be back and we can go to the park then. I bet Billy will be there."

"But I'm bored now."

Sunny understood boredom. It was her daily companion.

Eric heard the telephone ring first. He often received calls in the middle of the night and, despite his natural tendency to be a heavy sleeper, had trained himself to awaken quickly at that familiar sound. Expecting the hospital to be on the other end, he answered briskly, "Dr. Bergman." Sunny, finely attuned to the cries of a child, had learned to maintain a state of sleep through those calls, but something in Eric's tone broke through her sleep.

"I see," she heard him say softly. "When did it happen? No, of course, I'm sure you did everything you could." Quiet, and then Eric's voice again. "That would be a great help, thank you. We'll get the first plane out."

"What's wrong?" Sunny asked as she opened her eyes in the darkened bedroom.

"Sweetheart, I'm sorry."

"What are you saying? What's wrong?"

"Your mother. She's had a heart attack."

A state of disbelief seized Sunny. She bolted upright in bed and let herself be pulled into an embrace by Eric. "Is she okay?" she whispered, too afraid to speak the words loudly.

"No. I'm sorry. She passed away before the ambulance arrived."

"But … but … it can't be true. Mom's heart is fine. She's always been so strong."

"Sometimes it happens like that. With no warning." Eric held Sunny tight as the realization of her mother's death sunk in and her body shook from crying. A loud wail arose from her body. She kept shaking her head and murmuring, "No."

Eric stroked her hair until the sobs subsided.

"What will I do without her? She's my rock. I need her."

"I know."

"Who was on the phone?"

"Nancy. Your mother called her when she started having chest pains. She wanted to believe it was indigestion, but Nancy insisted she call 911. Only it was too late."

Nancy. Her mom's longtime friend. Almost like an aunt to Sunny.

Sunny tried to be strong, but tears erupted once more. Her father had died six years earlier. On her wedding day, when she walked down the aisle, she'd forced herself to hold back the tears that were so close to the surface because it wasn't her father by her side. "I have no one left," she said between sobs.

"You have me and Rachel."

"Yes, but it's not the same. I'm an orphan now. I've lost my history."

Eric stroked her arm and whispered comforting words to her. They didn't even try to return to sleep. He held Sunny in his arms until the outside light streaming through the blinds announced that a new day had begun.

The taxicab turned onto Aspen Road and Sunny felt her chest tighten. She had expected to return to her childhood home two weeks later for the Easter celebration. Her mother always waited in her plump window-side chair watching for her arrival. Now an empty house awaited her. Instead of a grandmother smothering Rachel with kisses, they'd walk into a deathly quiet home.

Nancy had made the funeral arrangements and contacted the few friends and family members who were left. Sunny had felt too numb to make decisions and was relieved to turn those responsibilities over to others. Now, as the taxicab turned into her driveway—her mother's driveway—tears once again began to roll down her cheeks.

"Don't cry, Mommy," Rachel said. "I'll kiss the boo-boo and make it all better."

Sunny wiped her wet cheeks with the back of her hand and wrapped her arm around Rachel. "You've already made it better. See? No more crying."

Eric paid the driver while Sunny and Rachel gathered their belongings and got out. The sun's rays were strong, the glare startling to Sunny. *That's wrong. It should be a gloomy day, not sparkling.* Yet everything did sparkle. The house, the lawn, the luxuriant gardens her mother had loved to tend. Holding Rachel's hand, Sunny unlocked the front door and stepped inside. Pictures of her family adorned the foyer walls.

Eric came in behind them. "Why don't you just relax? I'll call the funeral home and let them know we're here. We have a few hours before we're expected there."

It seemed surreal. Everything in the house looked the same as Sunny remembered: the gingham curtains in the kitchen that she'd helped her mother sew; on the dining-room table, the lace doily they'd picked up at a garage sale; the slipcovered sofa in the living room. Somehow, she'd thought it would be changed, different without her mother's presence. She walked from room to room, touching items in each. It gave her a sense of connection, connection to her mother, connection to her childhood.

The funeral service would be held the next day, a graveside service with just a small group in attendance. Her mother had retired from nursing a few years earlier and hadn't remained in touch with her former colleagues. "I want to travel while I'm still young enough to get around on my own," she'd said. And she did travel. Her first trip had been to New York, to visit Sunny. From there, she and Nancy flew to Paris. It had always been her dream to tour the Louvre, walk down the Champs Élysées, ride an elevator to the top of the Eiffel Tower. "It was everything I'd imagined," she told Sunny on her return. "Don't wait to travel until you're old, like me. Do it while you're young." She and Nancy had taken more trips after that, but the trip to Paris had remained special to her.

Sunny wondered if her mother would have begun traveling earlier in her life if she hadn't had her daughter to take care of. She'd been an older mother when she finally gave birth to Sunny, almost forty. The parents of Sunny's friends were still in their forties when their children went off to college, young enough to enjoy the freedom that brought. As Sunny walked through the house and fingered the knickknacks her mother had brought home from her travels, she wondered whether she had ever regretted being held down by a child. But as soon as the thought passed through her mind, it evaporated. Sunny knew that she had been the center of her parents' world, that they had loved every moment of their lives. Her mother had set aside her dream of traveling for something she cherished even more: her daughter. *How fortunate I was.* She settled onto the couch and looked at Eric and Rachel. She had postponed her own dream of becoming a nurse in favor of motherhood. As she watched her daughter snuggle in her father's lap, Sunny knew with certainty that she didn't regret her decision.

Chapter
18

Damn bureaucracies! Tommy had spent more than a week being shuffled from one agency to another and he'd gotten zilch. He'd hoped he wouldn't need to make a trip to Minnesota, but he'd gotten nowhere fast with the phone. Tomorrow he'd hoof it out there. Spring had finally arrived in New York. The incessant rain had stopped, the sun shone, and the golf course beckoned. He'd checked the weather forecast for Rochester, Minnesota, and it stunk. Wet and cold.

All his efforts had led to a state of gridlock as bad as anything that gripped Manhattan streets during rush hours. No movement forward, just sitting at his desk and twiddling his thumbs. Earlier that morning he'd gotten a call from the lab doing the testing on the note left tucked under his car's windshield wipers. The good news: The paper had yielded distinct fingerprints. The bad news: no match for them could be found in any of the databases.

Tommy wondered how Dani and Melanie were doing with their motion. There were only three ways to have certainty in this case: Exhume the body and find out definitively whether the child was Angelina Calhoun; find a record of her death in Minnesota; or find Angelina Calhoun, alive and well. That would be something, he thought, if she were still alive.

This case bothered him and not just because it involved a child. He'd been so convinced that this guy had handed them a load of baloney. Now he had doubts. Even if Calhoun had told the truth—and this was a big if—wasn't he still guilty of something? It must be a crime to abandon a sick child. Maybe if he hadn't, he would have found some way to get her medical treatment. Maybe she would have lived. And then there was that damned note on his car. What the hell was that about? There'd been no more nasty missives since he'd been back.

He looked at his watch and saw that it was after one o'clock. He sauntered to Bruce's office and stuck his head in. "Want to grab some lunch?"

Bruce looked at the clock on the wall and then at the papers strewn over his desk. "I probably shouldn't, but yeah, let's go. The weather's too nice to sit inside all day."

As they waited for the elevator, Tommy asked, "You ever miss not having kids?"

"Sometimes. When I'm at my sister's and her kids are running all over the place, all laughing and happy, I miss being a part of that."

"I know what you mean. It's great when they're young like that. You know, watching them at Little League and soccer, tumbling around on the floor with them, all that stuff. You can't believe how fast that changes. One day they're dependent on you for everything, and the next thing you know, they're embarrassed to admit you're their parents."

"Ah, the teenage years. I remember them fondly."

"Tommy Jr. is heading off for college in the fall. I don't know how Patty is going to handle that. She already gets weepy when she thinks about it."

"How about you? You ready for that?"

Tommy shook his head. "I remember what happened when I left for college. It was the beginning of moving out of the family into my own life. I know it's good for him. I know as parents we've got to let go, but still, it's hard to do. I guess that's why I'm so troubled by this Calhoun guy. I'm having a hard time letting Tommy Jr. fly the nest, and he's almost eighteen and healthy. How could Calhoun let go of his sick four-year-old? I just don't get it."

Bruce nodded. "It's hard to put ourselves in the minds of other people. We bring to these cases our own circumstances that make us the people we are. But we shouldn't judge decisions made by others who've had different life experiences. Unless they've broken the law."

"Well, the book is still out on Calhoun, as far as I'm concerned."

The elevator reached the lobby and they headed out the door into bright sunshine. "Well," Bruce said, "maybe after you get to Rochester, the answers will be as clear as today's weather."

"Maybe. I sure as hell hope so."

Tommy's plane landed at Rochester International Airport ten minutes early despite the driving rain. He wound his way through the airport corridors to the car-rental desk and then retrieved a Toyota Camry from the parking lot. He planned to check into his hotel and then start making visits. The first would be to the county Vital Records Office. He'd called the office, of course, one of the many fruitless calls he'd made. No death certificate could be found for an Angelina Calhoun. But she wouldn't have gone by her name. Maybe the first name would be the same, but if George had been truthful, he'd purposely stricken her real name from the medical records he'd hung around her neck.

Forty-five minutes later he stood at the front counter of the Vital Records Office. "Is Helen here by any chance?" he asked the heavy-set woman standing before him.

"Just left on a break. You can wait for her over there." She pointed to a bench against the wall.

"How long do you think she'll be?"

The clerk shrugged. She looked as if a smile would cause her face to crack into little pieces.

"Well, Anne? That's your name, right?" Tommy said, noting the name tag pinned to her shirt. "Maybe you can help me until she gets back. I need to check through your death certificates for a white female child between the ages of four and seven, dating back between sixteen and twenty years ago." Based on what Doc Samson had told him, Tommy figured that should cover the gamut of possible dates of death, assuming she'd succumbed to leukemia. It wasn't a perfect calculation, but there just wasn't time to expand the search.

Anne stared at Tommy with a blank expression.

"So, how 'bout it, Anne? Can you get me started on that?"

"You're joking, right?"

"Nope. Deadly serious."

"See those forms over there? Fill one out with what you're looking for. A search like that, figure six months or so. Maybe a year."

"I think I'll wait for Helen to get back," Tommy said and turned and walked to the bench against the wall. *Goddamn clerks. Do they go to school to learn how to drive people crazy?*

Ten minutes went by before a shapely young woman with straight black hair down to the middle of her back walked in. As she approached the front desk, Anne pointed at Tommy. "That man there was asking for you."

Helen turned and smiled warmly. "Yes? Can I help you?"

"I'm Tommy Noorland. We spoke on the phone a few days ago. Remember? About the little girl with leukemia?"

"Yes, of course. Come on back to my desk and we can talk there." Tommy followed her through the swinging door in the front counter to a desk in the back of the room. The first thing he noticed was a picture of Helen with a guy and a baby. *The good ones are always married,* he thought.

"As I told you on the phone, I'm not sure how much help we can be to you without more definitive information," Helen said as she settled into her chair. "You don't even know the child's name."

"Please tell me your records are computerized," Tommy said.

"Of course, back fifty years. Before that we'd have to go through the archives."

"Does your software have a search function?"

Helen nodded. "But I've never used it for anything other than searching a name."

"Could you try? You know how important this is."

"I do. And not just because your client is on death row. If the dead child isn't his, then it means some mother and father are out there who've spent almost twenty years not knowing what happened to their child. I can't imagine how agonizing that would be. So, yes, I do want to help you. If it's possible."

Thank goodness Helen had answered his initial phone call and not that sourpuss at the front desk. He was sure she'd have given him the brush-off. "Okay, so maybe we start with the year 1990, then narrow down results to where cause of death was leukemia, and then narrow those results to four-year-olds, and finally to females. And then do it the next year with five-year-olds. How does that sound?"

Helen had been fiddling with the computer while Tommy spoke. "I think it might work, but it's going to take some time. If you have some other things to do, I can work on this by myself and give you a call if I find anything."

Tommy gave her a big smile. "You're an angel. I owe you for this."

He wrote his cell number on the back of his card and handed it to Helen. As he headed out, he passed Anne behind the front counter. "Keep up the good work, sweetheart," he said and patted her fanny. He could have been wrong, but he thought he saw the barest hint of a smile.

Next stop—Olmsted County Community Services. If Angelina Calhoun had been abandoned in Rochester, Minnesota, someone would have called that agency to take her. Tommy had spoken to a few people there and mostly gotten a runaround. He didn't expect much more in person. By the time he arrived, the rain had finally tapered to a drizzle. After parking, Tommy walked into the building and scanned the directory for the right office. Five minutes later he sat at the desk of Roger Holmes. Roger looked like a throwback to the hippie generation: washed-out jeans, a T-shirt with a peace symbol on the front, bushy hair down to his shoulders, and a beard that should have been trimmed a decade ago. Tommy couldn't guess his age under all that hair, but he thought Roger was in his fifties. The nameplate on his desk had the initials "MSW" after his name.

Tommy had handed him Calhoun's signed release and a picture of three-year-old Angelina. Holmes sat staring at it. Finally he looked up. "I don't know what you expect me to do with this. You have no name of the child or the parents. And my crystal ball is out for repair."

"Look, I know I'm not asking for something easy. But maybe somebody here remembers a little girl being abandoned at the hospital."

Roger snorted. "You think that's unusual? I can't tell you the number of abandoned children we get. Not that it's an everyday occurrence, but enough so over the years that it's no longer shocking."

"This girl would have been different. She had leukemia. The parents left all her medical records with her."

Roger sat back in his chair and stroked his beard. "Let's see. Maybe Abby. She's old enough to have been around back in 1990. No." He shook his head. "I forgot she transferred here from up North." He continued stroking his beard, his lips moving silently as he rolled off names in his head. Suddenly his face brightened. "I know just who. She's not a caseworker, but Alice would know. She's been secretary to every director who's gone through these doors since 1979. Keeps track of everything that goes on in the office. If anyone remembers, it'd be Alice."

"Okay," Tommy said. "Let's go ask her."

Roger looked at the large clock on the adjacent wall: four thirty. He scanned the opposite end of the large open room and saw an empty desk next to the director's office. "You'll have to wait for tomorrow. She comes in at eight and leaves at four. She's gone for the day."

"Damn. I don't suppose you'd be willing to give me her home phone number."

Roger shook his head. "No can do, buddy."

"How about if you call her?"

"I wouldn't know her number. We don't share personal information here."

Tommy felt himself get irritated. He had a short fuse, a problem since his teen years. He'd gotten good at keeping it under control after he joined the FBI, but it still sparked now and then. "Look, somebody here's got to know her number. Don't you have a personnel office, or what do they call it now—human resources?"

"Sure, but they won't give you her phone number. What's the big deal about waiting one more day?"

"A man's fucking life. That's the big deal," Tommy said as he got up and left the office.

He'd had enough for one day. Flying always tired him out. He headed back to the hotel, where he took a long scalding-hot shower and ordered room service. While waiting for it to be delivered, he called Dani to report on his day.

"Please tell me you have good news, Tommy."

"Not yet. But it's also not hopeless. I've got a few things going here that might pan out. And I'm heading over to the hospital tomorrow."

"Well, we struck out today. The judge didn't even wait overnight to think about it. He ruled from the bench."

"You know, even though it's true that Angelina had leukemia, it doesn't mean our guy didn't kill her. Maybe it gave him more of a reason—he couldn't handle it. Or maybe he thought he'd save her from suffering in the end." He heard a sigh at the other end of the line. He pressed on. "You can't just ignore Sallie's confession. I mean, it's nineteen years later and she's still saying they killed their daughter." He appreciated how much Dani wanted George to be innocent. The thought of a parent murdering his child was abhorrent. But Tommy knew from his days at the FBI that most murders of children under the age of five were done by parents—fifty-seven percent. And the bulk of the rest were committed by other family members or family acquaintances. He would spend the time in Rochester looking for another answer, and he would do it diligently, but he didn't have high hopes that he'd find any trace of Angelina Calhoun in this city.

"She could barely look me in the eyes. There's no question she feels enormous guilt, but maybe it's over abandoning her sick daughter. Nineteen years of not knowing what happened to her. Not knowing whether she suffered a horrible death, all alone. Not knowing whether some stranger picked her up and did awful things to her. Yeah, I can see a mother feeling that she killed her daughter by leaving her the way they did."

Tommy would keep investigating and maybe he'd find something that would prove Dani right. He knew he'd never convince her otherwise.

Finally, the clouds were gone and sunshine greeted Tommy when he pulled back the heavy drapes in his room. The bright sky put him in a better mood. Not a great mood, just better. Being on the road, being away from his family, tired him. Lately, he'd thought about leaving HIPP and finding a steady security job, a nine-to-five life. He wasn't like the others there who were on a mission against capital punishment. He'd heard all the excuses criminals gave for their acts—their abusive childhoods, their alcoholic parents, their crime-infested neighborhoods. But for him it boiled down to this: Murderers should get what they gave.

He downed his usual breakfast—coffee and a cinnamon roll—and headed back to Olmstead Community Services to find Alice. An attractive young woman stood behind the counter with a welcoming smile. Her name tag read "Pam."

"You're a breath of fresh air to start the day with," he said.

Pam's smile dimmed. "Excuse me?"

"Just teasing you, sweetheart. I had a sourpuss wait on me yesterday over at Vital Records and you're a welcome improvement."

"Is there something I can do for you?" she asked, the smile now completely gone.

"I'm looking for Alice. Maybe Roger mentioned to you that I'd be back today?"

Pam's smile returned. "Oh, you're that investigator. Alice is all the way back in that corner," she said, pointing down the row of desks. "You can go on back. She's expecting you."

Tommy made his way past the various public workers, some busy at their desks, others chatting with each other. He passed one guy playing Freecell on his computer. As he approached Alice's desk, he saw a petite, gray-haired woman with thick-lensed glasses, dressed in a flowered blouse and a pleated skirt.

"Morning, Alice. I'm Tommy Noorland. Did Roger happen to speak to you about me?"

"You're the investigator, right? Asking about an abandoned child?"

"That's right."

"We've had a number of abandoned children who've come through these doors, but none that had leukemia."

"Are you certain? Have you gone back through the records?"

Alice's body stiffened. "I make it my business to know about the children that come through here. I can't remember the name of every one over the years, but I can assure you that I'd have remembered one who had leukemia. And such a pretty child, too. I certainly would have remembered that face."

Tommy couldn't say he was surprised. Step by step, his suspicions were being confirmed. George hadn't abandoned his sick daughter in Minnesota—he'd murdered her.

Last stop—the Mayo Clinic. His phone work back at the HIPP office had been helpful in working his way through the complex of campuses that made up the medical center. He knew just where he needed to go: If Angelina had been treated there, she would have ended up at either the Mayo Clinic Cancer Center or, more likely, Saint Mary's Hospital, where pediatric medicine was practiced. Tommy easily maneuvered through the streets of Rochester and arrived at Saint Mary's ten minutes later.

He'd called ahead and made an appointment with Dr. Jeffreys, head of the pediatric department. When he arrived, Jeffreys's secretary brought him into the doctor's office to wait for him. And wait. A half hour later, he started to get fidgety. He'd never had the patience to sit and do nothing. Just as he stood to leave, the door opened and a short, balding man with patches of red hair on the back and sides of his head walked in. Instead of hospital garb, he wore gray slacks and a navy blazer, with a blue striped shirt and a dark-red tie. He looked to be in his early forties, not old enough to have headed up pediatrics when Angelina was a toddler.

"I'm terribly sorry you had to wait so long," he said, holding out his hand. "I'm Dr. Jeffreys. Did anyone offer you some coffee?"

"No, but I'm fine. I already had my java for the morning. I appreciate you making the time to see me. I'm sure you're very busy."

"Well, yes, I am, of course, but I'm here now and so are you, so tell me, how can I help you."

Tommy handed the doctor Calhoun's signed release and took out a picture of Angelina. "Have you ever seen this child? It would have been about nineteen years ago."

"No," Dr. Jeffreys answered quickly. "But at that time I was still doing my residency at Yale Medical School. What's her name? I can check and see if there's a record of her as a patient here."

"Her real name was Angelina Calhoun, but she probably would have been registered under a different name."

"I don't understand."

Tommy filled him in about Calhoun's story.

"I'm afraid it's going to be hard to help you. None of the doctors in the peeds unit now were on staff back in 1990."

"Do you know if any are still in the area, maybe in a private practice?"

"Daniels moved to our center in Miami; Goldstein retired and I've heard he's moved, but I can't say where; and Blonstein, well, he passed away suddenly last summer."

It was like a broken record everywhere he went. Nobody knew anything. Was that the case because Angelina had never been here or because it was just too damn hard to search back nineteen years when he didn't even know what name she'd been given? Either way, he had nothing.

"I suppose I could post her picture in the doctors' lounge," Dr. Jeffreys offered. "If you have another copy of her photo, I could post it in the nurses' lounge as well. You never know."

"Thanks, Doc. Anything would help. But you know, we're running out of time here, so if someone recognizes her, they need to reach me ASAP." Tommy thanked the doctor and left.

As he walked to his carm his cell phone rang. "Tommy Noorland here."

"Tommy, this is Helen, from Vital Records. I just finished the search. I'm sorry. Nothing came up."

"Thanks, Helen. I appreciate you trying."

Well, that's it. I'm batting zero. If George was telling the truth, I don't think we'll ever find out.

*H*e'd stared at the computer screen for twenty minutes, transfixed by the half-column story in the Indiana Star. He'd almost missed it. Now he couldn't take his eyes off it. "Indiana State Superior Court denies bid to exhume dead child's body." That was the headline. He had just scanned the page when the name "George Calhoun" screamed out.

Okay. He had to calm down. It had been denied. They weren't going to dig her up. But he knew that rulings got appealed. Maybe this wasn't over. Damn! His hands were clammy. His chest felt tight. He struggled to take a breath. Was he having a heart attack? He almost wished he were. Then this would be over. The terror of being discovered would be gone.

Slowly, the tightness subsided and his breathing relaxed. He was okay. He would come through this. God hadn't spared him only to trip him up now, like some sort of cosmic joke. He thought about it. Was there another appeal? Maybe it was too late now. But if there were enough time, if they could appeal and the court let them exhume the body, then what? Even if they learned it wasn't the Calhouns' daughter, they still wouldn't know who was buried in that anonymous grave. Only he knew the name of the child. Only he knew he'd caused her death, burned her body beyond recognition, and discarded her like worthless trash.

He'd done what he had to to protect himself. And he'd do whatever needed to be done to continue protecting himself.

"I realize it's only been a week, but have you thought about what you're going to do with your mother's house?"

Nancy's question startled Sunny. She felt a rush of tears and struggled to hold them back. She couldn't bear parting with the house on Aspen Road. Not yet, at least. Later, when the pain of her mother's death wasn't so intense. She knew, though, that her reluctance stemmed from a secret wish that they would return to that house when Eric finished his residency. That was just a little more than a year away.

Byron was a wonderful place to raise a family, with its tree-lined streets, good schools, and neighbors who looked out for each other. Her mother had met Nancy when she lived in the house next door. They'd quickly become friends and remained so after Nancy and her husband moved.

"I don't want to sell it, Nancy. Maybe after Eric finishes here, when we know where we'll end up. But not yet."

"Don't worry about it. I know a handyman who can close it up. You know, drain the pipes and those sorts of things. I hope I'm not being too practical for you now, but there are some matters you should deal with right away."

"No, you're right. Is there something else I should be doing?"

"Well, you need to cancel the phone and cable service, things like that. And do you know if your mom left a will?"

"No. We never talked about that. I never thought that Mom might die. I mean, of course I knew it would happen someday, just not so soon."

"Well, whether she did or didn't, you'll need a lawyer to transfer the house into your name. Make sure everything is done proper and all. I can recommend an estate attorney if you'd like."

"You've been a godsend during this whole ordeal, Nancy. I don't know what I would have done without you."

After they finished their conversation and said their goodbyes, Sunny went back to cleaning up the breakfast dishes. She felt an ache in her chest when she thought of her mother, of their strong bond and their fierce love for each other. Her mother had been her best friend and now she was gone. Sunny's ties to Byron were severed.

Manhattan life seemed so different from life in Byron. No one smiled. No one made small talk when they passed in the hallway or rode together in the elevator. Thank goodness for play dates, when children got together while their mothers watched and gabbed. At least then she had some women to talk to. Not that they talked about anything serious. Sunny called it "empty talk." What movies they'd seen, what had happened on the latest installment of their favorite television shows, what gossip they'd heard. Sunny would never discuss with them the isolation she felt in this imposing city, how inadequate she sometimes felt raising a child, how she yearned to be living in a small town.

She'd had a wonderful childhood in Byron and wanted the same for Rachel. Instead of organized play dates, the children on her street would go door to door gathering friends. They'd ride their bikes up and down the block, make up games to play in their backyards, explore the nooks and crannies in each other's homes. When they were at Sunny's house, her mother would often be planted at the kitchen table, lost in discussion with Nancy. Sometimes Sunny would catch snippets of their conversation, so she knew they'd shared their deepest concerns and desires.

She heard rustling coming from Rachel's bedroom, a sign that she was stirring from her nap. Rachel usually awoke with a lusty cry, but if she saw Sunny sitting on her bed and stroking her arm, she awoke with a smile. Sunny headed to the bedroom.

"Hi, sleepyhead," she said as Rachel opened her eyes. "Want some ju-ju?"

"Yeth, apple ju-ju."

Sunny knew she meant apple juice. "Okay, scoot out of bed and let's go get some."

"And then play with Billy?"

"No, sweetie, not today."

"I want Billy," she whined.

How could she explain to her daughter that she was still too sad to sit with other women and engage in "empty talk." "We'll go to the zoo today. How about that?"

"And we'll see the aminals?"

"Yes, and you can feed the goats and sheep if you'd like."

Rachel's face glowed with her smile. "Yippee."

How easy to please a three-year-old, Sunny thought. *If only life stayed that way.*

Dani was exhausted. She and Melanie had worked around the clock. After filing the appeal of Judge Edwards's order denying exhumation of the body, they'd gone painstakingly through everything that had taken place before HIPP became involved and put together a petition, filed in the federal district court of northern Indiana, to set aside Calhoun's conviction on the basis of ineffective assistance of counsel. The papers had been submitted and now all they could do was wait for the hearing dates. Tonight was the first time Dani had been home in weeks without hours of work awaiting in her upstairs office.

With Jonah fast asleep, Dani lay entwined in Doug's arms on the living-room couch. It was honeymoon hour, but she was too tired to talk. She snuggled in his arms silently while he stroked her hair. The tenderness of his touch soothed her and she felt herself begin to unwind. "I think our papers are good, but they would have been so much stronger if Tommy had been able to get some confirmation of Calhoun's story," she said when her energy started to return.

"You can only deal with the facts you have."

"Well, obviously. I've been doing this for some time, you know. I'm not naïve."

"Ouch."

She sighed. "I know. I'm being irritable and I shouldn't. I'm just too tired to restrain myself."

"It's okay. I've been married to you for some time, and I know how you get. I'm not naïve."

"Ouch."

They both laughed, and suddenly Dani felt the heaviness she'd carried around for days leave her body. "Seriously, I'm worried about Calhoun's chances. It's so much easier when the appeal is based on DNA evidence."

"That's true. You've got a tough road here. Especially this late in the game. He's already been turned down on multiple appeals."

"Sure, but his lawyer did a half-assed job on those. And George hadn't offered an explanation for his daughter's disappearance back then."

"The court's not going to look too kindly on him waiting seventeen years to offer that explanation."

That's what troubled Dani the most. Seventeen years of silence. She understood Calhoun's reason. She appreciated the driving force to protect his child. Silence bought Angelina the possibility of treatment. It bought George hope that she would have a future. But once five or six years had passed, the time when it would be known whether the treatment had helped her or she had succumbed to the cancer, he'd still offered no explanation. Why? Dani had spoken to Calhoun on the phone many times since her first visit. When she asked that question, he said, "I didn't think anyone would believe me." And perhaps he was right. When he finally did broach it with his first attorney, Wilson ignored him.

"I know. My fear is they'll equate his silence with guilt. That's what Tommy thinks. He's sure George only gave us part of his story; that he mixed some truth with his lies to make him seem more believable. He knew we'd be able to confirm his daughter's medical history and then made up a story that would be impossible to check out."

"What does he think happened to Angelina?"

"He thinks George murdered her. Maybe because he felt over-whelmed by her illness, maybe because he thought it more merciful than letting her suffer."

"And you? Do you have any doubts?"

She thought about Doug's question. This was her first investigation. It had been her decision to take Calhoun's case. It would make sense for her to feel some uncertainty, but she didn't. "None. Absolutely none. And that's what makes this so hard. I believe Calhoun is innocent, but I'm not sure I can save him."

"So he will have sacrificed his life for his daughter's."

"Maybe, or maybe his daughter died anyway, alone and frightened. And maybe he deserves to be punished for that. But does he deserve to die?"

Doug, ever the professor, passed on the question. "What do you think?"

"No. Without reservation, no."

Each time the office phone rang, Dani hoped it was a court advising her of a hearing date. Her fingers were crossed that they'd hear first from the state court on the exhumation appeal. It would change everything if the girl found in the woods wasn't George's daughter. Of course, if she was Angelina, that changed things too. Not everything perhaps, because she could still appeal based on the inadequacy of Calhoun's counsel. But she had to ask herself: Would she still want to continue with the appeal if it was Angelina's body in the grave? She mulled over the scenario and realized she would. Before meeting George, she'd have said an emphatic "no." Now, hearing about Angelina's illness, knowing the despair George and Sallie experienced, made her realize she was wrong to have an absolute ban on representing child murderers. Even if Tommy was right about George, he didn't deserve to die. Perhaps if Wilson had done a better job, George would have received a sentence of life in prison rather than execution.

"Hear anything yet?" Bruce asked as he walked past her office.

"Not a word. Is it usual for it to take this long?"

"We like to think the judges share the same sense of urgency we do, but that's not always true."

"I can't seem to concentrate on anything else now."

"Your briefs are top-notch, you've gone over the oral argument dozens of times—it's out of your hands now. Let it go."

"Are you able to do that with your cases?"

Bruce smiled. "Never."

He left Dani's office and she pulled out an appeal she'd been working on for a different inmate. It was routine stuff: DNA evidence that had been unavailable when the client was convicted now proved his innocence. He had been convicted solely on one eyewitness's testimony. Eyewitness accounts were the least reliable evidence, she knew, but juries loved it. They gobbled up the words of someone sitting on the witness stand, saying, "He did it. I saw him do it." Nothing made them feel more comfortable sentencing a man, especially a black man, to the electric chair or to a lethal injection or whatever barbaric means a state chose to kill a convicted murderer. It didn't matter if the prosecution lacked forensic evidence to go with the eyewitness testimony or if the accused had an alibi, especially if the alibi was a friend or a family member.

Doug always demonstrated the unreliability of eyewitness accounts to the students in his Evidence class in dramatic fashion. Once, before Dani had begun working again, she sat in on his class to watch the lesson unfold. He began the lecture with a discussion of the case they were studying. In the midst of this discussion, a gun-wielding stranger burst into the classroom. "Don't move," he shouted in a loud staccato voice. He rushed over to Doug, grabbed him and pointed the gun at his head. "Anyone fuckin' moves, I shoot this guy. Hands on your desks—I wanna see them. Now," he screamed at the students, a note of hysteria in his voice. "You," he said to Doug, jabbing the gun against his temple, "hand me your wallet." After Doug reached inside his jacket and turned his wallet over, the intruder grabbed Doug's gold watch off his wrist and seemingly knocked him unconscious with the butt of his gun. Doug fell to the floor, the students gasped, and the intruder ran out. The entire incident lasted less than a minute. After a moment of stunned silence, a few students rushed from their seats to Doug's aid, but before they could get to the front of the classroom, Doug calmly stood up with a big grin on his face.

"Congratulations," he said to them. "You're all eyewitnesses to a crime. Who can describe the perpetrator?"

Amazingly, in a class of about a hundred students, he got almost a hundred different descriptions. When Doug first began his theatrical event, he used a third-year student to act the part of the robber. Soon, he realized that New York City probably had more unemployed actors than any place outside Los Angeles, many willing to work for peanuts, and he began hiring an actor to play the role. He used actors of all races and nationalities. Sometimes he dressed the actor in neutral nondescript colors; sometimes he had him wear one brightly colored article of clothing, perhaps a hat or a jacket. It didn't matter. Each time, the students argued vociferously about the color of his hair, his height, his weight, his age, the clothing worn, even the color of his skin. When the perpetrator wore a brightly colored article of clothing, it was frequently identified, but the students rarely reached agreement on other characteristics of the intruder. It was eye-opening for them; they all thought they were too smart to be mistaken.

The ring of the telephone broke Dani's concentration. She looked at the caller identification and, seeing an Indiana exchange, grabbed the phone before her secretary picked up. "Dani Trumball," she said into the receiver.

"Ms. Trumball, this is the clerk's office at the US District Court for the Northern District of Indiana. I'm calling to let you know the hearing on your petition is scheduled for Monday at 10:00 a.m. It's down for a day and a half. Will that be enough time?"

Her heart fell. Today was Thursday. Unless the state appeals court called by the end of the day, it looked like she'd be trying Calhoun's ineffective-counsel petition first. "Yes, that should be fine." After hanging up, she dialed Melanie on the intercom. "I just heard from the district court. We're on for Monday."

"Damn," Melanie said under her breath. "What do you think is taking the state court so long? Maybe we should call and remind them of the date of execution."

"I've been calling every day. I'm on a first-name basis with the chief clerk over there by now. She's sympathetic, but it's up to the scheduling judge."

"What do you need me to do?"

"Subpoena Bob Wilson for Monday morning. He's not going to be happy, but I'm sure he's expected this. And the doctor at Meadowbrook Hospital. I'd love for him to appear, but we can't compel him from another state. If he can't come to Indiana, then let's get his affidavit."

"Okay, I'll get on it."

"And I'll arrange for Calhoun to be brought to court. We'll need him to testify."

Dani hung up and put away the appeal she'd been working on before the call came in. Her full attention was now devoted to Calhoun and getting ready for court on Monday.

Fifteen Days

The federal courthouse in Fort Wayne, Indiana, was a granite-and-limestone modified Greek Doric edifice with marble floors and walls in its lofty vestibule. Tommy had joined Dani and Melanie for their trip back to Indiana, and they were all settled in the courtroom, ready to go. The assistant US attorney opposing the motion, Jolene Getty, was a mid-thirties woman dressed in a power suit: a black, pinstriped pencil skirt with matching jacket and a crisp ivory blouse. Unlike the female attorneys depicted on television, who showed up in court with cleavage-revealing sweaters, she evinced professionalism. Introductions had already been made, and they were awaiting the judge. George, hands and feet shackled, dressed in an orange prison jumpsuit, sat in the prisoner's box, a row of chairs reserved for men and women brought from various jails and prisons to participate in the proceedings.

As in the state court last week, the bailiff preceded the judge and told all to rise. Judge Arnold Smithson entered, seated himself, and indicated with his hands that everyone should be seated.

"Counselor," he said, nodding in Dani's direction, "are you ready to proceed?"

"I am, Your Honor."

"Go ahead."

Dani stood and pointed to several boxes laid out on a separate table. The boxes contained the complete transcript of each of Calhoun's trials and hearings as well as all exhibits entered in those proceedings. They also contained copies of all decisions rendered in his case. "I'd like to mark the documents in those boxes as Petitioner's Exhibit A."

"Any objections?" Smithson asked the opposing counsel.

"None," Getty answered.

"So marked."

The records were key to HIPP's claim that George had received ineffective counsel both at his trial and at all post-trial appeals. The relevant sections of the transcripts had been included in Dani's brief—a written argument to the court supporting her claim of ineffective counsel—which had already been submitted to the court. The brief laid out each of the points during the trial where the prior counsel's performance was deficient. There were a plethora of instances where he failed to object when he should have and where he failed to subject the prosecution's witnesses, especially Sallie, to meaningful cross-examination. However, the clearest evidence of Wilson's failure to provide effective assistance of counsel was not in the written record, so Dani needed to introduce those facts at this hearing.

"Do you have any witnesses?" Smithson asked.

"I do."

"Go ahead and call your first witness."

"I call Robert Wilson to the stand."

Wilson lumbered up to the witness box, clearly unhappy to be there. Dani walked over to him. "Mr. Wilson, you represented the defendant"—she pointed to George—"on charges of murder in the first degree, did you not?"

"I certainly did. And at substantially less than my usual fee."

"Have you represented other defendants in capital cases?"

"Sure have. Plenty of them."

"So you were familiar with the amount of work involved in a capital case when you accepted Mr. Calhoun as a client."

"Well, some cases take more work than others. Depends on the circumstances."

"And when you decided to take Mr. Calhoun's case, did you have an idea of how much work would be involved?"

"I made my estimate. Not much you can do when your wife confesses and implicates you."

"And in fact, you expected to enter into a plea bargain with this case, isn't that so?"

"Objection," Getty called out. "Leading."

"Let me rephrase," Dani said before the judge could rule. "When you agreed to take his case, did you have any expectations of the outcome?"

Wilson hesitated. "Well, I certainly thought it made sense to try and get a plea, take the death penalty off the table."

"And was an offer made by the prosecution for a plea agreement?"

"They sure as heck made one, but my client insisted he wanted to go to trial. Over my strong counsel to the contrary, I might add."

"Did he tell you why?"

"Said it wasn't his daughter they found in the woods."

"Would you tell the court what you did about his claim?"

"What I did? There wasn't anything to do. His wife had already said it was their daughter and that George there killed her and left her in the woods, where the police found her."

"Did you question Mrs. Calhoun as part of your preparation for trial as to whether the girl found was her daughter?"

"I had a copy of her videotaped confession. There wasn't any need to speak to her."

"Did you request any psychiatric testing be done on Mrs. Calhoun?"

"I asked around her neighborhood, where she worked. Nobody thought she was crazy."

"You didn't order a DNA test on the body found in the woods, right?"

"Didn't seem to be any point to do so. Like I said, Mrs. Calhoun had already admitted it was their daughter."

"DNA tests are expensive, aren't they?"

"A lot more than the Calhouns could afford."

"Did you apply to the court for funds to pay for a DNA test?"

Wilson sighed. "I keep telling you. There wasn't any point."

"What pretrial investigation did you undertake, then?"

"I spoke to his neighbors and his employer. I got them to testify to his good character."

"That was for the penalty phase, though, right?"

"Well, the trial outcome was pretty obvious. I tried to get some mitigating factors before the jury so they'd sentence him to life in prison, like his wife."

Dani returned to her table and looked through some papers before walking back to the witness stand. "You said Mr. Calhoun denied that the girl they found was his daughter. Did he tell you what happened to his daughter?"

"That's the thing. He wouldn't say a word. You can see how my hands were tied when he wouldn't explain his daughter's disappearance. After that, there wasn't much that any lawyer could do."

"You represented Mr. Calhoun on all his appeals, didn't you?"

"Everything up till you folks stepped in last month."

"And during all that time that you represented Mr. Calhoun, did he ever explain what happened to his daughter?"

"Never." He caught himself. "Wait. He did say one time, maybe about five years ago—he said something about his daughter being sick. About nobody helping her. I don't remember the details. It didn't make much sense. I thought I put the letter in his file, but I guess it got thrown away by mistake."

Wilson had changed his story to avoid reprimand by the judge. He knew all correspondence from his client should have been placed in his file, not wantonly discarded as he'd admitted to Dani when she first met him in his office. She let it pass. She didn't want to crucify Wilson.

"Did you ever follow up with Mr. Calhoun about his claim that Angelina had been ill?"

Wilson looked down sheepishly. He'd been told about Tommy's conversation with Dr. Samson at Meadowbrook Hospital. "I've got to admit, I didn't think it was real, his story. I just let it go."

She'd gotten what she needed from Wilson, and after a few more questions she turned him over to Getty.

The assistant US attorney walked to the witness box. "Mr. Wilson, on any of your capital cases prior to Mr. Calhoun's, had you ever sought DNA testing?"

"Not that I can remember."

"And isn't that because the science was still in its infancy at that time?"

"I believe that's true. Wasn't until years later it began to be used more often, and that was at first by the police. They started using it to tie up their evidence against the alleged perpetrator. It was after the prosecution began introducing it that defense counsel started using it to clear their clients."

"So considering all of the circumstances at that time, would you say that, using an objective standard of reasonableness, it was proper not to seek DNA testing?"

"Objection," Dani called out. "Calls for a conclusion."

"He's an attorney, and this is within his area of expertise," Getty said.

"Whether or not it was unreasonable to seek DNA testing is the ultimate issue in this case and for the court to adjudicate," Dani said.

"I'll allow it," Judge Smithson said.

"I can't imagine another attorney back then would have asked for DNA tests, especially given the facts of this case," Wilson answered.

Getty finished her questioning of Wilson and Dani stood up. "Just a few more questions. Do you know what the situation pertaining to the admittance of DNA evidence was five years ago?"

"Well, by then it was pretty much standard—that is, in cases where it was relevant."

Dani thanked him and he was excused. He left the courtroom and purposely avoided looking at Dani. She was sure she wouldn't be seeing him again.

"Do you have any more witnesses?" Judge Smithson asked.

"I do, Your Honor."

"Well, then, I think we'll break for lunch now. We'll reconvene at one o'clock."

Dani walked over to George. A guard waited nearby to take him back to a cell in the courthouse. "It's going well. You should keep your hopes up."

"Thank you," he said, his voice barely a whisper. He started to say something but stopped himself.

"What is it, George?"

"I wondered—I mean …" He stopped again and stared down at his feet. Dani saw that his hands were shaking.

"It's okay, George. You can ask me anything."

"It's just—I just thought you might have tried to find out what happened to Angelina. After we left her at the hospital?"

Dani put her hand on top of his. "I'm sorry. We did try, but we haven't been able to find anything."

George nodded and didn't say a word. As he left the courtroom, his head was slumped, his shoulders rounded. Before they'd gotten any ruling from this judge, their client was already defeated.

They found a small luncheonette two blocks from the courthouse and settled in for lunch. They got the last open table in the jampacked restaurant. Determined to be good, Dani ordered salad, dressing on the side, while Tommy and Melanie waited for their hamburgers.

"What do you think?" Melanie asked. "About this morning?"

"We got what we needed from Wilson into the record."

"Do you think it'll hurt us that they didn't use DNA testing much when George was tried?"

"I don't think it should. I mean, he didn't even ask for blood-typing tests to be done on the child's body. For all we know, their blood types were incompatible. He took whatever money George had and then went on autopilot."

"What happens if you lose this round?" Tommy asked.

Dani shook her head. Normally the next steps would be an appeal to the federal court of appeals and then, if they lost, review by the United States Supreme Court. But they were running out of time. Only two weeks remained before the scheduled date of execution. "I don't know. Try to get a quick appeal, I guess."

They ate their meals in silence, each of them aware of the clock running out.

They were back in court ten minutes early. When the judge arrived and all were seated, Dani called Dr. Samson as her next witness. She'd caught one lucky break: He'd been able to locate his medical records for Angelina Calhoun.

"Dr. Samson, are you familiar with the defendant?" Dani asked.

"Yes, that's George Calhoun. I treated his daughter, Angelina."

"What did you treat her for?"

"Acute lymphoblastic leukemia, usually referenced as 'ALL.' Evaluation showed she was pre-B-cell ALL."

"Can you tell the court what that means in layman's terms?"

"It means there are a large number of abnormal white blood cells in the bone marrow. Normal white cells protect the body from disease, but these can't because they are defective. *Acute* means the onset was rapid, and *lymphoblastic* refers to the type of white blood cells affected—that is, the lymphocytes. *Pre-B-cell* means the leukemia cells began in the B-cells but weren't yet fully mature."

"And what is the expected rate of survival for children with this type of cancer?"

"Well, now it's quite high. Back then, survival was more uncertain."

"How did you treat Angelina for her leukemia?"

"With chemotherapy. She underwent six months of treatment, after which she went into remission."

"Did there come a time when that changed?"

"Yes. About a year and a half later she began exhibiting symptoms. I performed a spinal tap and determined that the leukemia had spread through her central nervous system to her brain."

"What did that mean for her prognosis."

"It was very poor."

"Was there treatment available?"

"Yes, more chemotherapy and this time radiation as well. Her best chance of survival, though, was a bone-marrow transplant with an acceptable match. I agreed to waive my fee, but the hospital had previously extended credit to the Calhouns and weren't willing to do so again. He needed to raise funds to pay for the treatment. I never heard from the family after that."

"Dr. Samson, do you believe George Calhoun capable of murdering his daughter?"

"Objection. Calls for speculation," Getty called out.

"Your Honor, Dr. Samson has treated thousands of children with cancers. I believe he has expertise in how families react to such a diagnosis."

"I'll allow it. Go ahead, Dr. Samson."

"No. I don't believe he would have harmed his daughter. When families receive news like this, they become very protective of their child, and that was true of the Calhouns. It was clear to me that they loved their daughter very much."

"Thank you, Dr. Samson. No further questions."

Getty stood up. "Dr. Samson, would you describe what would happen to Angelina without treatment?"

"She would certainly die."

"And can you describe what she would experience in the late stages?"

"There would be loss of appetite with accompanying weight loss, significant bruising over her body, and considerable pain from the enlargement of her organs."

"So a parent devoted to his child and who couldn't afford treatment might want to spare his child that agony. Isn't that possible?"

"I can't see the Calhouns doing that."

"But is it possible?"

"I suppose it is."

"Thank you. No further questions."

Smithson looked at Dani. "Call your next witness."

She called George Calhoun.

"Mr. Calhoun, when you were arrested for the murder of the child found in the woods in Orland, Indiana, what did you tell the officers?" she asked.

"I told them it couldn't be my daughter."

"Did you tell them why it couldn't be your daughter?"

"No, ma'am."

"Did there come a time when you told your attorney, Mr. Wilson, that it wasn't your daughter found in the woods?"

"Yes, ma'am, the very first time I met with him."

"Did you tell Mr. Wilson why it couldn't be your daughter?"

"No, not then."

"At any time?"

"Yes, ma'am. About five years ago, when my last appeal was coming up, I sent him a letter and told him about Angelina, about her being sick and nobody willing to treat her."

"Is that all you told him?"

"Well, I also told him that we took her to the Mayo Clinic and left her there with all her records so that someone would have to treat her since she was all alone."

"Mr. Calhoun, you were on trial for murdering your daughter and burying her body in Orland, Indiana. The state sought the death penalty. Why didn't you tell your lawyer at that time what you had done with Angelina?"

Calhoun shifted in his seat and looked at the floor. "I was afraid if I told them where we left Angelina, they would take her back home, and then nobody would help her get better."

"Why did you decide to tell Mr. Wilson the truth about your daughter five years ago?"

"Well, I figured it was safe for her then. You know, if the treatment helped her, she'd have been all better. And if she'd lived, she'd be eighteen then, so she could decide for herself whether she wanted to see me and Sallie again."

"And if she hadn't survived?"

"Well, then, if the Mayo Clinic hadn't been able to help her, then it wouldn't of mattered anymore if I told the truth."

"Thank you, Mr. Calhoun. That's all I have."

Getty stood and walked to the witness box. "I have a few questions. How many times did you tell Mr. Wilson about your daughter's illness?"

"Just that once, in the letter."

"You never pursued it further with him?"

"No."

"Mr. Calhoun, I find it hard to believe that with your life hanging in the balance, you didn't try harder to talk to your attorney about that."

"Is there a question here?" Dani asked.

Getty smiled. "Sorry, I couldn't restrain myself from making that observation. I'll move on. Have you ever tried to find your daughter? Or find out what happened to her?"

"How could I do that? I was in prison."

"Please just answer the question."

"No."

"So you'd like us to believe that you left your sick daughter in another state, never told anyone, and never tried to find out whether she lived or died, is that right?"

"A day never passed that I wasn't thinking about my little girl. Everything I did was so she could have a good life."

"Very commendable, Mr. Calhoun, assuming your story is true. Her medical bills were very high, weren't they?"

"Yes, ma'am."

"If Angelina disappeared, then you wouldn't have to go into debt for her, isn't that right?"

"It didn't matter how much debt I'd have. I would have given every penny I had to make her well."

"But in fact you had no more money to pay for her treatment, isn't that right?"

George's eyes became misty. When he spoke, his voice was choked. "I tried everything I could. I begged for loans from every bank. I begged my boss for an advance. He would have too, but it was just too much money."

"Did you know how much your daughter would suffer as the disease progressed?"

George shook his head.

"You need to speak your answer, Mr. Calhoun."

"I could see how she suffered."

"Murdering Angelina would end her suffering, wouldn't it?"

"I would never have done that. Never."

"So you say. Seventeen years later and two weeks before your execution. Very convenient."

Dani jumped to her feet, outraged. "Objection," she shouted.

"No further questions," Getty said before the judge could rule.

"I have no more witnesses," Dani informed the judge.

"Ms. Getty, do you have any witnesses?"

"No, Your Honor."

"Okay, then. Let's have closing arguments tomorrow morning at 10:00 a.m."

Dani thanked the judge, gathered her files and, with Tommy and Melanie, headed to their hotel. She felt cautiously optimistic. She wouldn't allow herself to think of the alternative.

"Your Honor," Dani began as she stood before Judge Smithson, ready with her closing argument, "under the standard set forth in the Supreme Court decision in *Strickland*, we must show that Robert Wilson's representation of George Calhoun in his murder trial, and the appeals that followed, fell below an objective standard of reasonableness and that deficiency prejudiced the defendant. There can be no doubt that Mr. Wilson failed utterly in that regard. *Strickland* required him to make a reasonable investigation into the facts of the crime and his client's culpability. Instead, he made no investigation at all. This was a death-penalty case—his client's life was at stake. Yet over and over he accepted at face value the prosecution's flimsily constructed case. Did he look into Mr. Calhoun's insistence that the body in the woods wasn't his daughter? No. Not before his trial and not after he learned from Mr. Calhoun why it couldn't have been Angelina Calhoun. That alone is sufficient to rule that George Calhoun did not receive effective assistance of counsel, a right guaranteed him by our Constitution, a right especially to be guarded when the penalty upon conviction is death."

She paused. "Now, why did Mr. Wilson fail to investigate his client's claim? He says it was because Sallie Calhoun identified the child as theirs. Should her word be enough to contradict her husband's? No, not when Mr. Calhoun's life was on the line. A simple test—a blood test—might have ruled out George Calhoun as the father of that little girl. Mr. Wilson never asked for one. He never asked for a psychiatric exam of Mrs. Calhoun. He never even spoke directly to Sallie Calhoun. If he had, maybe he would have come away believing she harbored so much guilt over abandoning her daughter that it seemed to her that they had murdered her. Maybe he would then have cross-examined her more thoroughly on the witness stand and raised doubt in the jurors' minds as to what really happened.

"And then, when Mr. Calhoun finally confessed what had happened to Angelina, what did Mr. Wilson do? Nothing! He ignored the letter and never spoke about it to his client. Would a reasonable attorney look into Angelina's medical records to see if Mr. Calhoun told him the truth? Yes. Would a reasonable attorney ask for a DNA test then? Yes. Not Robert Wilson.

"Your Honor, there are so many more instances in the record of Wilson's abject failure to even marginally meet a standard of reasonable performance. His apparent belief in his client's guilt led him to willfully disregard just about every aspect of this case. As a result, Mr. Calhoun never received a fair hearing. He was tarred and feathered by his own attorney before a single witness testified.

"Did Mr. Wilson's failures prejudice the defendant? Without question. It goes without saying that had a simple blood test been conducted and shown that Mr. Calhoun could not have been the girl's father, there would not even have been a trial. And if DNA testing had been conducted five years ago and had shown definitively that he was not the father, Mr. Calhoun would be a free man right now. Do we know those would be the outcomes of the tests? No, because Mr. Wilson never asked for them. But the defendant doesn't have to prove that he wouldn't have been found guilty. He must only show that there's a reasonable probability that the results of the proceedings would have been different had Mr. Wilson done an effective job. Perhaps if Mr. Wilson had conducted the most basic investigation, which would have revealed Angelina Calhoun's medical condition, and informed the jurors of her cancer and the stress it placed on her family, the jurors might have imposed a sentence of life, instead of death.

"Robert Wilson's counsel strayed so far below the range of professional competencies as to be shocking. This court should recognize the travesty that has occurred and rule that George Calhoun's conviction be set aside. Thank you."

She sat down and Melanie leaned over to whisper into her ear. "Good job. Smithson seemed really intent on what you were saying."

Getty was dressed just as smartly today as yesterday, this time in a navy suit with a pink-and-white-striped shirt crisply tucked into her straight skirt. She stood and addressed the judge.

"Good morning, Your Honor. Defendant's counsel would have you believe that in order for an attorney to be competent, he must be prescient as well. She seems to think that Mr. Wilson should have known that, one day in the future, DNA evidence would be used in criminal proceedings, and urged the trial court to undertake the expense. She thinks that despite an outright admission from Mr. Calhoun's wife that the dead child was theirs, Mr. Wilson should have looked into his crystal ball and known that she lied. It's absurd. Sallie Calhoun is spending twenty-five years to life in prison because of her role in the death of that child. No reasonable attorney would think that she lied about something that would result in her incarceration for the remainder of her years. *Strickland* says that an attorney can make a reasonable decision that an investigation is unnecessary. Mr. Wilson did just that in this case.

"The other instances of alleged incompetence that Ms. Trumball references in her brief are all inconsequential. Even if Mr. Wilson erred, which I don't believe he did, those errors would have had no impact on the verdict.

"Now, five years or so ago, Mr. Calhoun, for the first time, offered Mr. Wilson a story that seemed so wild that any attorney would have been suspicious. The letter came as Mr. Wilson prepared Mr. Calhoun's last appeal. It seemed like a desperate move to him, as it would to most attorneys. Should he have dropped everything and said, 'Let's get a DNA test?' Hardly.

"Defendant's counsel is trying to convince this court that a DNA test could prove her client's innocence. But that's not what you're being asked to decide. The question before you is whether Mr. Wilson exercised his professional judgment in a manner consistent with other attorneys. The only answer to that is absolutely yes. Thank you."

"Okay, counselors," Judge Smithson said. "I understand the urgency of this case, and I'll do my best to give you a ruling as quickly as possible."

With that, the matter was finished. Once again all they could do was wait. They left the courtroom and turned their cell phones back on. Dani's phone beeped, alerting her to a message. She waited until they'd left the courthouse to retrieve the message. It was Bruce, letting her know that the state court had scheduled a hearing on the appeal of the exhumation case for Thursday. It made no sense to travel back to New York that night only to return the next day. She informed the others and they headed back to the hotel to extend their reservations.

"What's your assessment?" Tommy asked as they walked to the Holiday Inn.

Dani shrugged. No matter how well or poorly she thought a hearing had gone, the decision often surprised her.

"I thought Getty's closing was pretty weak," Melanie said.

"She made some good points," Dani said. "But it only matters what Smithson thinks. His reputation is good—smart, fair to both sides instead of a prosecutorial bias. But I'm worried. If he doesn't rule in our favor, we'll need to get a petition in to the court of appeals fast. Melanie, we'll have some time tomorrow. We should get started on that just in case."

Dani knew they were fighting an uphill battle. The chance of getting a convicted killer freed on grounds of ineffective assistance of counsel was small. Of the 107 death sentences handed down in Indiana since 1977, when the United States Supreme Court reinstated it as a potential penalty, only two men had been exonerated of their crimes, one of them two weeks before the scheduled execution and the other three days before. Yet she knew that many more on death row lacked the money to pay attorneys proficient in capital cases and lacked the resources to hire experts to refute those put forth by the prosecution. It wasn't the color of their skin that was the biggest hurdle to obtaining justice; it was the color of money.

They arrived at their hotel and, after arranging to extend their stay, retreated to their separate rooms. Each of them focused on preparing for the next task: getting a court to allow them to exhume the little girl's body. Hours went by until the ring of her cell phone interrupted Dani, who'd been absorbed in her work.

"Ms. Trumball?" the voice at the other end asked.

"Yes."

"This is May Collins, Judge Smithson's secretary. He'd like you to be at his court 10:00 a.m. tomorrow. He's going to read his decision from the bench."

"Thank you. We'll be there."

She hung up and wondered what it meant. Had Judge Smithson reached his decision quickly because their case was compelling or because he wanted to give them enough time to appeal? She called Melanie and Tommy to let them know. "Melanie, this means it's especially important to have our papers ready in case we need to appeal. It goes to the court of appeals in Chicago, so we'll need to overnight the papers as soon as they're ready. That is, if we lose tomorrow."

Melanie was chipper. "I really feel we're going to win."

"Well, just in case, get the appeal ready."

"Gotcha, chief."

Dani worked through dinner, ordering room service instead of joining Melanie and Tommy, but by nine o'clock she was bushed. It was just as well; it was honeymoon hour. She called Doug.

"How's it going?" he asked.

"I'll find out tomorrow morning. The judge will have his decision then."

"How are you holding up?"

"I'm exhausted. Not just physically. Emotionally too."

"It'll be over soon."

"Yes, but how? That's what's draining me. I know he's innocent, I just know it. Only I don't know if there's enough time to save him."

"We have an imperfect system. As long as there's a death penalty, some innocent men and women will die."

Suddenly, the combination of her fatigue and worry overwhelmed her, and she burst into tears. "It's wrong, it's so wrong," she said through her sobs.

Doug let her cry herself out. "It's better now than it used to be," he said after she calmed down. "At least in some cases there's DNA evidence to clear an innocent person. That wasn't always the case. Maybe twenty years from now there'll be some new scientific advance that can conclusively tell when a person is being truthful or lying. Maybe fifty years from now genome mapping will be complete, and scientists can figure out whether a person's genes make him capable of murder. Maybe if those things happen, or others that we can't even imagine, maybe then there won't be any innocents sitting on death row. In the meantime, you can only help one prisoner at a time. And for now, that prisoner is George Calhoun."

Dani dabbed her eyes with the napkin from her dinner tray. "If only we'd been able to find some evidence that Angelina had been left at the Mayo Clinic."

"And you're convinced she was?"

"Yes. Absolutely convinced."

"Then Calhoun is lucky he has a lawyer who believes in him."

"Now if he only has a judge who feels the same way."

"Maybe he does. You'll find out tomorrow."

By ten o'clock her eyelids started drooping. She said goodnight to Doug and got ready for bed. As she set the alarm, she felt prepared for whatever would happen tomorrow and each of the remaining days until Calhoun's execution date.

"I'm going to read my decision into the record," Judge Smithson said after they were all assembled in his courtroom. "Defendant has come before this court on a habeas corpus petition claiming that he received ineffective assistance of counsel in violation of the state and federal constitutions. This proceeding is the first time he has raised such a claim, but it is not unexpected, as his trial and appellate counsel were the same. The burden is on the defendant to show that his lawyer's performance fell below an objective standard of reasonableness and that there is a reasonable probability that the results of the proceedings would have been different if not for his attorney's errors. In looking at the reasonableness of the attorney's conduct, we must view it in light of the circumstances at the time of the proceedings. We may not apply subsequent knowledge or conduct to a prior period. Defendant claims that his attorney failed to perform a proper investigation into the facts during the pretrial stage. Yet defendant's own conduct led to such failure. Defendant's wife asserted the dead child was their own, and although defendant denied such was the case, he steadfastly refused to inform his attorney as to the whereabouts of his daughter. Given those facts, it was not unreasonable for his attorney to forgo an investigation. Nor was it unreasonable for him not to seek exhumation of the child's body twelve years later in order to conduct a DNA test. Once again, the defendant's conduct over those twelve years would lead a reasonable attorney to believe his claim was 'grasping at straws.'

"The remaining claims of ineffective assistance do not rise to the level of prejudicial conduct. For these reasons, defendant's petition is denied and he is to be remanded back to Indiana State Prison."

Dani's hands shook. She willed herself not to cry. It wasn't over yet, she kept telling herself. Not for thirteen more days.

Indianapolis was home to the state court of appeals. Dani felt as if they'd come full circle from their visit there just a few short weeks ago. Their case wasn't scheduled until the afternoon, so she'd decided to visit Sallie once more at the Indiana Woman's Prison. Dani was already seated in the interview room when the door opened and Sallie entered, still gaunt, still lifeless.

"Hello, Sallie. Do you remember me?"

She nodded. Like she'd done during the first interview, she stared down at the table.

"I've been speaking to George, your husband."

She looked up. "Is he still alive?"

"Yes."

"Tell him I'm sorry," she said, her voice barely a whisper.

"Sorry for what?"

"He'll know."

"Sallie, George told me what happened to Angelina."

Tears started to roll down Sallie's cheeks. She remained silent as she rocked back and forth. Finally, she said, "We killed her."

"How did you kill her, Sallie?"

"George knows."

"George told me Angelina was sick, that she had cancer. Do you remember that?"

"We killed her."

"But how, Sallie?" The frail woman sitting across from Dani looked ghostly, with her white pallor and skin so translucent that her bones showed. *She believes she killed Angelina. She's so cut off from reality that she can't tell the difference between murder and abandonment. Unless George lied to us. Could they have killed her out of a misguided sense of mercy? To spare her more suffering?* "Do you remember that Angelina's cancer came back?"

Sallie stopped rocking. "They wouldn't help her. We couldn't pay them, so they wouldn't help her. How could they do that? How could they turn a child away?"

"They should have treated her. It was cruel."

Sallie nodded. "You see. You understand."

"Yes, I understand. You had no choice. Tell me what you did."

Suddenly, a wail of anguish erupted from deep within Sallie. She wrapped her arms around her body tightly. "We were supposed to care for her. We were her parents. She needed our comforting, our little baby, our precious little girl. She needed us."

Dani said nothing for a while and left Sallie alone with her memories. When her rocking stopped, she asked, "Did George kill her to end her suffering?"

"We didn't end her suffering. We did worse, much worse."

"Did you leave her at the Mayo Clinic?"

Sallie nodded.

"Was that George's plan?"

Another nod.

"You didn't want to do that?"

Sallie shook her head.

"Is that why you said you and George killed her?"

Sallie stared at her, her eyes alive for the first time with a burning intensity. "We did kill her. We left our baby alone and sick with no one around to love her and take care of her. That's murder, isn't it?"

"No, Sallie," Dani said. "I don't know whether it was right or wrong, but it wasn't murder." She let the words sink in. "Did you want to be punished for what you and George did, for leaving Angelina at the hospital?"

"Yes."

"Do you think George should be killed for doing that? For making you go along with it?"

Sallie remained silent for a long time. Again, her arms were wrapped tightly around her body, the skin under her hands beginning to turn purple with bruises.

"Sallie? Can you answer my question?"

Sallie looked at Dani with lifeless eyes. "I will hate George for the rest of my life for what he did." She stood up to leave, and Dani thought she was finished, but she stopped at the door and turned to her. "Yes, I think George should die," she said and left the room.

Dani had nurtured a dim hope that, with the truth out in the open, Sallie would agree to give her an affidavit, a sworn statement that confirmed what she and George had done with Angelina. But it was obvious that she wouldn't, and Dani didn't even ask. Instead she now knew that George's tale was absolutely true. Had there been a kernel of doubt that she'd pushed away, it no longer existed. Now it wasn't her *belief* that George was innocent—it was a fact.

Three robed judges sat behind a raised mahogany bench. The small courtroom had only six rows of seats behind the swinging gate. Dani, Melanie, and Tommy sat in the third row. Their case was fourth on the court's calendar, and they waited while oral argument took place in the cases before theirs. Two of the cases were civil, one a criminal matter. As Dani listened to the arguments, it became apparent that this was a "hot" bench—the judges had read the briefs submitted beforehand and were actively engaging the attorneys in questioning.

"*People versus George Calhoun*," the bailiff called out sooner than Dani expected. She and Melanie took their seats at the defendant's table. Ted Landry seated himself at the prosecutor's table.

"Are you ready?" asked the chief judge, sitting between the two other judges.

"Yes," Dani said. She walked to the lectern between the two tables and arranged her note cards.

"Let me remind you that when the yellow light comes on, you have only one minute left. When the red light comes on, your time is up."

"I understand. Your Honors, George Calhoun has been on death row for seventeen years, convicted of murdering his daughter, after the body of a young girl, estimated at between three and four years old, was found in the woods in Orland. From the very beginning, Mr. Calhoun has consistently and repeatedly denied that the child's body was his daughter. At the time of his trial, DNA testing was not widely used. That's no longer the case. Now—"

"Isn't it true that Mr. Calhoun's daughter had disappeared about the same time?" asked the judge on the right, a woman with brown hair pulled back into a bun.

"Yes, that's true, and although my client failed to explain her disappearance at that time, he had compelling reasons for doing so."

"Yes, I've read your papers. He now claims he abandoned her at the Mayo Clinic as an act of mercy."

"More like an act of desperation. His daughter was dying and needed treatment that he couldn't pay for and that no one would provide without payment."

"Doesn't Medicaid pay the medical costs for indigent families?" asked the judge on the left, an elderly man with dark horn-rimmed glasses.

"His income was too high to be eligible for Medicaid but too low to afford insurance. Although the state of Indiana now has a program to provide low-cost health insurance for children whose parents fall into that category, it didn't exist nineteen years ago. DNA testing is now routine and widely accepted. Even with bones that are nineteen years old, it can conclusively determine whether the child was Angelina Calhoun. Shouldn't—"

"How long would it take for DNA results to come back?" the right-side judge asked.

"It's possible to obtain results in five days."

"Assuming the lab isn't backed up, isn't that right?"

"Yes, of course."

"It seems to me," the chief judge said, "that you have a fundamental problem. The defendant has already exhausted his direct appeals. Even if we ordered the body to be exhumed and the results of the DNA test excluded Mr. Calhoun as the father, where does he go with that?"

"This would be newly discovered evidence. It would give rise to a new appeal."

"How is it newly discovered evidence? If what Mr. Calhoun says is true, he's known from the beginning that it wasn't his daughter. At every step of his proceedings, this issue could have been raised. Hasn't he waived the right to ask for the body to be exhumed now by his own silence?"

Dani saw the yellow light come on. She had only a minute left to persuade these three judges to rule in her favor. "Your Honors, if there is incontrovertible evidence available which could show that the child in the woods was not Angelina Calhoun, then the prosecutor's case disappears. Their only basis for convicting Mr. Calhoun was the identification of that child as Angelina. Justice mandates that he have access to the evidence. If he has no appeals left—and I don't believe that's the case—then the governor of this state would be able to right a cruel wrong by commuting George Calhoun's sentence and setting an innocent man free."

"Your time is up, Ms. Trumball."

"Thank you, Your Honors."

She sat down and a sense of numbness enshrouded her. Landry stood at the podium now. Dani saw his mouth move but heard nothing. She felt exhausted from the preparation, from the performance, from the ever-present sound of the ticking clock. She felt like a wooden soldier marching steadfastly toward a steep cliff and the inevitable fall to the chasm below. A poke in her arm jolted her back to the proceedings.

"Dani, are you okay?" Melanie asked.

She looked up and saw that Landry had left. Two men in neatly pressed suits were waiting to take her place at the defense table. The next case had been called. It was time to leave.

The flight back from Indianapolis departed on time. Dani was anxious to be home, to be enveloped in the safe cocoon of her family. Her already great respect for Bruce had grown exponentially. He'd handled capital appeals from beginning to end for ten years now and, at least during the time she had worked there, never seemed to lose his equilibrium. It wasn't so for her. There had been moments, alone in her hotel room, when she'd wanted to run away, crawl under the covers, escape the hell of representing an innocent man condemned to die. When she handled only the appeals, she didn't bond with the inmate in the same way. She wrote words on a page and then argued law and principles in a court. It had changed now. She was connected to George Calhoun. She was his lifeline.

They circled LaGuardia Airport for twenty minutes before being cleared for landing, typical of congested New York City airports. When they finally landed, they all checked their voice mail.

"Hey, I got a message from a nurse at the Mayo Clinic," Tommy said after closing his phone. "She saw the flier posted in the nurse's lounge. Says she may have some information for us."

Dani couldn't believe what she'd heard. Proof that Angelina had been left at the Mayo Clinic would change everything. "Call her back. Right now."

"Already tried. Got her voice mail. I'll keep trying. This may be just the break we need."

Please let it be so suddenly became her mantra. *Please let it be so.*

Eleven Days

Tommy hoped the perfect weather in Rochester, Minnesota, portended that something good would come of his meeting with Jody Melnick. Instead of the drenching rain that had greeted him on his last visit, a few puffy white clouds dotted the crystalline blue sky and the temperature stayed at seventy-two degrees. He'd finally reached Jody last night. She wasn't certain her information would be helpful but had agreed to meet with him the next day when her shift ended. Tommy had caught the first plane out in the morning and now waited for her in the hospital cafeteria.

"Mr. Noorland?"

Tommy looked up and saw a middle-aged woman in starched white scrubs. Her name tag read "Jody Melnick, R.N." "Ms. Melnick," he said as he stood up and extended his hand to shake hers. "Thank you so much for meeting with me. And please call me Tommy. You sounded a little cryptic on the phone."

"And call me Jody. I appreciate you coming out to speak to me in person. I hesitated to call at all. Trudy and I worked closely together for many years. I wouldn't want to get her in trouble. I can't even be sure we're talking about the same girl."

"Why don't we sit down? Can I get you something to eat? A cup of coffee maybe?"

Jody shook her head. "No, thank you, I'm fine."

"Why don't you start from the beginning? Tell me why you think you know something about Angelina Calhoun."

"Well, Trudy and Ed never had children of their own. Trudy worked with me as a surgical nurse. We weren't friends outside the hospital, but you know how it is. When you work with someone a long time, you talk to each other about things. Only some things Trudy never talked about. Oh dear, I think I'm rambling already."

Tommy patted her hand. "It's okay, dear. You tell the story any way you want."

"Well, as I said, Trudy and Ed had been married for ten years or so and never had any children. Then one day Trudy calls in sick at the last minute—really, she should already have started her shift. We had to scramble to find a replacement. But she said a family emergency had come up. A full week passed before she came back, and when she did, she told everyone that her sister and brother-in-law had been killed in a car crash. Their daughter survived and had come to live with Trudy and Ed. I thought it peculiar then, because Trudy had never mentioned a sister. Trudy missed a lot of work after that, for a few years at least. She said the niece had lingering injuries from the accident and she took time off to get her treatment. I remember asking how old her niece was, you know, when the accident happened. And Trudy said four years old. Wasn't that the age of the little girl you're asking about?"

"Yes, about that. Do you know the name of her niece?"

"Sunshine. I always remembered that because it was such an unusual name."

"And her last name?"

"Well, that's the strange thing. She should have had the last name of Trudy's brother-in-law, but she didn't. She used Trudy and Ed's last name. Harrington. And whenever Trudy brought her to our annual picnic, Sunshine would call her 'Mommy.'"

"Did she look like the girl in the picture on the flier?"

"Well, years passed before Trudy actually took her anyplace public. I'd always assumed it was because of her injuries. So when I first saw Sunshine, she must have been around six or seven years old. But yes, I think there's a similarity. It was a long time ago, so I'm not absolutely certain. But I think so."

"Is Trudy still working here?"

"No. She retired a few years ago. I think she lived in Byron. At least she did when she worked here. Maybe human resources can give you her address."

Tommy thanked Jody profusely. Finally, a solid lead. After Jody left, he took out his cell phone and dialed information. "Do you have a listing for Edward or Trudy Harrington in Byron, Minnesota?" he asked the operator.

"There's a Trudy Harrington on Aspen Road."

"I'll take that—and before you go, do you have a house number?"

"It's 4. Hold on and I'll connect you."

The phone rang twice and a computer voice came on. "The number you have reached is disconnected. Please try again or check your number for accuracy."

"Damn."

But at least now he had a name. He decided to see if Dr. Jeffreys were available and rode the elevator to his floor. He walked down the hallway in the direction he remembered and opened the outer door to the secretary's desk. "Any chance Dr. Jeffreys is in?" he asked the young woman sitting there.

"He's off today."

"Can you reach him at home? It's important."

The young woman studied him. "You're the investigator who was here last week, right?"

"Yes, ma'am."

"About the little girl?"

"Right."

"Dr. Jeffreys is at a medical conference in Paris. He'll be back in two days. Normally, he doesn't work on Sundays, but he plans on coming in to check on his patients and catch up with paperwork. Can it wait?"

Tommy put on his most winsome smile. "I wish it could, sweetheart, but I really need to speak to him. Can you give him a call?"

The secretary looked at her watch. "It's after eight there. I could try his hotel, but he's probably out to dinner by now. And his cell doesn't work overseas."

"What's your name?"

"Mandy."

"Mandy, I need to see if you have records of a little girl treated here twenty years ago. Is there any way you can help me with that? I have a release from the girl's biological and legal father." George took a copy of the release from his briefcase and handed it to Mandy.

Mandy looked it over. "Is this the girl's last name? Calhoun?"

"No. It would be Harrington. Sunshine Harrington."

"Well, to begin with, I wouldn't have access to that database. But I don't think anyone will do a search for you without proof that the person who signed the release is her father."

"And who does have authority to access the database?"

"Probably Mr. Oxblood. He's the executive director of the hospital. But he's out too. His father passed away two days ago. The wake is going on now, and the funeral is tomorrow, so he'll be back on Monday. And don't even ask. I wouldn't dream of disturbing him during this time."

"Who's covering for Dr. Jeffreys while he's away?"

"That would be Dr. Burroughs, but she wouldn't okay a search of the database without Mr. Oxblood's go-ahead. And neither would Dr. Jeffreys. Not with the name on the release being different."

Tommy understood that getting angry wouldn't get him anywhere. As difficult as it was, he needed to be patient. There were other avenues he could pursue in the meantime. "Okay, Mandy. Can you get me in to see Dr. Jeffreys first thing in the morning when he gets back?"

Mandy penciled him in for 8:00 a.m., before the doctor would begin his rounds.

If Tommy was right, he didn't need to call Helen at Vital Records or Abby at County Community Services. It seemed that Angelina hadn't succumbed to the leukemia, so there wouldn't be a death certificate.

And he didn't think anyone had turned her over to foster care. If he couldn't get anywhere with his search, he'd double back to both places and have them check the name of Sunshine Harrington. But he suspected that the person who found Angelina Calhoun at the Mayo Clinic, alone and frightened, was Trudy Harrington, on her way to work. He figured she'd read the records tied around Angelina's waist and made an instant decision: She would take care of this child, get treatment for her, and raise her and love her as her own daughter. Dani may have had George Calhoun pegged from the start after all. *Damn, I must be losing my touch.* Now he needed to find Trudy Harrington to confirm his theory.

The hour was getting late and he was tired. He decided to call it a night and take a drive out to Byron the next day to poke around and see what he could find.

After his morning stop at Dunkin Donuts, Tommy found a bookstore that had street maps for Olmsted County. He mapped out a route to Aspen Road, got in his car and thirty minutes later stood in front of the beige, vinyl-sided house at 4 Aspen Road. After he knocked on the door and received no response, he walked to the front window nearest the door. Curtains covered the windows, but it appeared that no lights were on inside. He walked to the back of the house and still saw no evidence of movement. *Well, this is what legwork is about.* He walked to the house to the right of No. 4, identical in all respects except the color, and knocked on the front door. A young woman, her hair pulled back in a ponytail, opened the door, and Tommy could see two toddlers sitting on the floor inside, hunched over toy trucks and making *vroom* sounds.

"Yeah?"

"Excuse me, miss. I'm looking for the folks who live next door," Tommy said as he pointed to the beige house.

"What about?"

"It's a personal matter."

"Well, I can't help you anyway. I'm just a baby sitter."

Tommy thanked her and moved on to the next house. A middle-aged woman dressed in casual pants and a loose-fitting sweater answered the door with a bright smile.

"Good morning, ma'am. I'm looking for Trudy Harrington. She lives at No. 4 over there. Do you know where I might find her?"

The woman's smile disappeared. "Are you a friend?"

"No, ma'am. I'm an investigator, and it's urgent I find her or her husband."

"Well, I'm sorry to tell you, they're both deceased. Ed passed away a number of years ago, but Trudy just died recently, maybe ten or so days ago."

Tommy's face dropped. "Do you know their daughter?"

"Sunshine?"

"Yes, I need to find her."

"Can I ask what this is about?"

"It concerns an inheritance."

"Her daughter was just here, for the funeral, I assume. I wasn't really friends with Trudy, just knew her to say 'hello' to." The woman pointed to a home across the street. "The woman who lives there was friendly with Trudy, I think. Her name is Laura Devine. She might know something about Sunshine's whereabouts. But she works on Saturdays. I usually see her car in the driveway around six."

Tommy thanked her and moved on. His years of investigation work taught him that it was often painstaking. He knocked at each of the homes along Aspen Road. The street was in the process of turning over from families who had lived there for decades to new families seeking their first home in the suburbs. Where someone answered his knock, the newcomers knew little about the family at 4 Aspen Road. Older residents weren't able to tell him much more than he'd already learned. He made a note to come back that evening to speak to Laura. Nothing more could be done until then.

At exactly seven o'clock, Tommy knocked on Laura Devine's front door.

"Hi."

"Ms. Devine, my name is Tommy Noorland."

"You're the investigator, right?"

Tommy nodded.

"My neighbor told me about you. I figured you'd come back to find me. I'm really the only one of Trudy's friends left. There were a whole bunch of us from the block who were close when our children were young, but you know how it is. The kids grow up, the parents move on. Winters are so hard here that a lot of folks head to warmer areas when they retire. I've still got a few years to go, but you can be sure I'll be heading to Phoenix when I'm done. Come on in. I've got a pot of coffee just made. Can I get you a cup?"

"Thanks. I'd appreciate that."

Laura led Tommy into her kitchen, which clearly had never been remodeled. Tommy guessed the homes on Aspen Road had been built in the early '70s, when ornate dark-wood cabinets were in vogue, along with avocado-green appliances and linoleum tile floors. He took a seat at the table. Laura brought over two mugs of coffee, along with cream and sugar, and sat across from him.

"So, what's this about?"

"It involves an inheritance."

Laura reached behind her to the formica counter and grabbed a pack of cigarettes. "Mind if I smoke?"

"Go right ahead."

She walked to the stove and lit a cigarette with a gas burner. After two long, deep puffs, she put out the cigarette and turned back to Tommy. "Sorry, every now and then I just need a few drags. I'm trying to quit. I figure if I don't finish them, eventually I'll be able to give it up entirely. I started with six puffs and now I'm down to two. Pretty good, don't you think?"

"Sure."

"Okay. Let's talk now about what you're really here for. I doubt it's about an inheritance. Neither Trudy nor Ed had any siblings, and their parents are long gone."

"It's nothing that anyone's in trouble for."

"You've got to give me more than that."

Tommy sized up the woman. His years in the field taught him to do that—make snap decisions about whom he could and couldn't trust. He didn't see a downside to being honest with her. He'd reached a dead end anyway, so he told her about George, about his upcoming execution, and about his claim that he'd left Angelina at the Mayo Clinic. As he spoke, Laura didn't say a word, just listened intently. "So, yesterday, I met with a nurse over at the Mayo Clinic, and she says Trudy suddenly showed up one day with a four-year-old, claimed it was her niece whose parents had just been killed in a car crash. And she says the little girl was injured or sick or something. Now, here I am, trying to find out if Sunshine Harrington is really Angelina Calhoun."

Laura took another cigarette out of her pack. "I need another drag to process what you've just said. I almost found it more believable that you were here about an inheritance, except you couldn't have made up a story like that."

"You now know everything I know."

"Well, I may be able to help a little, but that's all. I moved here when Sunny was about eight. I remember because she's a year younger than my daughter. She seemed perfectly healthy all the time I knew her. She got married a few years ago, to a medical student. They moved away from here when he finished school, I guess for his internship or residency. I don't remember which. Trudy may have told me where, but frankly I don't remember. And if she told me her son-in-law's name, I don't remember that either. I saw Sunny last week, when she was here for her mother's funeral, but we never talked about where she lived now. Oh, and she has a daughter. Rachel. She's almost three. Trudy never told me she adopted Sunny, so whether she could be your Angelina Calhoun, I have no idea."

"Do you know any of Trudy's friends? Anyone she might have confided in?"

"There was one woman, Nancy Ferguson, used to live right next door to her. She moved away four or five years after I bought this house. They were real tight. Nancy was here last week too. I'm pretty sure she handled the funeral arrangements."

"Do you know where Nancy lives now?"

"Up in Minneapolis."

"And her husband's name?"

"Gone. Left ten years ago. She and Trudy used to travel together, since both were singles."

"That's a help."

"If Trudy confided in anyone, it would be Nancy. Find her and you may get your answer."

Tommy thanked her and left. Before he pulled away, he called information. There were two Nancy Fergusons in Minneapolis and one in a nearby suburb. Tommy reached two by telephone, neither of whom knew Trudy Harrington. At the third number, he got a machine. He left a message, stressed the urgency of a return call and headed back to his hotel, where he planned to get good and drunk.

The ringing of Tommy's telephone woke him. The bedside clock read 8:30. "Shit." He'd missed his 8:00 a.m. appointment with Jeffreys. Normally an early riser, he shook himself awake and grabbed his cell phone.

"Hello." His voice sounded thick.

"Mr. Noorland? This is Mandy, Dr. Jeffrey's assistant. You had an appointment with him at eight this morning."

"Mandy, I screwed up and overslept. I can get there in thirty minutes. Any chance he can squeeze me in?"

"He's got appointments all morning. But I told him what you were looking for, and he said he could squeeze you in at lunchtime, say around 12:30?"

"You're a sweetheart. I'll be there."

His head ached from tying one on last night, something he hadn't done in years. When he was at the Bureau, the guys would go out drinking on Friday nights, and he always downed quite a few those evenings. He left that behind when he joined HIPP. He shuffled to the bathroom and turned on the hot water in the shower. He brushed his teeth while the room steamed up and then stepped into the tub. The hot water streaming down his face and body felt good, and gradually the ache in his head subsided.

He'd expected to see Dr. Jeffreys first and then drive up to Minneapolis. There wasn't enough time to reverse the order. He'd just have to wait to try to find Nancy Ferguson. He tried calling the third number one more time and still got only her voicemail.

Before he knew it, the morning had disappeared, and he made his way to the Mayo Clinic. He arrived with time to spare for his meeting with Dr. Jeffreys. Mandy ushered him into the office with a promise that the doctor would be back soon. She was good to her word. Five minutes later, Dr. Jeffreys walked in.

"Sorry about this morning, Doc. I appreciate you rescheduling."

"Not a problem. Sorry you had to wait two days. So tell me, how does Sunshine Harrington fit in with Angelina Calhoun?"

Tommy filled him in on his conversation with Jody. "So there's a real possibility they're the same person."

"It's possible. The problem I have is getting around the patient privacy laws."

"I've got the signed release from her father."

"Yes, but we don't know he's her father. And won't know unless I show you her file, which gets us back to the privacy problem."

Tommy thought for a moment. "Were the privacy laws in effect twenty years ago?"

Dr. Jeffreys hesitated. "Probably not as federal law, as it is now. But we still had a policy of respecting a patient's privacy."

"We know that Angelina was treated for leukemia back in Pennsylvania. If Sunshine's the same age and was treated for the same thing, isn't it probable that they're the same person?"

"Leukemia is pretty generic. And it's the most common cancer in young children."

"Wait a minute." Tommy opened his briefcase and riffled through a copy of the medical records for Angelina Calhoun that he'd received from Dr. Samson. "Here it is. She had acute lymphoblastic leukemia, pre-B-cell. Does that help?"

"Actually, it does. Pre-B-cell is a less common form."

Tommy handed Dr. Jeffreys a stack of papers. "These are copies of her medical records from Pennsylvania. It shows her treatment before the cancer reoccurred."

Dr. Jeffreys leafed through the papers.

"So how about it, Doc? Can you take a look and see if Sunshine Harrington was treated here? And if she matches up with Angelina's records, can you share it with me?"

"I'll check with our lawyers, but I think that should work. Why don't you get back to me tomorrow?"

Tommy grimaced. "You know, most of the time when someone says, 'Every minute counts,' it's bullshit, but in this case it's true. If I'm right about Sunshine, then in nine days a man's going to be executed for murdering someone who's now married with a child of her own. I don't want to live with that. You gotta help me, Doc."

"I'll do my best. Give me a call at five o'clock."

The drive to Minneapolis took a little over an hour. Tommy drove directly to the address he'd been given for the third Nancy Ferguson. The new-looking, high-rise apartment building had no doorman and no security, something unheard of in New York City. He searched the mailboxes for her apartment number and then rode the elevator to the twelfth floor. He followed the winding corridor to her apartment and knocked. No answer. He banged harder. No answer, but this time he thought he heard a cat meow. *She can't be far gone if she left her cat behind.*

As he'd done on Aspen Road, Tommy began knocking on her neighbors' doors. He got lucky—or maybe it was unlucky—with the first one. The woman who answered the door knew Nancy Ferguson. "Nancy's on a little trip right now," she told Tommy. "I'm taking care of her cat for her. She'll be back next week."

"Do you have a number where you can reach her?"

"Well, I have her cell number, but she's on a rafting trip, on the Colorado River. I don't expect there would be cell service there. It's something she always wanted to do but kept putting off. Then a good friend of hers died a week and a half ago and she said to me, 'I'm not going to put anything off anymore. Life's too short.' She up and went, just like that."

"If she calls you, would you give her my phone number? It's extremely urgent that I speak to her as soon as possible."

Tommy handed her his card and the woman looked it over. "As I said, I don't expect to hear from her, but if I do, I'll give her your message."

One more dead end.

Just before five o'clock, Tommy dialed Dr. Jeffreys's number. When Mandy answered, Tommy asked, "Is the doc in?"

"He had an emergency come up, but he gave me a message for you. He got the go-ahead on searching the records, but because it's so long ago, it's not on the computer. One of the file clerks is doing a manual search, but so far—nothing. He'll give you a call if he finds something."

Tommy felt as if he were continuously butting up against a wall. Each morsel of information led to a dead end and further frustration. There wasn't any more reason to stay in Minnesota. Time to go home.

G*od had watched over him again. Or maybe it was just dumb luck, his calling the detective at just the right time and learning that he was heading to Minnesota. A nurse knew something. A lead. From the beginning, he'd known it was important to make the detective his friend. Now he pumped him for more information, learned where and when the meeting with the nurse would take place. He got there first and waited. A pasted-on mustache and sideburns helped to disguise him. He was good at waiting. Security probably thought he was a distraught parent who just needed some air.*

He didn't know what he'd learn when the investigator arrived. He only knew he had to prevent him from exonerating George Calhoun. That was his salvation. George's death for a crime he'd committed meant he'd remain free. If the lead was good, if it proved George's innocence, he had to stop the investigator before he acted on it. He thought about killing him. It would only delay the information—someone else would probably follow up with the nurse—but delay was all he needed. Eleven days. Surely, eliminating the investigator could buy him eleven days.

Tucked away in his inside jacket pocket was his brother's badge. Even though Charlie had bullied him ever since they were toddlers, he missed him at times. It made sense that Charlie had become a police officer—he could bully plenty of people without anyone blinking an eye. Still, he hadn't deserved to die. It had been an accident, really. Just like the child.

It had been his eighteenth birthday. They were both juiced up, having downed shots at the bar all night. The law said he couldn't drink until he turned twenty-one, but Charlie was the law, and no bartender refused him drinks for his little brother. When they left, Charlie began ragging him again, calling him a no-good loser over and over. He'd taken enough from him, and when he swung his arm around and his fist connected with Charlie's jaw, he thought, "Good, that'll shut him up for a while." Charlie just lay there, his face buried in the gravel, his arms under his body. "Get up, you big jerk," he'd yelled at him. "You don't like it when your little brother gets the best of you, huh? Well, tough shit. Just lay there like the stupid-ass coward you are." When Charlie didn't move, he helped him to his feet. As he lifted his brother off the ground, he caught a glimpse of the knife in his hand. He managed to swerve just as Charlie spun and came at him, the blade glistening in the moonlight. Instantly, he sobered up. "Hey, bro, put that thing down," he said. Charlie glared at him, his eyes black with hatred, and rushed at him again. He grabbed his hand and managed to wrench the knife away, but that inflamed his brother even more.

Charlie then swung at him and caught him in the gut. He doubled over, gasping for breath. "You fuckin' crybaby," Charlie said. "I'll teach you to fuck around with me." Charlie pulled him up and punched him several times before losing his balance. He took advantage of the slip and fell on top of Charlie, hitting him hard over and over. When Charlie no longer fought back, he rolled off him, exhausted. When he got up and offered a hand to his brother, Charlie's face was a bloody pulp. "You look like shit," he said. But Charlie didn't move. His dead eyes stared up at him, frozen with the realization that he could no longer push his little brother around.

"C'mon, stop playing games." He crouched next to his brother and laid his head against his chest. He heard nothing. He picked up Charlie's wrist and checked for a pulse but felt nothing. Charlie was dead.

He knew everyone would blame him. Charlie was a cop. It didn't matter that he was a bully, had always been a bully. It didn't matter that they were brothers and they'd both been drunk. He knew he'd go to jail for this. He had looked toward the bar. A few stragglers were still inside. The loud music had drowned out the fight.

He did what he had to do. He drove Charlie's car to Devil's Turn, the aptly named road that curved sharply around the hill, nothing but cliff on the other side. It was late and no one was around to see him get out of the car, place Charlie in the driver's seat and push it over the cliff. After it landed at the bottom, he scrambled down, rolling part of the way so his body would be bruised, and lay just outside the car as if he'd been thrown from it. A tragedy, everyone said. Charlie had had such a promising future.

Charlie's badge had been at his house. He'd told the precinct he couldn't find it, but that wasn't true. He'd kept his brother's badge as a reminder of what he'd lost.

Now that badge would come into use. He spotted the investigator in the parking lot and watched him walk into the building. He followed him to the cafeteria, keeping a safe distance. He didn't need to hear what the nurse said to him. He'd find out later. When the nurse left, he followed her into the elevator. "Ma'am, I'm a detective from the Hammond, Illinois, police," he said and flashed the badge. "The man you were talking to, he's a person of interest to us. We need to know what you told him." The woman readily cooperated. He didn't need to follow the investigator. He knew just where he would go next: to the home of Trudy Harrington.

After getting Trudy's address from the information operator, he got in his car and headed to Byron. No one was home at 4 Aspen Road, so he waited and watched. Having spotted no activity by nine o'clock, he checked into a local motel. At 6:00 a.m., he returned to Aspen Road. When the investigator finally showed up, he watched him ring the Harringtons' doorbell and then walk around the house. He watched him go up and down the block, knocking on doors. He watched him leave.

He retraced the investigator's footsteps, showing his badge at each door, asking about their conversation. When he left each home, he cautioned the residents not to tell anyone about his visit; otherwise they'd jeopardize his investigation. He learned enough to figure out that the investigator would be back after six to talk to Laura Devine. He returned at 5:30 and waited in his car a discreet distance away. He watched a woman drive up a little after six *and enter the home, and an hour later he saw the investigator drive up. The investigator stayed inside for longer than he had at the other homes, and when the investigator drove away, he knocked on the same door.*

He used the same introduction and gave the same caution he'd given at the other homes. Laura told him about Nancy, told him where she lived. He made some calls, got an address, and didn't wait to drive to Minneapolis. There he knocked on doors near Nancy's apartment and hit pay dirt at the fourth door. The occupant of the apartment, a friend of Nancy's, told him all about her trip, even showed him the brochure for the tour company. She had been thinking of taking the same trip herself, but Nancy's decision to go was too sudden. She couldn't get away on such short notice. He took the brochure with him. There was so much information on the web that he could probably figure out exactly where Nancy would be without even talking to anyone from the tour company.

Yes. God had watched over him again.

Four Days

Dani wondered if George, sitting in his jail cell, felt as if the hands of the clock were speeding toward Tuesday, the day the state of Indiana had set for his execution. Unless she succeeded in getting him freed, or at least obtaining a stay of execution, he would be placed in a special cell Monday. He would be provided meals of his choice all day. If he should so desire, a clergyman would visit him. Dani would be there that day as well. She would sit with him in his cell and hold his hand. Sometime after midnight, he would be taken to the room of his death, where he would be prepared for the three injections that would kill him. Indiana law mandated that the execution take place before 6:00 a.m. By custom, it would occur shortly after midnight. She would take her place in the viewing room and watch him die.

For Dani, the hands of the clock were painstakingly slow. She awaited a decision from the federal court of appeals on the denial of the writ of habeas corpus. They did not want to hear oral argument; the papers were sufficient, they said. She didn't know whether that boded well or ill for George. She only knew it was agonizing to sit and wait for the call from the clerk's office.

Today was Friday. The loss of their appeal to exhume the child's body had been devastating. If they lost the appeal on the writ of habeas corpus as well, their last hope would be the Supreme Court. Unless a stay were issued, that meant an emergency petition to the highest court of the land, a rarely successful gambit. The tragedy was compounded by the fact that time—the same time that was speeding forward for George and had slowed to a crawl for Dani— was the salvation they needed. Time for the Mayo Clinic to uncover Sunshine Harrington's medical records; time for Nancy Ferguson to return from her rafting trip; time for Tommy to find Sunshine Harrington—or whatever her married name was; time to run a DNA test to confirm what they all now believed to be true: that Sunshine was the daughter George and Sallie Calhoun sacrificed their lives for.

Busywork spared Dani from utter paralysis, but it didn't stop her from looking at the clock every five minutes. The papers for an emergency writ to the Supreme Court were completed, should she need them. No pressing matters were on her desk. Still, she couldn't leave.

"Go home, Dani," Bruce had said an hour ago, obviously able to see her exhaustion. He knew that, should they lose, there would be no rest for her until Tuesday had passed. "I can't," she'd told him. He understood.

As the hands of the clock inched toward five o'clock, Dani's heart sank. Could the decision be sitting in a pile on the desk of a clerk who was unaware that time was slipping away? Perhaps she was thinking about her child's birthday party the next day or was going through a stack of decisions in the order they'd been put on her desk, routine decisions given the same priority as life-or-death decisions. Whatever the reason, it seemed inconceivable to her that the court would leave this undecided on the Friday before his execution.

She picked up the phone and dialed the clerk's office. A male voice answered. "This is Dani Trumball with the Help Innocent Prisoners Project. We have an appeal pending on a capital case. I just wondered if there's been any decision yet."

"Hold on a moment."

A crisp female voice came on the line. "Ms. Trumball, I was just dialing you when you called. I have the decision and I'll fax it over to you now."

"Can you tell me—how was it decided?"

Her voice softened. "I'm sorry. It was denied."

"And the stay?"

"Also denied."

Dani sat in Bruce's office, sobbing. He was perched on the edge of his desk, facing her. He handed her a tissue and tried to console her. Dani knew she should remain professional. She understood the importance of keeping her emotions in check in order to best represent her client. And she was keenly aware of being considered "soft" because she was a woman. None of it mattered now. The news devastated her.

"You'll file your petition with the Supreme Court first thing Monday morning," Bruce said. "It's not over yet."

Bruce was being kind. They both knew that the odds of getting the Supreme Court to review the case, much less overturn it, were minuscule.

"Go home. Put this out of your mind for tonight. Tomorrow we'll both come in and tighten up the petition to the Supremes," he said.

As she stood to leave, Tommy walked in. "You're not going to believe this," he said. "I just got off the phone with Jack—you know, the guy from the Sharpsburg police who ran the fingerprint check for me on that note left on my car. He decided to send it over to the FBI, since they have an expanded database. The prints were run again and a partial match came up. With Stacy Conklin."

"Isn't that the little girl who disappeared around the same time as Angelina?" Dani said.

"You got it."

"How would a young child's fingerprints get into a database?"

"My guess is her mother or father took her to one of those mall events where kids get fingerprinted in case something bad should happen to them. It helps the police if they've got them on file. It was pretty commonplace back then."

"So it's Stacy's fingerprint on the letter?"

"Not hers. Only part of it matched. But the person who threatened me is related to her, closely related. Her mother or father, most likely."

"Oh my god! You just met with them the day before. You obviously struck a nerve." Dani practically danced with excitement. "Now we know who's buried in that grave. It's Stacy Conklin. It must be."

"Hold your horses," Bruce said, ever the pragmatist. "Don't get carried away with yourselves too quickly. It's possible that, losing their own daughter the way they did, the thought of a child-murderer getting off on what they might view as a technicality was too much to bear."

Her joy deflated.

"Why don't you call the cop that handled that investigation?" Bruce said to Tommy. "If he bites, then he can ask a local judge for an order to exhume the body. If it's part of an ongoing police investigation, he shouldn't have any trouble getting it."

"Sure. I always had a bad feeling about Mickey Conklin, so I've been keeping in touch with Cannon all along."

Bruce turned to Dani. "And you should start reaching out to the governor. Let's alert her to what's going on and ask her to be available on Monday to consider at the least a stay." Colleen Timmons was the governor of Indiana, the first woman elected to that position in that state. She'd run as a tough-on-crime candidate and hadn't changed since being in office. Dani hoped it wouldn't come down to relying on her compassion.

She and Tommy headed to their respective desks. With Indiana time an hour earlier than New York time, they were hopeful they'd still be able to reach the people they were looking for. Dani pulled out her reference guide to each state's gubernatorial office and dialed the number for Joe Guidry, the governor's chief of staff. He answered the phone directly. She identified herself and filled him in on what had happened with George Calhoun. She finished with her purpose in calling: "Joe, this guy is innocent, and if we have one more week, I'm sure we can prove it beyond any doubt whatsoever. We're hoping that Governor Timmons can stand by on Monday in case the Supreme Court turns us down."

All she heard was Joe's breathing.

"You still there?"

"Yeah. I'm just thinking. Let me understand. You've been turned down by two federal courts; your request of the state court for exhumation has been turned down; and if the big Court turns you down, you want the governor to put her neck out there and give this convicted child-murderer a break. Does that about sum it up?"

"It's not exactly how I'd put it. I'm not asking her to let the guy go free, not yet anyway. All I need is seven days. Seven days to wrap it up with a nice bow and ribbon, and I'll throw in the real murderer, who's been living unpunished for nineteen years." Dani realized she'd probably gone too far. Bruce was right; she shouldn't jump to conclusions about the Conklins. Still, she didn't pull back the pledge. If that's what it took to get a stay, she'd say anything at this point.

"I don't know what the governor will want to do. The best I can promise you is that she'll listen to you on Monday. Call us after the Supreme Court rules."

It was the most she could hope for—Governor Timmons would hear her out. She walked back to Bruce's office and saw Tommy inside. "Did you reach Cannon?" she asked.

"Nope. Just got his voice mail. I left an urgent message, then called the general number for the sheriff's office and left a second message. Hopefully he'll call me back."

Dani filled Tommy and Bruce in on her conversation with Joe Guidry.

"There's nothing more you guys can do tonight. Go home and get some rest," Bruce said.

As if she could.

***

It was almost 8:30 when Dani arrived home. An accident on the FDR had slowed the usual Friday-night exodus from the city to a standstill. By the time she pulled up to her house, her body ached from head to toe. Doug greeted her at the door with a glass of wine.

"Rough day?"

"A rough six weeks."

He put his arm around her and led her to the couch. On the cocktail table lay a platter of her favorite cheeses with crackers. Next to it was a bowl of ruby-red cherries, her favorite fruit.

"Where's Jonah?"

"Sound asleep."

Dani settled into the couch and let the wine relax her. The windows were open and a soft breeze moved the curtains like ripples on a lake. It felt so good to be home.

"Do you want to talk about it?" Doug asked.

"No. Not tonight. Tonight I want to pretend that I'm back in law school, that last year, when I was excited about entering the legal profession. I remember how I thought I would do so much good as a lawyer. Everything seemed black and white then, remember? Bad guys were convicted, good guys were never even arrested. Wasn't that how it was supposed to be?"

Doug cut a piece of cheese and placed it on a cracker and handed it to her. "I don't think even then we were that naïve."

"I was. I thought the law really meant something. That truth and justice were the goal, not wins and losses."

"Truth and justice are the goal. But finding the truth is difficult. You're sure your client is innocent, that all the facts you've uncovered prove he is. But the people opposing you believe in a different truth. They believe your facts are suggestive, perhaps, but not conclusive. And to set a convicted child-murderer free, there must be indisputable facts. Whose truth is right?"

"Okay, different people look at facts differently. I get that. But death is irreversible. When there isn't agreement on what is the truth, then keep the prisoner alive while the search for the truth—a truth that can't be challenged—goes on. How can anyone be comfortable with killing a man who might be innocent?"

"You and I aren't comfortable with that. But others may argue that those instances are so rare they shouldn't change what is just punishment for atrocious deeds."

Dani leaned her head back into the couch and felt her eyes drift closed. She spread herself out on the couch and Doug covered her with a blanket. She was too tired to talk anymore. She was too tired for their honeymoon hour. Sleep overtook her and she welcomed it; she welcomed her escape from a world of gray.

Dani returned to the office Saturday. Waiting at the fax machine was the decision from the federal court. Two of the judges on the three-judge panel had denied the habeas petition as well as the stay. The third had dissented, agreeing that George had received ineffective assistance of counsel at his trial. The majority's opinion was succinct: "Nothing in the record below supports defendant's claim of ineffective assistance of counsel. Defendant has not shown that his attorney's performance affected the outcome of his trial. Rather, defendant's own silence concerning the whereabouts of his daughter, despite the urgings of his counsel to explain her disappearance, are likely to have played a greater role in the verdict than any act or failure to act of his attorney. Nor does the allegedly new evidence support a reopening of his case. His motion for a writ of habeas corpus is denied, as is his request for a stay of the execution." The lone dissenter was equally succinct: "The majority's blind eye to the possibility of executing an innocent man is tantamount to the commission of murder by the state."

Dani couldn't have agreed more.

Her work was finished and she was ready to leave when she got a call from Tommy.

"What are you still doing at work? Go home and play with your kid."

"I was just about to do that. What's up?"

"Cannon called me back. I filled him in on the fingerprint results and he was pretty skeptical."

"But will he follow up on it?"

"He won't go for an exhumation, not yet. But he did say he'd take a ride over to the Conklins' and talk to them. I think I can push him some more, but we need time."

Each time Dani heard that word—*time*—it felt like a sucker punch to her gut. "That's the one thing we don't have."

One Day

Dani had planned to take an early Sunday flight to Indianapolis, drive to Michigan City the same afternoon, and be refreshed for her stay with George on Monday. When tired, her emotions rose to the surface too easily. She needed to keep them in check for George. She needed to be strong for him.

Plans go awry. She'd sat at the departure gate at LaGuardia for three hours. Weather, they'd said. Torrential downpours and gusty winds, to be more exact. Her flight hadn't landed until nine o'clock, too late for her to drive to Michigan City. Instead, after picking up her rental car, she had called around for a hotel room near the airport, settled into the room, and quickly drifted off to sleep.

The ringing of her cell phone woke her at 6:45. She didn't mind being awakened. She'd set her alarm to go off soon anyway.

"I didn't wake you, did I?" Tommy asked.

"No, I was up."

"Good. I wanted to give you an update on Cannon. He went out to their house yesterday. The wife was there, but not the husband. According to the wife, he's a pharmaceutical salesman and is on the road now."

"Did she say anything useful?"

"Well, Cannon asked if they'd ever had their daughter's fingerprints taken. At first the wife got excited, asked if they'd found Stacy. Cannon said no, then told her about the partial of Stacy's prints on a threatening letter. Which is pretty stupid if you ask me. Doesn't the guy know how to run an investigation? Anyway, the strange part is that the wife said they'd never had her fingerprints taken."

"She has to be lying."

"Or maybe the husband did it without telling his wife."

"Maybe. But one or both of them doesn't want us stirring things up with Calhoun's case."

"Cannon is still on the fence with this. He wants to believe the partial is wrong, that it's not a match for someone in Stacy's family. After all, it's not a complete match."

"So what's he going to do?"

"Wait for the husband to get back, then talk to him."

It wasn't the response Dani had hoped for, but she couldn't do anything about it. She downed a quick breakfast and checked out of the hotel. The roads were clear and she made good time on Interstate 65, arriving at the prison by eleven o'clock. She'd already arranged with Warden Coates to spend the day with George, a stark departure from the usual prison practice. Despite the daily violence in the other sections of the prison, where seventy-five percent of the inmates were there for murder and where even the visiting chaplains wore protective vests, death row was relatively tranquil. As a precaution, she'd been required to sign a waiver of liability protecting the prison against any lawsuit, despite Coates's confidence that George wouldn't harm her.

Melanie stood by in the office and waited for a ruling from the Supreme Court. Dani had the phone number of Joe Guidry, the governor's chief of staff, programmed into her own phone. A push of a single button would reach him.

There was no cell-phone service in George's cell, so the warden had agreed to get her when Melanie called his office with word from the Supremes.

After Dani was processed through the visitor's entrance, a guard escorted her to George's jail cell. The concrete corridors had a musty odor, and her nose twitched as she held back a sneeze. She endured the expected catcalls as she walked past the cells. The roominess of the enclosures surprised her. Then she remembered Coates's telling her that death-row inmates, who occupied their cells alone, were given more space because the rooms encompassed their entire world. No job duties, no library, no group meals. Just their cells all but a half hour each day. She passed a cell whose walls were covered with paintings as good as some she'd seen in museums. Another cell looked like a greenhouse, with dozens of plants below a small window. At the end of the row, she heard a squeak as she passed, and looked up to see a snow-white rabbit sitting on a small table and an open cage in the corner.

"The prisoners are allowed pets?" Dani asked her escort.

"Only on death row. These men, they know they're going to die. It helps some keep depression at bay."

Dani passed through a security gate at the end of the row and was led down a separate corridor where inmates were placed within twenty-four hours of their execution. Unlike the other sections marked by a constant hum of blended noises, this area was eerily quiet. George looked up as he heard footsteps approach, and a hopeful smile broke out on his face when he saw Dani.

"I don't have any news for you yet," she told him after the cell door had closed behind her and the guard had left. "But Melanie will get word to me as soon as we hear from the Supreme Court."

George nodded slowly. "I don't expect much."

"There's still time. Executions have been stopped with just hours to go."

George's hands rested on his lap. He had a look of determination on his face. "I'm ready for it to be over. I did what I had to and I'm okay with that."

She hadn't told George about the nurse at the Mayo Clinic. She felt torn. She didn't know how he'd react. Would it heighten his anguish to think his daughter was alive and not be able to find her? Or would it bring him peace? Dani concluded that it was wrong for her to withhold information from him.

"George, it's possible that Angelina is alive."

George's shoulders shot back and his body became taut. "Have you found her?" he asked in a choked voice.

"No, not yet."

"But she's alive?"

"We're not certain. But we believe she may be."

Dani told him about the nurse at the Mayo Clinic. She described the efforts they'd made to track down Sunshine Harrington. As she spoke, George slumped into his chair as if a pin had been stuck into his body and all the air had escaped.

She put her hand on his. "I'm sorry."

George sat upright again. "No, it's good. It's good. My beautiful angel is alive. It means what I did meant something. It mattered."

They didn't know yet if that were true, but if George did walk to his death tonight, Dani preferred that it be with the belief that Angelina had survived.

Unlike the cells she'd passed along death row, this one was bare. A bed, a small table and wooden chair, and a toilet in the corner—nothing more was needed in quarters meant to be used for less than twenty-four hours. Every now and then a guard walked by, his footsteps echoing in the hallway. Once, a chaplain appeared and asked George if he needed anything. George shook his head.

The hours passed slowly. George didn't speak much. Dani could only imagine what his thoughts must be. Her life wouldn't end tonight, yet she felt the same helplessness he must have felt. She tried to engage him in conversation, as if by doing so she could drag the thoughts of death from his mind.

"Do you have any family?" she asked. "Parents? Siblings?"

"My dad died about ten years ago. Heart attack. Very sudden."

"I'm sorry to hear that."

"It was the stress, my being here, that did it to him. Every time he'd come visit, I could see it in his face."

"And your mother?"

"She's still alive."

"Will she be here tonight? In the visitors room?"

George's face tightened. "She came yesterday. We had a good visit. I told her don't come tonight. I couldn't bear my mom seeing me all strapped up like that. My folks, they understood. They knew what I did for Angelina. Never once did they doubt me."

"They sound like good parents. Tell me about them."

"Dad, he taught me everything I knew about cars. He could take apart any car and build it right back up like brand new. He worked on the factory line, though. Cars were a hobby for him."

"How about your mom?"

"A boy couldn't have had a better mom. She would have done anything for me. I had no brothers or sisters. I'd come home from school and she'd always have something fresh baked for me. Always." A smile crossed his face. "She wasn't educated. Never even finished tenth grade. As soon as my dad finished high school, she ran off and married him. Mom thought everything I did was right. Never once did she use harsh words with me. It breaks my heart to see what this has done to her, but she puts on a strong show for me. Every time she visits, she tells me I did what I had to do."

"She must love you very much."

"Yes, ma'am, she does." George stopped talking for a moment and then said, "If you do find Angelina, will you make sure she gets to know her grandma? That would be a real good present for my mom. Not that it'll heal her broken heart over me, but it would help. I know it would, if she had a granddaughter to love. So, will you?"

"Of course."

"You've got to promise me."

"I promise you, George."

At 3:45, a guard came to take Dani to Coates's office.

"Your associate is on the phone. Do you want some privacy?"

"Yes, please."

She was afraid to pick up the phone. The odds were small that the Supreme Court would stop this travesty, and she didn't want to hear the words she dreaded. But she couldn't avoid it.

"Melanie, have you heard something?"

Melanie's voice was weak, as if the elasticity had been strained out of her vocal cords. "It's bad news. They denied a stay and they denied cert." *Certiorari* was the term used when the Supreme Court agreed to decide a case.

Dani's legs shook. She'd been through this before with other inmates. It never got easier. "I'll call the governor's office. There's still hope in that corner."

She got off the phone and dialed Joe Guidry's number.

"Joe, the Supremes have turned us down. Governor Timmons is the last hope to stop the execution of an innocent man."

"Look, I've read the stuff you've sent me, and I agree there are doubts in this case. But she's all about law and order. She needs something solid."

"Give me one week. That's all I'm asking for. One week and I'll get you something solid."

"Hold tight. I'll go speak to her."

The line was quiet for ten minutes before Joe came back. "One week and you need to produce the daughter. That's the deal. If you don't have Angelina Calhoun or a valid death certificate for her in one week, then she won't do anything more for you. Understand?"

"Joe, she won't regret this."

"We'll see. I'm faxing the stay over to the prison now."

Dani hung up, elated. One more week. It was a lifetime.

If he weren't so goddamn tense, he might have appreciated the beauty surrounding him. *The red rock encasing the Colorado River as it snaked its way thousands of feet below truly was majestic. Maybe when this was over, he'd take his wife for a vacation here.*

The website listed on the brochure told him exactly when and where Nancy's trip would end: Marble Canyon. It even said where they'd spend their last night before being whisked to Las Vegas for their flights home: Marble Canyon Inn. He had arrived two days earlier and settled into a room at the same lodging. He'd used another name and showed a false driver's license. It had been easy finding someone to make it, no questions asked. There wasn't much to do while he waited for her, so he'd taken in some of the sights: a boat ride up Lake Powell, a hike along the north rim of the Grand Canyon, a visit to Navaho Bridge. All spectacular, he thought. Even so, his next move was always in the forefront of his mind. Nothing he saw or did could shake it from there. He was prepared to kill Nancy Ferguson.

He hoped it wouldn't come to that. Maybe she didn't know anything. Or maybe she knew that Sunshine Harrington wasn't the Calhouns' daughter. That would be fine. Then she'd mosey on home from her adventure vacation *and he'd go back to his wife. But if not, well, he'd had to clean up problems before. He wouldn't shy away from it now.*

Although he'd been away from home for five days now, he wasn't cut off from what was happening back home. The hotel had a computer for guests, and each night he logged on to The News Dispatch, *Michigan City's daily newspaper. And last night he'd seen it: George Calhoun's execution had been stayed for seven days. He knew what that meant. They were waiting for Nancy to get back from her trip, waiting for her to lead them to Sunshine Harrington, waiting to determine if she was George Calhoun's daughter. If that happened, if it turned out to be true, they'd start wondering whose body was in that grave. He couldn't let that occur.*

He sat in the hotel lobby at a seat near the front desk, a local newspaper held up to his face, waiting for Nancy's arrival. The police badge was tucked into his jacket pocket and his nerves were in check. Shortly after three o'clock a bedraggled group of twelve arrived and began checking in. There were a family of four, three couples, and two single women. One woman looked to be in her twenties, the other considerably older. The older one must be Nancy, he thought. His guess was confirmed when she took her turn at the desk. "Nancy Ferguson," she told the clerk, and he handed her a room-access card.

He carefully folded his newspaper and followed her group into the elevator. When she got off on the third floor, he followed, watching which room she entered, and continued down the corridor. He didn't want to be seen talking to her. There couldn't be anyone who might identify him later, when her body was found—if it came to that. After the corridor had cleared, he walked back to her room and knocked on the door.

"Ms. Ferguson?" He showed her his badge. "I'm a detective and I have a few questions about an ongoing investigation. May I come in?"

Nancy stood there in the open doorway, with her arms folded. "What investigation?"

"I'd prefer not to talk in the hallway."

"Then I guess you'd better tell me what this is about."

"It's a murder investigation and it concerns Sunshine Harrington."

Nancy's hand flew to her mouth. "No! Has she been killed! Please tell me that's not so."

"No, no, she's fine. But she may have information that will be helpful in connection with an old unsolved murder."

Visibly relieved, Nancy invited him in. He closed the door behind him.

"How could Sunshine know anything about an old murder? She's too young."

He cleared his throat. "I understand you were close friends with her mother."

Nancy nodded.

"Did Mrs. Harrington ever tell you how she came to raise Sunshine as her daughter?"

Nancy looked at the floor. "She was her brother's daughter. He and his wife were killed in a car accident."

"We know that's not true. A man's life is at stake now." He raised his voice. "This isn't a time to preserve secrets. If I learn that you're lying to me, you're guilty of obstruction of justice. That's a felony. You'd be looking at serious jail time."

After some hesitation, Nancy said, "She found Sunshine sitting in a chair at the Mayo Clinic. She was a very sick child, abandoned by her parents. Trudy couldn't bear the thought of this little girl being shuffled through the foster-care system, so she took her home. She saved Sunshine's life."

"And where is Sunshine now?"

Nancy gave him Sunshine's address. It was the last thing she ever did.

The Final Week

T he phone rang in Tommy's office and he picked it up immediately. Everyone was on edge this week, waiting—no, praying—for one of the various lines they had floating out there to pop up with the missing answers. "Tommy Noorland here."

"Tommy, this is Dr. Jeffreys, from the Mayo Clinic."

"Doc, please tell me you found something."

"Yes, finally. Sorry it took so long, but it was buried in our closed-files room. I hope it's not too late."

"We got a reprieve. Just for one week. So tell me, is it the same girl?"

"There's no way I could tell you that definitively without DNA testing, but I can tell you this: Their medical records are identical. Same type of leukemia, and the medical history entered into the charts is exactly what's in the medical history you got from Angelina Calhoun's doctor."

If they'd been in the same room, Tommy would have gotten down on his hands and knees and kissed the doctor's feet. "Doc, I owe you big time. You ever need anything from me, just call and it's yours."

"Just let me know how it turns out, okay?

"You got it, Doc."

Tommy walked to Dani's office.

"You're smiling like a Cheshire cat, Tommy."

"I just got word from Dr. Jeffreys. The medical histories match. They've got to be the same girl."

Dani leaned back in her chair and frowned.

"I thought you'd be ecstatic."

"I am. I just don't think it'll be enough for the governor. They need the girl. Or woman, now, I guess."

"The mother's friend, Nancy—she'll be back from her trip soon. She's got to know where the daughter is living. After all, somebody had to contact Sunshine when her mother died, and it was probably Nancy."

"When is she due back?'

"Tomorrow."

"And you left a message on her voicemail to call? In case the neighbor forgets?"

"All done."

"Then we just have to wait."

"We'll find her, Dani," Tommy said,

"I hope so."

By Friday, Tommy still hadn't heard from Nancy. Everyone in the office was on edge. Each ring of the phone on his desk felt like a jolt of electricity to his nerves. He fumed each time it turned out to be someone other than Nancy. He was of no use to anyone, including himself, and decided to get out of the office. He'd left his cell-phone number on the message to Nancy. She could reach him wherever he went.

Before he left, he made one more call, a call he'd made every day that week. When Cannon picked up the phone, Tommy said, "Hey, it's me again. Any news?"

"Yeah, he got back late last night. I'm going over there today to speak to him."

"Hank, I know I sound like a broken record, but what's the harm in getting a judge to sign a court order? If it's not done today, then it'll be

Monday before anything happens, and that's too late to get DNA testing done."

"The harm is what it'll do to that family. They've suffered enough without having suspicion turned on them for their daughter's disappearance. Before that happens, I want to make damn sure there's good reason."

"Isn't the fingerprint enough of a reason?"

"Look, I've been working with that family for eighteen years. I'm the one who cleared them as suspects. I need to look Mickey in the face and ask him about it. I'll know whether he's lying to me. And in my book, a partial fingerprint showing up on a piece of paper could be something or nothing at all."

Tommy knew he wouldn't convince him otherwise. All week he'd tried, to no avail. "Just do me a favor and call me after you speak to him, okay?"

"Sure, I'll do you that favor. One cop to another."

Tommy let Bruce know he'd be out for the rest of the day and took the subway up to Central Park. He entered at 59th Street and began walking north. Joggers, bicyclists, and roller skaters of all sizes and ages scooted past him. The smell of summer was in the air, even though it wouldn't officially arrive for another month. The fragrance of the spring flowers mixed with the warm air. Despite the hordes of people in the park, it was a place Tommy could go to ease the tension. And he was filled with tension.

He headed along the east side of the park to The Dene, an area with rolling hills and valleys. Carolina silverbell, a white flower shaped like a bell, was in bloom. The flower always reminded him of weddings. At 76th Street he started walking to the west side, stopping first at the Azalea Pond. The bird-watchers were out in full force, and so were the azaleas and barberry bush. He stopped to smell the California wild rose, with its delicate pink coloring. Friends were always surprised when they learned of his interest in flowers and gardening. Apparently, it didn't match his image as a tough guy. "Tough guys can be tender too," he'd tell them. Gardening relaxed him—digging up the dirt to plant the flowers, pulling the weeds so they didn't crowd the plants. It satisfied him to work with his hands to bring something to life.

When he reached the area of the park known as the Shakespeare Garden, at West 79th Street, he climbed up the hill, found a bench, and sat down. The other spring flowers were in bloom: the yellow daffodils, day lilies, and crown imperial, the purple crocuses and irises, purple and yellow primrose, pink and red tulips, and the exotic-looking hellebore and knapweed. His wife had given him a book on flowers and plants one Father's Day, and over time he'd learned to identify them.

He'd needed to get out of the office, get away from the pall that hung over everyone. The death penalty had always made sense to him. An eye for an eye—that's what the Bible said. But bureaucracy seemed to get in the way of that simple principle. It wasn't an eye for an eye when the person being executed was innocent. He'd never had to face this before at HIPP. Many clients were exonerated based on DNA evidence. Some were freed or got new trials for other reasons. And for some, HIPP's involvement made no difference at all; the prisoner remained incarcerated or went on to be executed if it was a capital offense. In those cases, though, guilt or innocence hadn't been so certain. People viewed things differently, and who was he to argue with that? But he had to agree with Dani on this: The little girl's body found in the woods was not Angelina Calhoun, and that meant George did not murder his daughter. And unless Nancy Ferguson returned his call soon, it looked like an innocent man would die.

It was after six o'clock when Tommy returned to his home in Flatbush. He'd stopped at his favorite tavern for a few drinks first. The scotch had helped, as had the banter with Nick, his bartender and friend. The kids were already scattered, the two youngest playing Nintendo Wii on the television, the older ones out with friends.

"Job getting to you?" Patty, his wife, asked as she warmed up his dinner.

"This is a tough one."

"You can't take it personally."

"No? Then who should take it personally? The governor? The judges? Don't they all go to sleep at night saying they can't take it personally? Maybe if I'd pushed harder I could have gotten Cannon to move on it. Maybe if I camped out at Nancy Ferguson's doorstep I'd get an answer from her. So, yeah, I take it personally."

Patty came over to Tommy and began massaging his neck. "You're so tight," she murmured.

"I'm sorry. I shouldn't take it out on you."

"Go ahead. I'll bounce back."

"Everyone feels so goddamn helpless. And you know what the funny thing is? The calmest one is Calhoun. He's okay with what's going to happen."

"He's been in prison a long time. Maybe he's just ready for it to be over."

"It's not that. He believes his daughter is alive. Hell, we all believe she's alive. But for him, it's some sort of redemption. He's totally at peace now."

The oven timer pinged. As Patty placed the food on the table, Tommy's cell phone rang.

"Mr. Noorland, this is May Oliver, Nancy's neighbor."

"Have you heard from Nancy?"

"Oh, it's the most awful thing," she said, her voice choked. "Her daughter just left. She's dead."

Tommy didn't follow. "Who's dead?"

"Nancy. She must have slipped on the rocks and fallen into the cavern. Out in Arizona. They said her neck was broken. Some hikers found her yesterday. I didn't know if I should call you, but you made it sound so urgent. I can't believe it. She was so young for this to happen."

Tommy thanked her for calling and sunk into his chair.

"What's wrong?" Patty asked. "You look awful."

"It's over," Tommy said. "We're out of options."

He knew he had to tell Dani but dreaded making the call. "Do me a favor, doll, put the food back in the oven. I'm gonna take a shower."

Feeling no more refreshed after the shower, he dried himself off and dialed Dani's number.

"That's it," Dani said after he'd told her. "The ties to Sunshine Harrington have all been cut. As far as anyone in authority is concerned, it's as though she doesn't exist."

Tommy couldn't get Sunshine Harrington out of his thoughts. Everyone at HIPP believed she was George and Sallie's daughter, including him. The medical records didn't lie. Even though Dr. Jeffreys wouldn't say with absolute certainty that the two girls were one and the same, it was too coincidental to be otherwise. No, it all pointed to one conclusion: Sunshine Harrington was Angelina Calhoun.

But how could they find her? It was his job to investigate, to look for clues, put them together and get results. He pushed the food around on his plate, unable to eat. Patty talked to him, but her words were a blur. Suddenly, he had one more idea, a long shot but worth a try.

Trudy Harrington's neighbor Laura Devine had told Tommy that Sunshine was married. Somewhere there had to be a record of a marriage license. "Patty, I can't eat now. Maybe later. I'm just not hungry."

Patty nodded as he headed down the hall to his den. He sat in front of the computer and typed "marriage licenses" into the Google search bar. A string of websites appeared, all offering access to marriage records. He chose one and typed in the name "Sunshine Harrington." He clicked the box for all states and then clicked on "Search." Nothing. That's what the screen said. "There are no results for this name. Please try another name." *Damn*!

Sunshine Harrington had grown up in Minnesota. Chances are that's where she'd have married. It was one hour earlier in Minnesota. There was still time. He placed a call to the Minnesota Department of Health, Section of Vital Statistics. "What do I need to do to check a marriage record?" he asked when a female voice answered.

"Where was the party married?" she asked.

"Not sure, but maybe Olmsted County."

"Then you need to call the local registrar in Olmsted County. They'll send you a form to fill out and you send it back with an eight-dollar fee. You'll have to provide a form of proof of your kinship to the married couple. It can be a driver's license or birth certificate. A few other things, but it's all spelled out on the application. Do you need the phone number for the registrar's office?"

"No thanks, I'm set." Tommy knew it would be fruitless to start dealing with a new bureaucrat at this stage. Instead, he dialed Helen at the Bureau of Vital Statistics in Rochester. She'd gone out of her way for him before and he hoped she would again.

He caught her in the office. "I need a big favor," Tommy said after they'd exchanged greetings. He filled her in on everything he'd learned since she'd tried to help him. "So now that we know what happened to Angelina Calhoun, we're stuck trying to find her. I thought maybe if I knew her married name, I could do an Internet search for her."

Helen remained silent awhile. "I'm not supposed to do this," she finally said, "but if ever there was a reason to bend the rules, this is it. Hold on and I'll check our computer records."

Tommy waited nervously for Helen to get back on the phone. Even if she found the name of Sunshine's husband, would that be enough? Despite the astounding amount of information on the web, there were gaps. And even if he had the name, was there enough time to track her down?

"Tommy, you still there?"

"Tell me you have a name for me." Tommy wondered if she could hear the desperation in his voice.

"I'm sorry. If she's married, it wasn't in Olmsted County. There's no marriage license for her in our records."

He had failed. It had happened on occasion before, both with the FBI and at HIPP. There were times when he did everything right, when he explored every avenue, and still came up empty. He knew it wasn't his fault that Sunshine couldn't be found. And he knew an innocent man would die.

Mickey Conklin had expected Detective Cannon's visit. Janine had asked him whether he'd ever had Stacy's fingerprints taken. He'd forgotten all about it. They'd been walking through the mall and saw a sign that read, "Help Us Help Your Child." He went to the booth to see what it was about. A registry of children's fingerprints, in case anything happened to them. A surefire way to identify your child. He'd thought it was a good idea at the time.

"I'm really embarrassed to be asking you about this," Cannon said. He was sitting on a couch in Mickey's living room, a cup of coffee in his hand. "That investigator from New York keeps pushing me, and, well, I'm just here to get him off my back."

"It's fine. I'm glad you're doing your job. I don't mind you checking it out. I'd forgotten all about it. But I don't get it. How could the fingerprints on some letter match Stacy's?"

"It wasn't Stacy's fingerprints. Let me explain. Everybody has a unique set of markers on their fingerprints. A couple of those markers matched Stacy's but not all. Sometimes that means it's a close relative of Stacy's."

"You mean me or Janine?"

"That's what the investigator is saying. But I'm sure it's just a mistake."

"How does that happen?"

Cannon put down the cup of coffee and leaned toward Mickey. "I wish I could tell you the feds were infallible, but they make errors just like anyone else. And remember, it was just a partial match. Maybe a few of the markers were the same and they called it Stacy's, but it could just as easily have belonged to someone else."

Mickey nodded. "Well, I hope they get it straightened out."

Cannon coughed and squirmed in his seat. "Listen. I hate to ask you this, but I wouldn't be doing my job otherwise. Do you remember where you were the day after that investigator visited you?"

Mickey thought for a moment. "Wait, let me check my appointments." He pulled out his smartphone and scrolled to his appointment calendar. "Do you have the exact date?"

"April 15. Tax day."

"Here it is. I was on the road that day. I called on a couple of accounts in Cleveland."

"I'll just need those names."

Mickey laughed. "It's a good thing I wasn't carrying on an affair. You could really get me in trouble if you checked and I wasn't there."

"Ah, Mickey, you know I'm not trying to cause you problems. Look, with my schedule, I probably won't even get to this for a few weeks. If then. I just had to ask."

"Don't worry, Hank. You've been great to our family. We really appreciate it."

Cannon took out a notepad to write down the people Mickey had seen on his trip and then searched through his pockets for a pen. "Now, this is embarrassing. I don't have anything to write with. Can I borrow a pen?"

"Sure," Mickey said. He walked into the kitchen and came back with a pen. Cannon wrote down the names Mickey gave him and then stood up to leave. As Mickey walked him to the door, he asked, "So what's happening with that guy on death row? The one the investigator is working for?"

"Oh, it's going to be over for him soon. His time is up."

When Dani arrived home, Katie met her at the door. "I didn't want to bother you at work. I know how wrapped up you are now. But Jonah's coming down with something, I think. He's had diarrhea all afternoon, and his stomach is really bothering him."

"Any fever?"

"No, ninety-nine even."

She went upstairs to Jonah's room. As a child with Williams syndrome, he was more prone to illnesses than other children. It was one of Dani's reasons for avoiding taking on cases from the investigation stage. She hated being away from home when he was sick.

Jonah lay on his bed with his eyes closed and an open comic book next to him. Dani started to leave and then heard a moan. "Jonah, are you asleep?" she whispered.

"No, I'm conscious. My stomach is feeling awfully unpleasant, though."

"Katie told me." She sat on his bed and felt his forehead. "What did you eat at school today?"

"Pizza."

"Nothing else? Did you take food from anyone?"

Jonah shook his head and suddenly bolted upright and scooted off the bed. "I have to depart now," he said as he rushed to the bathroom.

When he came back, Dani got him settled into bed again and then left to call Dr. Dolman.

"Give him Immodium AD or Pepto-Bismol and watch him over the weekend. If it persists, call my office on Monday and tell them I need to see him then."

Monday. She was supposed to leave Sunday and fly back to Indiana. She was supposed to sit with George Calhoun one more time to wait as the clock ticked down. Doug could take off Monday to stay with Jonah, but did she want that? Dani wondered if fathers, even those as actively involved in their children's lives as Doug, felt the same tug between work and family. When Jonah was sick, she wanted to be near him, to comfort him. And although in most instances Jonah was perfectly content to be with his father or even Katie, when he was sick he wanted his mother. All she could do was hope he'd feel better tomorrow.

She went back downstairs and sat in the kitchen. Katie busily prepared dinner for them—meatloaf and mashed potatoes—and Dani enjoyed chatting with her while she did so. "How is Megan doing?" Dani asked.

"That girl will be the death of me, I swear. If I weren't her mother, I'd wring her neck."

"What's she up to now?"

"Claims she needs a break from college and is going to spend next year volunteering to teach poor children in Nicaragua. Can you imagine that? We skimp and save every extra penny to send her off to college, and she up and decides to quit."

"Why do you say she's quitting? It sounds admirable to me. And then after a year she can go back to her studies."

"Now, that's easy for you to say. Jonah is nice and safe here in his home with both his parents around. All those poor people she'll be around—who's to say they won't be jealous of the pittance she has and rob her in her sleep? Or worse."

"Megan is so independent. She'll be able to take care of herself."

"Humph!" Katie turned her back. Clearly, Dani hadn't offered her the answer she'd hoped for. No doubt she wanted Dani to say she was right, that Megan should stay at home. She wanted Dani to understand her need to protect her child. And she did understand. Sometimes, though, it was beyond a parent's control.

Jonah was awake most of the night, running to the bathroom at irregular intervals. Dani made a bed for herself on the floor of his room so she could be near him. He was such a good child, rarely complaining, and it ached her to see him suffer so much. They both fell asleep around 4:00 a.m., and the morning sun woke Dani two hours later.

She checked Jonah's forehead as he slept and it still felt cool. She tiptoed to her own bedroom and slipped in beside Doug. He murmured something unintelligible and resumed his rhythmic snoring. Dani's mind swirled with confusion. Should she stay home with Jonah and send Melanie in her place tomorrow? She'd been George's lifeline these past few weeks. How could she abandon him now? Yet, in the end, lawyers were fungible; mothers were not.

Underlying her unease was the awareness that Williams syndrome children were prone to celiac disease, an autoimmune disorder caused by an intolerance to gluten. The symptoms include diarrhea and nausea, just like Jonah had been experiencing. She and Doug had been grateful that Jonah seemed to have escaped that added burden. He loved his pizza and Katie's homemade cookies that awaited him on his return from school, and Cap'n Crunch cereal in the mornings. If he had this condition, there were so many other foods he'd need to avoid. It was hard enough to explain to a child with the normal range of intelligence that certain foods were forbidden. How would she make Jonah understand the importance of eliminating foods he loved?

Dani tended to do this, imagine the worst before it became a reality. She didn't know why. For herself, she turned a blind eye to any symptom that might pop up, but with Jonah and Doug, the opposite occurred.

At 8:00 a.m., with Jonah and Doug still sleeping, she slipped out of bed and called Dr. Dolman's answering service. He called her back fifteen minutes later.

"Dr. Dolman, I know I'm being a worrywart, but could this be the onset of celiac disease in Jonah?"

"I gather he still has symptoms."

"Yes, he had a difficult night."

"It could be celiac, or it could be a stomach virus, or mild food poisoning. He hasn't developed celiac disease yet, so that wouldn't be my first guess."

"I'm supposed to be somewhere else tomorrow and Monday. I'm afraid to leave him."

"Mrs. Trumball, Jonah is not in serious danger. Can your husband be home with him?"

"Yes."

"Then go and don't worry about him. To be on the safe side, keep him away from wheat and grain products until I see him on Monday. But if he's still having symptoms, he probably won't be too hungry anyway. Just make sure whoever's with him keeps him hydrated."

She thanked Dr. Dolman and hung up.

When Jonah awoke, Dani could see from his whitewashed pallor and the perspiration beading his forehead that he was still sick. She fixed him a breakfast of scrambled eggs, but after two forkfuls he said, "My tummy needs a respite." The day proceeded slowly, with Jonah lethargic and only reluctantly sipping the hot soup and drinking the warm tea Dani prepared for him.

By the time Jonah finally fell asleep that night, Dani felt drained. "I don't think I should go tomorrow," she told Doug during their honeymoon hour. "Jonah prefers when I take him to the doctor."

"Whatever is going on with Jonah is not going to change if I take him to see Dr. Dolman."

"Sure, but—"

"I know. You'll feel better if you're with him. But do you really think it'll be the same for George if Melanie is by his side instead of you?"

Dani sighed. Doug was right, of course, infuriatingly right. Once again she felt the tug of war raging within her. Mother or lawyer? Which came first? Motherhood, of course. Jonah's well-being always took precedence. But if she was honest with herself, she knew he would be fine with his father.

She lay her head on Doug's shoulder. "It's so hard for me to let go."

"I know. "

Dani looked up at the clock. She needed to call Melanie before it got too late if she wanted her to fly to Indiana in Dani's place. As she lowered her eyes, she spotted Jonah's backpack on the chair across from the couch. The one he'd used in kindergarten had sported pictures of Barney, the giant purple dinosaur. Now it was the Jonas Brothers. *He's growing up. I've got to accept that.* Dani lifted her head and looked at Doug. "I'm going to Indiana tomorrow. You're right. That's where I need to be."

Two Days

Once again, Dani flew to Indianapolis, this time with no airport delays. She arrived early enough to get her rental car and drive to Michigan City the same day. Being away from home so often had been hard for her, but handling a case from the beginning had given her a connection to the client that she'd missed when only handling the appeals. That was both good and bad. Her connection to George Calhoun was so strong that the thought of losing her battle for his freedom devastated her. She pulled up to the Holiday Inn and found a parking spot right in front. With her overnight bag in hand, she approached the front desk.

"Ms. Trumball, nice to see you back here," said the young lady behind the counter.

"Thank you, Angie," she said, reading her name from the tag pinned to her shirt.

"I have Room 229 for you. That'll be two nights, right?"

"Yes."

"If there's anything we can do for you while you're here, just call down to the front desk."

Dani thanked her and went up to her room. She unpacked her toiletries and placed them on the bathroom vanity. She turned on the TV and watched CNN for a few minutes before turning it off. It was too early to eat dinner, and she was too nervous to relax. She picked up the phone and called Tommy.

"We're missing something," she said to him when he answered.

"What do you mean?"

"There has to be something else we can do to find this woman. I just keep thinking there's something we should have done, and it's right there in front of me and I'm missing it."

"Look, I know what you're going through. I've been second-guessing myself all weekend. But we've done everything we can. The courts have failed us, that's what's happened. And it's not because you weren't brilliant. Your arguments were strong and you presented them well. The system just got it wrong this time."

"What about the funeral home, the one that buried Trudy Harrington? They must have an address for Sunshine."

"Already checked and came up empty. Nancy was their contact person."

"The woman who lived across the street, the one whose daughter was friends with Sunshine—maybe her daughter kept in touch and knows where she is now."

"Checked and checked. *Nada*."

"Social media sites?"

"I didn't expect to find anything without her married name, but I tried anyway. Facebook, Twitter, LinkedIn. A bunch of smaller ones too. Nothing."

Dani knew she was grasping at straws. She'd asked to have Tommy on her team because he was the most thorough investigator in the office. Top drawer all the way. Of course he had followed up on any possible strand.

They were both silent for a moment. "Tommy?"

"Yeah?"

"Do you think it's strange that Nancy died in an accident? I mean, she was the only person who could lead us to Sunshine, and before she returns home, she goes out on her own and just happens to fall over a canyon ledge? I'm not usually a conspiracy nut, but still."

"It's been bothering me too. I keep thinking that Mickey Conklin is somehow involved in this. It had to be him that left the threatening note on my car. He's been trying to stop us, and Nancy's death sure as hell slammed the brakes on finding Sunshine. I can't figure out how he'd know about Nancy, though. And if somehow he did know she held the key, how would he know where to find her?"

"He followed you once. Maybe he followed you back to Byron, learned about Nancy the same way you did."

"I've thought about that. But that would mean he followed me back to New York, kept tabs on me until I went back to the Mayo Clinic, then followed me out there. He'd have to be awfully good to do that without me catching on."

"He didn't need to. Cannon could have told him where you were going."

"Shit. Of course. I practically gave Cannon a blueprint of my plans."

"The answer's out there, Tommy. I just know it."

"Dani, don't get your hopes up."

"I won't. But Tommy …"

"Yes?"

"It's just—we've had our differences on this case. I know you thought I was crazy for believing George. But I want you to know that I couldn't have done this with anyone but you. Thank you."

"Get some rest, Dani. You need to be strong tomorrow."

After she hung up, Dani decided to go for a walk. She'd been sitting all day, in the airport terminal, the plane, and then the car. Daylight would last at least two more hours, and she used that time to wander the streets of Michigan City. The stores were closed, but she stopped now and then to look at the merchandise in the windows. It was mindless walking, and that was what she needed.

As it approached seven o'clock, she realized she was hungry. She began walking back in the direction of the hotel, looking for a restaurant that seemed welcoming. She hadn't paid attention as she walked and was surprised when she heard someone call her name. She looked up and saw Warden Coates.

"You look lost," he said.

She smiled. "Deliberately lost. I needed to clear my mind, and just drifting along seemed to do the trick."

"No hope left for tomorrow?"

Dani tried to look stalwart. "I'm afraid not."

"Mr. Calhoun seems prepared for what's coming. I find that's often the case when the day draws near. The inmate accepts the inevitable."

"Maybe I would sleep better if I saw his execution as inevitable. Nothing about this injustice seems inevitable to me."

Coates looked at Dani kindly. "Do you remember our first conversation? I told you I was glad Mr. Calhoun had contacted you. That death-row inmates who insisted they were innocent should have every chance to prove their case. He's had that now. You've advocated for him in every possible way. Now it's time to accept that, with every case, there comes a time for argument to end."

"I do remember our conversation. You also said you sleep better knowing something wasn't missed. Something has been missed here: the true identity of the girl buried in that grave. It wasn't Angelina Calhoun. I'm certain of that."

"Then we'll both have a sleepless night tonight," he said, a look of sadness on his face.

They parted ways and Dani continued her search for a restaurant. Finally, one looked promising, and she went in. It was a homey southern Italian restaurant with only ten tables, each covered with red-checkered tablecloths. She ordered linguine with white clam sauce and a glass of Chianti. Dani loathed dining by herself. She found it impossible to avoid staring at the other patrons, whether they were couples enjoying an intimate evening, families struggling to keep the younger children quiet, or a group of friends getting together. She didn't want to, but staring into space didn't work either. So she pulled out a book to read while she sipped her wine and waited for dinner to arrive. When it did, the food tasted as if it had come from the freezer section of a supermarket. She downed it quickly and returned to the hotel.

By the time she got to her room, it was almost nine o'clock, time for her call home. Doug reported that Jonah's stomach had returned to normal. Once more, they seemed to have escaped a greater medical issue.

"By the way, Jonah's camp package came in the mail today. It tells what he should bring for the summer," Doug said. "Jonah's been poring over it and making a list of all the new things he'll need."

Dani's heart stopped. The mailman. The person who filled the mailbox standing next to their driveway with reams of catalogs; tons of bills; occasional greeting cards; and, once in a rare while, a letter from a faraway friend who still cherished the written document. Their mailman's name was Joe. Every Christmas they gave him a card with a cash gift, thanking him for his dedicated service. If Dani were home when he delivered a package or a letter needing her signature, he'd greet her by name and ask how Jonah was doing. She suspected he knew more about their family than the neighbors next door just from sorting the mail sent to their house.

Was it possible? Trudy's neighbor, Laura, said Sunshine had grown up in the house on Aspen Street. Could the same mailman who had known her as a child still be delivering mail to that block? Could he know where Sunshine was living? Dani quickly got off the phone with Doug and dialed Tommy.

"The mailman," she practically shouted when he picked up. "We never tried the mailman."

"What the hell are you talking about?"

"Sunshine grew up on that street. If she sent her mother cards, you know, for her birthday or Christmas and put her return address on it, the mailman might know where she is."

"Uh, Dani, you're the lawyer, but aren't there privacy laws about that? I mean, are mail deliverers allowed to look at the letters they deliver?"

"They're people. And they have to look at what's written on the envelope to deliver the mail. Isn't it possible that he might have noticed where Sunshine's mail came from? Or even her married name?"

"Do you realize how many homes are on each route? How many pieces of mail these guys deliver every day?"

Dani was too agitated to sit. The cord on the hotel phone wouldn't let her walk far, but she paced as far as she could. "I know it's a long shot. We have nothing else. Can you call the Bryon post office first thing in the morning?"

"Nobody's going to talk to me on the phone. Even in person it'll be a tough sell."

Dani looked at her watch—9:20. There was no chance of Tommy's getting a flight out tonight. Even if he could get on an early-morning flight, he'd arrive in Byron after the mailmen had left the post office. Waiting for the right one to return at the end of the day would make it impossible to follow up in time on any information they might get. "Try anyway, Tommy. Please."

She heard a long sigh. "I'll see what I can do. Just don't get your hopes up."

"You're wrong, Tommy. I have to get my hopes up. It's the only way I'll get through the night."

As soon as he got off the phone, Tommy turned to his wife. "This is so goddamn frustrating. We believe she's out there but have no idea where."

"Tell me what you've tried."

Tommy ran through the list of avenues he'd searched. When he finished, Patty turned away from him and went into the kitchen.

"Hey, where're you going?

"Be right back." A minute later, she returned to the living room with a small book in her hand. "I couldn't get by without my address book," she said, a big smile on her face. "Everybody I've ever known is written down, with their phone number and address. I even keep a record of birthdays in here. I know the young people now all have their Blackberrys and such, but our generation? We like the old paper-and-pencil record."

"Shit! I can't believe I didn't think about that. I'm losing my goddamn touch."

"You have to go out there and check the house."

"It's all locked up, you know."

"Tommy Noorland, I've heard enough of your stories from the FBI days to know that a locked door never stopped you."

Tommy chuckled. Patty was right. He could be on the first flight out in the morning. Breaking into someone's house in broad daylight wasn't ideal, but he still remembered his skill with a pick. And if some neighbor called the cops, he'd already be inside and have had a chance to look for an address book. Besides, his credentials as former FBI and the reason for the break-in were bound to get him some professional courtesy, if it came to that.

He rushed to the computer and booked a 6:20 a.m. flight to Rochester. As he got ready for bed, his first flicker of optimism was tempered with the realization that someone did not want HIPP to find Sunshine and may have already killed to make sure of it.

He got to Trudy's home at 10:15. The street was empty of people, but Tommy went around to the back door anyway. He slipped a pick out of his pocket, slid it into the small hole in the doorknob, and with three turns heard a click. He turned the knob and entered the kitchen of Trudy Harrington. It was bright enough outside, even with the windows covered in curtains, that he didn't need to turn on any lights. Patty kept her address book in a kitchen drawer, and that's where he began his search. "Try the drawer closest to the telephone," she had told him. He scanned the room and saw an old-fashioned phone on the wall under a kitchen cabinet. The nearest drawer was filled with loose papers, a stapler, restaurant menus, and a plastic bag filled with business cards. He opened the next drawer. Sitting on top of an Olmsted County phone directory was a blue address book with a photo of a dog on the cover. Tommy grabbed it and, after saying a quick prayer under his breath, opened it. He turned to the "H" page, hoping Trudy had just crossed out Sunshine's maiden name and written over it with her married name. No luck. He started at the beginning. As he turned the page from the A's to the B's, he caught his breath. Right at the top was Sunny Bergman. He stared at the page,

He couldn't believe it. Sunny Bergman lived in Manhattan. Not only Manhattan but just a few blocks from the HIPP office. Quickly, he took out his phone and called Melanie. "I found her," he said as soon as she answered the phone.

"Who?"

"Angelina. Or at least Sunshine Harrington."

"How? Where?"

"I'll explain the how later, but she's in Manhattan on East 16th Street. You've got to get over to her apartment right away."

"Oh my god! This means—"

"That's right. This means we might be able to save him."

Eric was right. They'd needed a vacation, an escape from the city. Although it was only May, the heat had started to build, trapped by the tall buildings that surrounded the small island of Manhattan. It was the last weekend before the Hamptons officially opened to the hordes that descended on them from Memorial Day to Labor Day, and the beaches were blissfully empty. Sunny had been unsure when Eric told her of his friend Ken's offer of his East Hampton home for the weekend. Her mother's death remained ever present, a heaviness she carried with her every day. Eric had insisted, though, and she was happy he had. They drove out of the city Thursday afternoon and wouldn't go back until Monday. The air smelled fresher here at the end of Long Island, and the weight of her mother's death seemed lighter in the salty air. Even Eric seemed relaxed, more so than he'd been in weeks.

The ocean, which seemed to go on forever, was a new experience for Sunny. The house they were using, a three-bedroom home styled after a beach bungalow but filled with expensive furniture and knickknacks, was just steps away from it. The morning sun and the crash of the waves awakened Sunny early. Each morning while the others slept, she'd gone for a long walk along the water's edge, picking up shells for Rachel along the way. Rachel loved playing in the sand, loved burying herself in it. She'd laugh when she tumbled over the sand castles she'd built. A digital camera hung around Sunny's neck at all times, ready to capture photos of Rachel. She'd asked her mother once why there were no pictures of her from before her sixth birthday party. "They were lost during our move to this house," her mother had answered. Now Sunny's computer was filled with pictures of Rachel, and the full memory cards were locked away in a safe deposit box.

The weather had been glorious. Cloudless sunshine every day. The ocean water still felt too cold for swimming, but she and Rachel had dipped their toes in the foamy surf.

They'd visited South Hampton and window-shopped in the expensive stores. Eric bought each of them matching T-shirts that read "Fabulous Hamptons." They had lunch at a restaurant that claimed "World's Best Hamburgers," and Sunny thought they must be, they were so delicious. Eric was certain he'd spotted Paul McCartney ducking into a bakery, but Sunny thought it couldn't have been him. They drove along the ocean roads gawking at the huge mansions. "We'll live in one of those someday," Eric said, and Sunny just laughed. Before going back to the house, they stopped for ice cream so creamy that it too must have been the world's best.

Today, the last day before they had to return to the soot of Manhattan, they were going to the very tip of the island, to Montauk Point.

"Wake up, sleepyhead," Sunny said to Eric. "Time for breakfast."

Eric rubbed his eyes and looked at the clock—8:55. "Why'd you wake me?" he groaned. "I haven't slept late in a lifetime. And I was having the nicest dream."

"What about?"

Eric pulled Sunny onto the bed and put his arms around her, nuzzling his nose into her neck. "Let's see. You were in it, of course. It couldn't be a nice dream without you. We lived in a cozy cottage with a white picket fence around it and our very own swimming pond. And there was the most delicious odor of pancakes, blueberry pancakes, coming from the kitchen."

Sunny punched him in the arm. "Silly, you smelled my pancakes. They're waiting for you in the kitchen. Rachel already ate hers."

After Eric finished breakfast, they headed along Montauk Highway to their destination. The two-lane road offering periodic glimpses of the ocean seemed worlds away from the congestion of Manhattan. For the first time, Sunny could see herself living in another place than Minnesota. She thought it would be lovely if Eric joined a practice in a seaside community. She and Rachel could take walks in the sand every day. They'd start a collection of seashells, all different colors and shapes. Eric could go deep-sea fishing on his days off. What a beautiful way to live.

Thirty minutes later they arrived at the Montauk lighthouse, sitting atop a bluff with the Atlantic Ocean on three sides. In the gift shop, Eric picked up a brochure. "Listen to this," he said. "This is the oldest lighthouse in New York and the fourth-oldest active lighthouse in the entire United States. What do you think of that?"

"Wha' 'ighthouse, Daddy?"

"See those boats out in the water? Well, it's hard for their captains to see at night, so there's a light at the top of this tower and it flashes every five seconds. That helps the captains see where they're going and steer their boats."

"I wanna see 'ight."

"We'll walk all the way to the top and you'll see it."

They set off up the winding stairs. After just one flight, Rachel held up her arms to be carried. Once they reached the lookout point, the view was breathtaking. "I could stay here forever," Sunny whispered to Eric. It had been a long time since she'd felt so happy, so carefree.

After a while, they made their way back down and drove to a petting farm. Rachel ran up and down the rows of baby animals. There were goats, sheep, rabbits, calves, turkeys, pigs, and beautifully colored pea-cocks. Sunny bought a baby bottle filled with milk for Rachel to feed to the goats. Rachel laughed gaily as a goat grabbed on to the nipple and hungrily emptied the contents.

Later, they stopped at a local market and bought food for a picnic. They set up a blanket on the beach and, while they ate their lunch, watched the seagulls swoop to the sand, looking for scraps. On the way back, they stopped to pick up porterhouse steaks for dinner. By the time they returned to the house, they were all spent. As Rachel lay down for her nap, so did her parents.

When Sunny awakened, Eric was no longer by her side. She got out of bed and followed the aroma of charcoal. "Mmm, that smells delicious," she said as she stepped onto the deck, where Eric was grilling the steaks. "It reminds me of home. Dad used to barbecue almost every night during the warm weather."

"Funny, it seems it's always the dad that's barbecuing."

"I think there's a gene somewhere on the Y chromosome that gives men a special talent for it," she said and laughed.

"You've enjoyed this trip, haven't you?"

"Oh, yes. I love being here. Rachel does too."

"Maybe Ken will let us use it again after Labor Day. Or we could take a weekend and go down to the Jersey shore over the summer. How about that?"

"Sounds dreamy." Everything about their stay out East had been dreamy. It had helped push away the nightmare of her mother's death.

After dinner, they put Rachel to bed and sat on the deck, sipping wine in the cool night air. When she got up to stretch her legs, Eric pulled her onto his lap and kissed her, first softly, then hungrily. He led her into the bedroom and they lay down on the queen-size bed.

They undressed each other and then made love. It had been a long time since they'd last done so. Eric's hours at the hospital and her tiredness from running after Rachel all day had conspired to keep them apart. Eric's touch was gentle; he knew the spots to touch on her body to arouse her, and he expertly brought her to a climax.

Afterward, lying in Eric's arms, Sunny felt her eyelids grow heavy. Before she drifted off to sleep, she realized how happy she was. She loved Eric, she loved Rachel, and she was loved in return. If only she had her mother, her life would be perfect.

Thirteen Hours

Ten minutes after Tommy's call, Melanie stood in front of the address she had for Sunshine Harrington Bergman. She rang the buzzer for her apartment but was met with silence. She waited outside for someone to leave the building, and when a man finally opened the locked door to the lobby, Melanie slipped inside. She took the elevator to the eighth floor and walked down the hallway to apartment 8-C. She pressed her thumb against the ringer and held it for two seconds. Still no response.

Melanie didn't know whether Sunshine hadn't heard the bell or was away. She didn't have time to wait for the answer. Instead, she rang the bell at 8-D. For a long time she heard no response. Just as she was about to leave, she heard some shuffling inside and then the turning of several locks. A man standing at least six-four and weighing well over 250 pounds opened the door. "I know this sounds corny, but it really is a matter of life and death. Do you know if your neighbor next door is away from home?"

"You're fucking waking me up to find some guy?"

Melanie looked at her watch. It was 11:40. "I'm sorry I disturbed you. And it's not what you think. A man is hours away from execution and she's the only person who can stop it."

"Listen, lady. I just got to sleep two hours ago. I don't care if it's the fucking Queen of England that's gonna die." He slammed the door shut.

Melanie didn't care if she woke up more people. She continued to knock on doors, beginning with 8-A, and worked her way down the row.

When she reached 8-F, a teenage girl with long brown hair and longer legs below her shorts opened the door. Melanie went into her standard opening, rote by now. "Sorry to bother you, miss, but I'm looking for Sunshine Bergman, who lives in 8-C."

"Oh, sure. Sunny. I baby-sit Rachel sometimes."

"You don't happen to know where she might be, do you?"

"The whole family went away for the weekend. They might be back tonight, I think."

Melanie stopped in her tracks. Each step of the way in this case, they seemed to come so close only to butt up against an obstacle. She turned back to the girl. "Do you have a cell-phone number for her? Or her husband?"

"Sure. I need it for when I baby-sit. You know, in case something happens."

"Can you give it to me? It's urgent that I reach her."

The girl thought for a moment. "I … I don't think I should. In fact, I'm not sure I should even be talking to you."

As she started to close the door, Melanie stuck her foot inside to block it. She took out her HIPP identification and showed it to the girl. "What's your name?"

"Leanne."

"Okay, Leanne. There's a man who's going to be executed in thirteen hours for a crime he didn't commit. I don't know if Sunny Bergman here is the woman I'm looking for, but if she is, she's the only one who can save his life. I've got to speak to her immediately."

Leanne looked Melanie over. "I don't know. I keep hearing about all these scams. How do I know you're not some con artist? Or some kind of freak?"

Melanie's heart did flip-flops in her chest. "Please, give me her phone number, I'm begging you."

"I don't know what to do. My mom would be furious for me to even be talking to you."

Melanie kept her foot in the doorway. "How about this. Would you call her for me?"

Leanne hesitated. "Okay, I guess I can do that. Wait here while I get my phone."

Moments later she came back holding a hot-pink cordless phone. She punched in some numbers and Melanie could hear the phone ring. When it was answered, Melanie heard static on the line.

"Sunny, it's Leanne. There's a woman here who says it's urgent that she speak to you. Can I put her on the phone?"

Leanne handed the phone to Melanie. "Ms. Bergman, I'm with the Help Innocent Prisoners Project, and right now there's a man who's going to be executed in a few hours who's innocent. We need your help."

Through thick static, Melanie thought she heard her say, "Why me?"

"It's too complicated for the phone. Where are you?"

Melanie could make out the words *Long Island Expressway, traffic,* and *accident.*

"How long do you think it'll take you to get back home?"

More static and then, "Three more hours."

"I'll be waiting here for you."

Why did good news and bad news always come together? It seemed miraculous that Tommy had found Sunshine Harrington, but now she had to wait three precious hours for a DNA sample.

She thanked Leanne and headed back to the HIPP office, stopping along the way at the corner delicatessen to pick up a coffee and a Danish. She went into Bruce's office and sat down.

"Tommy found Sunshine Harrington."

Bruce's face broke out into a wide grin. "Did she give him a swab for DNA?"

"Let me rephrase. He found where she lives. I just got back from there. Tommy's on his way back from Minnesota."

"Minnesota? When did he go out there?"

"I don't know the details. He called earlier and gave me her address. I haven't made contact yet. Sunshine's on her way back from a vacation. And naturally stuck in traffic on the LIE. She doesn't expect to be back here for another three hours." A seventy-one-mile highway between Manhattan and Riverhead, the gateway to the Hamptons, the Long Island Expressway was often referred to as "the Long Island Distressway." Bumper stickers attesting to the travails of traveling the roadway were rampant. Melanie's favorite was "I drive the LIE. Please pray for me."

"Will it be enough for the governor if we produce Sunshine without DNA proof that she's Angelina?" Bruce asked.

"Dani has an affidavit from Jody, the nurse who put us on to her, and another from Dr. Jeffreys saying their medical histories match. Maybe that'll be enough."

"Does Dani know about Sunshine?"

"I don't know. Tommy called me right away so I could get over to her apartment."

"Call Dani. She needs to get in touch with the governor's chief of staff and give him a heads-up on our progress, smooth the way for at least postponing the execution until the testing comes back. I'll call the lab and make sure they'll stay late for us."

It took twenty minutes for Dani to reach the phone. Once again, Coates sent a guard to bring her from George Calhoun's cell to the warden's office.

"Dani, have you spoken to Tommy today?" Melanie asked when she picked up the phone.

"No. Did he learn anything? Did the mailman come through?"

"I don't know how he got it, but Tommy called me this morning with Sunshine's address, and I've been to her apartment. She's right here in Manhattan. The bad news is she's not at home. But I talked to her and she'll be back around 2:30. And get this—she lives just a few blocks from HIPP."

"No! Are you serious? She was right in our backyard all along?"

"Yep."

"I think I'm numb from shock."

"Listen, will producing her be enough for the governor? I don't think it's possible to run DNA before midnight."

The lab had already run a DNA swab from Calhoun. Now they just needed a sample from Sunshine to confirm she was his daughter. Because of backlogs, DNA testing in a crime lab could take anywhere from weeks to months, but the process itself was quick. Depending on the equipment, preliminary results could be gotten in as little as twelve hours or as many as thirty-six. HIPP had an arrangement with a private lab. If results needed to be expedited, the lab accommodated.

"All Guidry said to me was that they need a body. I'll give him a call right now. And Melanie?"

"Yes?"

"When you meet with Sunshine, be gentle. This has got to be a shock for her."

"I think it's going to be a shock for a lot of people."

Dani called Joe Guidry and the words rushed out of her mouth like a swirling tornado. "We've found her, Angelina Calhoun. We can prove she's not the girl found murdered. You can't let the execution go forward. He's innocent, just as we've said."

"Whoa. Slow down. You have someone who claims to be Angelina Calhoun?"

"No, not exactly. She probably has no memory of her first few years. But you've seen the affidavit from that nurse at the Mayo Clinic. And we've gotten word from the doctor who treated Sunshine Harrington that her medical records match Angelina Calhoun's."

"So you have Sunshine Harrington."

"Yes, sort of. She's on her way home. She lives in New York, just two blocks from our office. Isn't that incredible? My associate spoke to her and she's waiting at her apartment."

"That's all interesting, but without DNA, how can you be certain they're the same person."

"Well, we can't, of course. Not a hundred percent. But how could the governor let an execution go forward now? You have to give us time to get the DNA tested."

"How much time?"

"One more week. That should do it."

"I'll have to get back to you."

Dani gave him the phone number for the warden's office. She was torn between waiting for Joe's call and going back to the cell to let George know the latest development. She decided to wait. She didn't want to raise George's hopes only to deflate them if they didn't get the extra time. She went outside the office to let Coates know she was off the phone.

"So, what's the story?" he asked.

"We found a woman we believe is George's daughter, Angelina. That means the little girl found in the woods is someone else and George didn't kill her."

Coates went into his office and sat at his desk. He motioned for Dani to take a seat across from him. "So, does this mean the governor will stop the execution?"

"I'm waiting to hear back from her."

The warden opened his bottom right desk drawer, thumbed through some files and pulled two out. "These are the reasons I was happy George Calhoun contacted you." He placed both folders in front of Dani. "Both of these men were on death row in this prison. The first one, Johnny Tubbs, was before my time here. He'd been convicted on eyewitness testimony. His attorney came from the public defender's office, a kid still wet behind the ears. He never investigated Tubbs's alibi, never examined the prosecution's evidence. After a two-day trial, the jury sentenced Tubbs to die. He spent five years on death row. The kid was lucky, though. Two weeks before his execution date, some good-hearted attorney who'd volunteered his time got Tubbs a stay, then a new trial. He showed that none of the prosecution's evidence supported Tubbs as the perpetrator. If this attorney hadn't taken on Tubbs's case, Indiana would have executed an innocent man." Coates pointed to the second file. "Carl Jones. I was already working here, assigned to death row. Carl had been on death row fifteen years by the time I arrived. He was a quiet man, meek almost. He'd been convicted of murdering a shop owner and customer in the course of a robbery. When decent lawyers got involved, they were able to show that the witnesses against him had lied. Jones came within two days of execution before he got a stay and retrial. If a lawyer hadn't believed in him, it would've been my job to walk him to the room where he'd get a lethal injection. I would have been escorting an innocent man to his death. That's a hard thing for a man to live with. So"—he took a deep breath—"you and I are on the same page now. I'd welcome the governor calling and telling me to hold off so you can get your testing done. Like I told you the first time we spoke, I like a man to get every chance possible to prove he's innocent."

Just as the warden finished, his phone rang. He answered it and handed it to Dani. "Joe Guidry," he whispered.

"Joe, give me some good news."

"I'm just calling to let you know I haven't been able to reach the governor yet. She's been tied up in a meeting. I had a note sent in to her, but she hasn't come out yet. I don't know how much longer she'll be, and I didn't want you waiting around without knowing what's happening."

"Thanks, Joe. Call me as soon as you know something."

It didn't make sense to continue to wait in the warden's office. Dani thanked him for the use of his office and followed a guard back to George's cell.

He sat on his bed and stood quickly when he saw her. "Anything?" he asked.

"We've found your daughter."

George sat down again, placed his hands over his face and rocked back and forth. When he finally stopped and looked up at Dani, she saw that his cheeks were tear-stained.

"She's alive," George whispered. "My angel is alive."

Dani hated to give him bad news right now, but she had to. "I don't know whether this is sufficient for the governor without the DNA. I'm waiting to hear back from her. We're not out of the woods yet."

George stood again and paced. "She has to give me time. I thought it would be enough just to know she's alive, but it's not. I want to see my daughter. I want to hold her in my arms."

Dani nodded. Of course he did. He'd sacrificed so much for this child. She reached out and took his hands. This man had endured seventeen years of isolation, almost twenty years of not knowing if he'd made the right decision, twenty years of silence about that decision. Was he wrong to risk a death sentence for only the smallest possibility of saving his daughter? Dani didn't know what she would have done. She only knew that George deserved to see the results of that decision. He deserved to be part of Sunshine's life.

"There's something else, George. You have a granddaughter. She's just about three years old."

George fell back onto his bed and began to cry again. Dani sat next to him and they waited together for the governor's call.

An hour later, Dani was summoned again to the warden's office. The phone was off the hook, waiting for her, and the office was empty. She picked it up, expecting to hear Joe's voice, and was surprised to hear a woman speak.

"Ms. Trumball, this is Governor Timmons. Joe has filled me in on your request for a stay and your reasons for believing Mr. Calhoun is innocent. Frankly, it seems rather tenuous. It seems a leap to go from a nurse harboring suspicions about the appearance of a daughter in her colleague's life to assuming that girl is Angelina Calhoun."

"Madame Governor, the girl's medical records are the same as Angelina's."

"Isn't leukemia the most common cancer in young children?"

"Yes, but—"

"I'm sorry. I don't mean to cut you off, but I've left an important meeting that I have to get back to. The bottom line is I'm not convinced you've given me enough to postpone the execution."

"But DNA testing would be conclusive. Then there'd be no doubt."

"If it comes back the way you think it would. If it doesn't, the state would have postponed the execution a second time, at considerable expense."

"Please, Madame Governor," Dani begged, struggling to hold back tears. "We just need a little more time."

There was silence for a few seconds. "Executions are mandated to take place before 6 a.m. The practice has been to conduct them just after midnight. I'll instruct the warden to hold off until 5:50. Get your DNA proof before then. That's all I can give you."

"Thank you, Madame Governor."

Dani hung up the phone and sat down, stunned by the governor's decision. Now she had to go back downstairs and face George.

By 3:00, Sunshine still hadn't shown up. Melanie had made herself comfortable sitting on the floor in front of her door, but now her legs were starting to cramp. She stood and looked at her watch once more. She had to stop that. Checking so often wasn't going to make the minutes move any faster.

She'd heard from Dani. They had only until sunrise to get her DNA run. Bruce had worked his magic with the guys from the lab. They'd stay all night to work on it. But first they needed to get it. And for that they needed Sunshine.

Twenty minutes later she heard the elevator door open. Walking toward her was a blond woman, her long hair pulled back in a ponytail. Her red cheeks looked like two apples, and her slate-blue eyes were fringed with thick brown lashes. The little girl holding her hand looked like a carbon copy of Angelina Calhoun at the same age.

"Ms. Quinn? Sorry we're so late. Traffic was impossible." She introduced her family and unlocked their apartment door. "Please, come in." The family walked inside and Melanie followed. "Let me get Rachel settled and then we can talk." She took the little girl into the kitchen, removed a bottle of apple juice from the refrigerator, and poured it into a sippy cup. "Eric, would you take Rachel into our room and turn on the TV for her?"

"Sure."

Sunshine turned back to Melanie. "Please sit," she said, pointing to a chair. She sat down on the sofa across from her. "So, what's the big emergency?"

Melanie didn't know how to start. This woman had grown up believing her parents were the Harringtons. How could she tell her that everything she knew had been built on a lie? Maybe if she'd had more time she could have brought someone with her, someone more adept at easing into the truth. "Mrs. Bergman—"

"Please, call me Sunny."

"Sunny, there's a man on death row who's going to be given a lethal injection just before 6:00 a.m. tomorrow morning. He was convicted of murdering his daughter, a four-year-old girl named Angelina Calhoun. From the very beginning, he's always claimed that the body of the child they found wasn't his daughter. I'm telling you this because ... we believe you're Angelina Calhoun."

Sunny sat before her in stunned silence, her hands gripping each other.

"I know this is hard to take in," Melanie continued, her voice soft. "But the only way to stop the execution this coming morning is to take a DNA sample from you and have it tested."

Sunny shook her head, her hands still locked together. "Why are you saying this? My parents were Ed and Trudy Harrington."

"Those were the folks that raised you. But we don't believe they're your biological parents."

Hugging herself, Sunny began to rock and stared at the floor. "No, no, no," she said over and over.

"Do you remember being sick as a child?" Melanie asked.

Her rocking stopped and she became still. Sunny looked up at Melanie and whispered, "Yes."

"You had leukemia. Your biological parents tried to get medical care for you. At first they were able to, but then the leukemia came back. You needed a bone-marrow transplant, but they had no insurance and no one would treat you."

"I remember being in the hospital. I remember how much it hurt."

"You would probably have died if you didn't get treatment. Your parents loved you very much, so much that they made the ultimate sacrifice. They brought you to the Mayo Clinic and left you there, hoping that the county would take you in and get you the help that they couldn't provide. They need your help now."

Tears rolled down Sunny's cheeks. Eric walked back into the living room, sat next to Sunny, and put his arm around her. Sunny lay her head on Eric's chest and sobbed. He held her tightly. "What's going on?" he asked.

Sunny lifted her head, wiped away her tears, and recounted what Melanie had told her.

"Why Sunny?" Eric asked Melanie. "Why would you think it's her and not some other child treated at the Mayo Clinic?"

"There's no time to go into the complete investigation. We've got to get a DNA sample to the lab right away. But I'll tell you this—your daughter is the spitting image of Angelina Calhoun at age three."

Sunny slumped back on the couch. "What do I have to do?"

"I'll just take a swab of the inside of your cheek. That's all. And then I'll bring it to the lab. DNA is exact. It'll tell us definitively whether you're Angelina Calhoun."

Sunny nodded. "Okay. You can take it. But this man, this man you say is my father—"

"I can tell you all about him and your mother too, but later. If I don't get to the lab fast, then—well, I just need to get there."

"Yes, I understand."

Melanie took out a swab kit, scraped the inside of Sunny's cheek and carefully placed the buccal swab in a plastic baggie. She said goodbye and then sprinted down the stairs, too impatient to wait for the elevator. She grabbed a cab to take her to the lab's midtown office and arrived just before 3:30.

"Got it," she said to Stan, the technician waiting for her at the front desk. "Can it be done? Can you get results by 5:00 a.m.?"

"It'll be tight. We should be able to get preliminary results at least."

Melanie put in a call to Dani to let her know the lab had gotten the sample. There was nothing left for her to do. Nothing but wait.

Sunny went through the motions of making dinner, still numb from the bombshell that had exploded in her living room. *How could this be?* Yet she knew it was true. The absence of any pictures of her as a baby and a toddler now made sense. Instead of inspiring anger toward the parents who raised her—anger that they'd kept this secret from her—Melanie's revelation intensified her love for the Harringtons. They had taken in a desperately sick child and loved her as if she were their own. But her biological parents? She didn't know how she felt about them.

"Are you okay, honey?" Eric asked as he came into the kitchen. He'd been asking her the same question every fifteen minutes.

"I'm not sure." She held out her hand to show that it was shaking. "How am I supposed to feel about my parents? The ones who left me?"

"I don't think there's any one way you're supposed to feel about them. And there's no reason for you to figure out now how you do feel. Give it time; let it sink in."

"But that woman—she said my father will be executed in the morning. Because of me. Because they think he killed me."

"We don't even know for sure that he is your father."

Sunny looked up from the mixing bowl. "I know. He's my father. And if he dies, it'll be because of me."

Eric took Sunny's hands and led her from the kitchen. He sat her down on a chair at the dining table and then sat down next to her. "Listen to me. If he is your father, if the DNA tells you that, he made a decision to give you a second chance at life. He did that out of love for you. Tell me, is there anything you wouldn't do for Rachel?"

Sunny shook her head.

"Whatever happens next, always remember, your parents made that decision. Not you. And you're not responsible for the consequences of their decision."

"I don't know how I can live with those consequences."

"You live with them to honor their sacrifice."

Sunny nodded. Somehow, she knew that's what her parents would want. She also knew it would not be easy.

Five Hours

It felt like déjà vu to Dani. She could only imagine what it felt like for George. They were back together, enduring the long wait. Only this time it was taking much longer. Coates had bent his rules even further and allowed her to stay in George's cell overnight. He'd brought in a cot and a blanket for Dani. "Hell, the rules say it's supposed to happen right after midnight. If that can be changed, I don't see any reason why I can't allow him your company overnight," he'd said. Coates stayed in his office overnight as well, ready to answer the phone if the test results came back.

Dani encouraged George to try to sleep, but he couldn't, and neither could she, so they talked quietly.

"You should have seen Sallie when I first met her. We were in high school together, both freshmen, and she really was the prettiest one in the whole class. I almost passed out cold when she said she'd go out with me, I was so surprised. She could've had her pick, but she chose me. . . . I know it sounds corny, but she's the only girl I ever loved."

"There must have been something about you that attracted her."

"I suppose. It's funny, we were so worried back then in high school that she'd get pregnant. We'd seen it happen to buddies of ours and it sure messed them up. We couldn't have been any more careful. Then, when we wanted to have a baby, it took us the longest time. But, oh, Angelina was worth waiting for. What a beauty! People just stopped us on the street all the time to ooh and aah over her."

"I suppose all parents think their children are beautiful, but I have to admit—I've seen pictures of Angelina, and she was exceptionally pretty."

"You have kids of your own?"

"I do. A son. His name is Jonah."

"I bet he means the world to you."

"Yes, of course."

"You know, I never blamed Sallie. Not once. It was grief that made her say we killed our Angelina. I think she believed we did."

"Have you had any contact with Sallie since the trial?"

George stared in the distance and shook his head slowly. "I tried writing to her, but she never answered. My mom went to visit her once, drove a long time to get there too, but Sallie wouldn't see her." He turned to Dani. "You've seen her, haven't you?"

I nodded.

"Is she doing okay? I mean, is she holding up inside?"

"She's been treated well by the other women, but it's been hard for her. Not prison. I think she feels she belongs there. But I don't think she's ever been able to reconcile leaving Angelina."

They were both quiet for a while.

"Are you afraid of dying?" George asked.

"I suppose so. I try not to think about it."

"They wanted me to speak to the preacher, but I said no. God is either going to understand what I did or not, and there's nothing I can do about that now."

"I understand what you did. And I think your daughter will understand too."

"That's all that matters to me."

Feeling herself getting sleepy, Dani knew she needed to move around to rouse herself. She wanted to be awake for George, whether he needed to talk or just silently contemplate what was to come. As she stood, she heard the faint ring of the telephone in the guard's station down the hall. Moments later, footsteps approached. "Ms. Trumball, there's a call for you in the warden's office."

Her heart did acrobatics in her chest. It was 4:00 a.m. The call could mean only one thing: The DNA results were in. George looked up at her, his eyes moist. "Whatever happens, thank you for believing in me," he said. Dani nodded and followed the guard upstairs to Coates's office, where she found him at his desk, looking anxious. Unlike he had done with her earlier phone calls, he remained in the office.

"Dani," Bruce said. "It's a match. One hundred percent certainty. Sunshine Harrington is George and Sallie's daughter. I'm faxing over a copy of the report to you right now."

She was too overwhelmed to respond. She looked at Coates and nodded. He understood. They both knew what this meant. George Calhoun would live.

One Week Later

"All rise," the bailiff intoned. They were all back at the LaGrange County Courthouse again, Melanie, Tommy, and Dani. This time, in the courtroom of Judge Andrea Hermann, and this time with both George and Sallie sitting in the prisoners row—the first time they'd seen each other in seventeen years. "You may be seated," the bailiff said after Judge Hermann had taken her seat.

"I understand the state has a motion," the judge said.

The assistant prosecutor stood up. "We do, Your Honor. The people move to dismiss all charges against George Calhoun and Sallie Calhoun based on exculpatory evidence that has just come to light."

"I understand Mr. Calhoun came within hours of the needle," the judge said. "I'm grateful our system didn't fail him."

Dani didn't see it that way. Seventeen years in prison for an innocent couple seemed like a failure to her. But it was one in which the Calhouns shared culpability.

"I hereby order that George Calhoun and Sallie Calhoun be released from custody as expeditiously as possible, but in no event later than one week from today." Judge Hermann turned to the Calhouns. "I want to wish you both the best of luck. I understand there's someone with whom you have some catching up to do."

"Yes, ma'am, I hope so," George said.

Sallie had been quiet all morning. When Dani had visited her in the holding cell, she'd seemed to be in a state of shock, unsure of what had happened. It would take time to reorient herself to freedom.

The guard came to take George and Sallie back to their holding cells. They had to be transported back to their respective prisons for purposes of paperwork. Before they'd walk out the prison doors, counselors would try to prepare them for the changes they would encounter. Dani knew how difficult it was for exonerees to adjust to the outside world. For George and Sallie, the time they'd spent inside had been so long that the adjustment would be monumental.

Before the guard led him away, George turned to Dani. "I never believed this would happen," he said, his voice barely above a whisper. "Is this real? Am I really free?"

"You will be soon, very soon."

"When I wrote to you, I didn't mind dying. I'd come to accept it. I just needed to know if there was a purpose for it. That Angelina—" He shook his head. "I keep forgetting that's not her name anymore. Sunshine. It's a good name."

"You shouldn't have had to make that sacrifice, to choose between your life and Angelina's."

"No, ma'am. No one should. But at least it had a purpose. At least she's had a good life."

The guard, who usually brusquely whisked prisoners back to the jailhouse cell, waited patiently by George's side. It seemed to Dani he understood that an innocent man had spent seventeen years behind bars and was entitled to the few extra minutes he needed.

George took Dani's hand in his. "Thank you." He didn't need to say more. He nodded at the guard and was led out of the courtroom, back to a cell that had changed from a waiting room outside death's door to a last step toward freedom.

As soon as her plane from Indiana landed at LaGuardia, Dani headed to Sunny with the news of her parents' exoneration. The quiet in the apartment seemed out of place in the middle of Manhattan. Rachel had gone to sleep shortly after she'd arrived, and although Eric had chatted with her earlier, he'd retreated to his bedroom. It was just Dani and Sunny.

Dani had met with Sunny and her family several times since Melanie broke the disquieting news of her parentage. Up close, the differences between Rachel and the pictures Dani had seen of three-year-old Angelina Calhoun were apparent. But the similarities were strong enough that she suspected they would be unsettling for George and Sallie, a stark reminder of the little girl they'd loved so dearly. If Sunny could let them into her life, perhaps seeing their granddaughter would give them a second chance to watch a child they loved as she grew up.

"It should take a week, no more, for George and Sallie's release," she told Sunny. Dani didn't refer to them as her parents. Sunny wasn't ready to embrace them as such.

"Where will they go then?"

"Back to Pennsylvania. Your grandmother still lives there. George is moving in with her. And Sallie, she's moving into sort of a halfway house."

"But why? Aren't they still married?"

"Yes, but they've had no contact with each other during all those years in prison. They've both changed. It's best for them to first adjust to their freedom. Then maybe they can try to reconnect with each other."

Sunny stood and began pacing. She was a striking woman, but now her body looked caved in, as if it couldn't bear the burden of the past week. "It's my fault. I did this to them." The tears she'd held back filled her eyes and fell down her cheeks.

Dani put her hands on Sunny's shoulders and turned her so that they faced each other. "No, Sunny. It's not your fault that you got sick. It's not your fault that the hospital wouldn't treat you. And it's certainly not your fault that your parents left you alone in Minnesota."

Sunny stopped pacing and stared at Dani. She looked like a frightened child, not the mother of a little girl. "I don't know whether to hate myself for what happened to them or hate them for leaving me. I just can't get my head around it. I don't know what's right for me to think."

"There's nothing 'right' for you to think. And there's nothing 'right' for you to feel. Give yourself time. When you're ready, if you want to meet them, I'll take you there. Until then, just keep remembering that their decision allowed you to have all this," Dani said, spreading her arms.

Sunny sat back on the couch. "Tell me, what are they like?"

For the next hour, Dani filled Sunny in on what George had told her about his and Sallie's life, from the time they'd met in high school to the fateful decision to leave their daughter at the Mayo Clinic. "But most of all," she finished, "George always struck me as very courageous and very strong. I didn't spend much time with Sallie, so I can't tell you as much about her." She didn't want Sunny to know the extent of Sallie's damage from years of believing she and George had been responsible for Angelina's death. That could come later.

After leaving Sunny, Dani stopped by the office to pick up some files. Her work had piled up over the past seven weeks. There were motions to file, briefs to write, and letters to answer from inmates around the country, men and women claiming to be innocent and for whom HIPP was the last hope, the only hope.

Before she knew it, it was almost eight o'clock. She needed to go home. With any luck, she'd get there before the honeymoon hour. She'd lie on the couch and let Doug massage the knots in her neck. She'd forget about the stress of the past seven weeks. And she wouldn't think at all about the murderer of a young child who remained unpunished.

Mickey Conklin had expected the knock on the door all week. As soon as he read in the newspaper that Angelina Calhoun was alive, he knew it was over. When Cannon showed up, it was almost a relief. He followed him willingly to police headquarters, waived his Miranda rights, and waited patiently for the questioning to begin. He sat across a small table from the beefy detective. He knew that others were watching on the other side of the mirrored wall. But in the room, it was just him and Cannon. No one to play good cop.

"You must have had a good laugh stringing me along all these years," Cannon said after he settled himself into the chair across from Mickey.

Mickey just shook his head.

Cannon took a sheet from inside a folder and held it in front of him. "You know what we did after we found out the child in the woods wasn't Angelina Calhoun? We went and got an order to dig up the grave. Guess what we found?"

Mickey shrugged.

Cannon slammed his fist onto the table and screamed at Mickey. "You know goddamn well what we found! It was Stacy. Your precious daughter that you've been mourning for two decades. The one you said couldn't have been Stacy when we brought you in for an ID."

"What makes you so sure it's Stacy?" Mickey knew he'd cleansed her room of any remnants that could identify her.

"'Cause, jackass, I decided to go check our evidence kit from back when she went missing. And sure enough, we'd collected some of her things, including her hairbrush."

Mickey remained silent. Talking wouldn't help him, only hurt him.

"So, how did she die, you son of a bitch?"

Silence.

It went like that for two hours, with Cannon pushing and Mickey remaining quiet. Finally, Cannon said, "We have you on this; you're gonna be booked for murder."

"You have nothing. So what if it's Stacy? Somebody grabbed her and killed her. I was too much in shock to identify her body. You know, denial. I didn't want it to be her."

Cannon leaned back in his chair. "You're wrong, Mickey. We have plenty. Explain the note you left for the investigator from New York."

"I don't know what you're talking about."

"Sure you do. We checked. It's your fingerprints all over it."

He knew the note had been a mistake. He'd been too impulsive. Shit.

"You're bullshitting me. My fingerprints aren't in any system to compare."

Cannon nodded. "That's true. But they were on the pen you gave me last time I was at your house. A perfect match. So, my only question is, did you kill her on your own, or was Janine in on it?"

Mickey practically jumped out of his seat. "You leave her out of this!"

Cannon smiled a slow grin that grew bigger and bigger until all Mickey saw were two rows of yellowed teeth.

"Why? You do it all by yourself? You been lying to Janine too all these years?"

It was over. He needed to come clean. It wasn't murder. Maybe Cannon would understand. With his voice barely above a whisper, Mickey began his story. "I never meant to hurt Stacy. I loved her. But, see, I'd been working double shifts back then, raking in the overtime. I'd come home so damn tired and just fall into bed. Janine would already be asleep. I never woke her. She was always a deep sleeper. When Stacy was an infant, before she slept through the night, it was me who woke up first. I always had to nudge Janine awake."

Cannon didn't need to take notes. The tape recorder was running, and cameras were capturing the whole thing.

"I came home wired one night. See, there was this woman at work—Darlene. She was new at the plant and worked the night shift, too. When she first flirted with me, I thought it was a joke and played along. But that night, it went beyond joking. She cornered me when I came out of the john and asked when I'd finally get around to kissing her. I acted like a dumb fool, all fumbling and mumbling. She must have thought I was an idiot. But I didn't kiss her. When I came home, though, I was rattled, and so instead of going to bed, I had a couple of beers first, maybe more than a couple.... I'd been dreaming when I first heard Stacy's cries. Dreaming about Darlene. I still remember that dream all these years later. I keep thinking my head would've been clearer if I hadn't been dreaming of her. But you can't control your dreams, right?"

"Keep going. You're helping yourself now. That's good."

"I was annoyed that the dream had been cut short, annoyed at Stacy for waking me up. I went over to her room and turned on the light and sat next to her on her bed. 'What's wrong, pumpkin?' I said. I soothed her for a while, but all the time I was seething.

"'I want a glass of water,' she said.

"'Stay in bed. I'll get it for you.' I told her. I walked out of her room and was by the steps when I heard her whimpering behind me.

"'Don't leave me alone,' she said.

"I yelled at her. 'Go back to your room.' She just stood there crying. I said, 'Be quiet. You'll wake up Mommy.' She didn't move. I don't know what happened. I just felt this fury flood over me, fury that Stacy had gotten out of bed, fury that it wasn't Janine taking care of her, fury that I didn't kiss Darlene back even though I wanted to so badly. I smacked her behind, just a little, just to let her know

I meant business. It was just a tap. She must have lost her balance, 'cause she fell down the stairs. I just stood there. And then it was so quiet. I ran down the steps. Her body was limp. Her eyes were wide open, but she didn't move. I kept tapping her face—I knew I shouldn't move her. But she didn't wake up. She must have broken her neck in the fall."

"You're telling me it was an accident?" Cannon said.

"I swear to God."

"Then why didn't you call the police?"

"How could I explain to Janine that I'd killed our daughter? How could I explain to the police? They'd see the empty beer bottles, they'd test my blood-alcohol level. They'd never believe it was an accident. I couldn't breathe life into Stacy. The only thing I could do was save myself. I wrapped a blanket around her and put it in the trunk of my car and drove to a forest an hour north of town, where I used to go deer hunting. I walked into the forest and buried her. What was the crime in that? A father's allowed to bury his daughter."

"Well, for one, you were guilty of impeding a police investigation. Filing a false police statement. I could keep going. I'm sure I could come up with a long list of crimes."

"I wasn't thinking straight. I'd just lost my little girl."

"Go on. What did you tell Janine?"

"When I got back to the house, the sky had just begun to brighten. It was still dark but a grayer shade of dark. I slipped into bed and waited for Janine to wake up. My mind kept racing with thoughts of what I had done. I knew my life would never be the same, that I'd never forgive myself. Only God could forgive me.... I must have fallen asleep. Janine woke me by shoving me, screaming, 'Wake up. Stacy's missing. Wake up. We've got to find her.' The rest of that day and the next few days were a blur. Hysterics and sirens—those are the sounds I remember. I was too afraid to say anything when Janine told the police we'd left her window open for some air. I let everyone think she'd been snatched from her room by a stranger. After a week went by, I started worrying that I'd picked a forest too close to home. I drove back and got her body. I unwrapped the blanket and poured gasoline over her and then dropped a match and watched as she burned. I kept saying to myself, 'It's just a shell, it's not my daughter,' over and over. I didn't want her to be found; I didn't want her to be recognized. I'd seen enough police shows on TV to know a lot could be figured out with forensic evidence. I couldn't take a chance. If the police knew it was Stacy, they'd see she had a broken neck. They'd figure I killed her on purpose. I wrapped her body in a new blanket, a store-bought blanket Janine wouldn't recognize, and drove to the next state. When I passed a forest, I pulled off the road and buried her again."

"You knew that another man was sentenced to death for murdering her," Cannon said. "How could you let that be?"

"I thought it was a sign. A sign that God had forgiven me."

"You're a sick son of a bitch."

Mickey looked Cannon straight in the eye. "I know I did something despicable. But I didn't murder my daughter. You can't charge me with that."

Cannon leaned forward in his chair, his face inches from Mickey's. "Maybe not. But it's a different story with Nancy Ferguson, isn't it?"

How could they know about that? He had to think fast and keep his mouth shut.

"Want to tell me about that?"

Mickey didn't respond.

Cannon's grin turned into a sneer. "Don't worry. You don't need to talk. See, we've been busy while we waited for the DNA on your daughter's body to come back. I showed your picture to some of Ms. Ferguson's neighbors. Seems like one remembered speaking to you. Said she gave you a brochure for Nancy's trip. So I decided to call the last hotel Nancy stayed in before she died, and guess what."

Mickey remained silent.

"Oh, come on. Give it a guess…. No? Well, I faxed over a picture of you and it turns out they had cameras in the elevators. They had a real clear shot of you riding up in one with Nancy Ferguson. And here's the kicker: The police there did a thorough dusting of Nancy's room and found a set of your fingerprints on the wall in the bathroom. I guess the maids don't clean everything, do they?"

Mickey's heart raced and his head spun. He couldn't think up a story fast enough to satisfy Cannon. *Say nothing, say nothing, say nothing.*

"Cat got your tongue? Well, here's the best news—for me, that is. For you it's the worst. I've got an order of extradition to Arizona for you. Seems they've charged you with Nancy Ferguson's murder. I'm going to escort you there myself. And by the way, Illinois has suspended the death sentence, but not Arizona. It took a long time, but you're finally going to get what you deserve."

A groan escaped Mickey's lips. God hadn't forgiven him. He'd just waited until he could exact greater retribution.

EPILOGUE

Two Months Later

Sunny and Dani sat at American Airlines' Gate 39 at LaGuardia Airport, waiting to board their flight to Pittsburgh. She'd called Dani two days ago and told her she was finally ready to meet George and Sallie.

"What made you change your mind?" Dani asked.

"I've been seeing a counselor. She's helped me sort through what I'm feeling."

"And?"

"And I guess I'm a little clearer now. It was all so jumbled before. I had these wild swings between anger and guilt. Anger at them for abandoning me. Guilt for what they suffered. Everyone told me I wasn't responsible for what happened, but those feelings wouldn't go away."

"What changed?"

"The counselor helped me understand that some of my guilt came from not having any feelings at all for them, for the Calhouns. I mean, after all, they gave birth to me. I thought I should have felt more gratitude for what they sacrificed. But they're strangers to me. I don't remember them at all. So instead, I felt guilty. And angry. Now I want to get to know them. And I want them to be part of Rachel's life. I'm ready for that."

"I'm glad."

They sat quietly reading, Sunny a Nicholas Sparks novel, Dani a newspaper.

"Sunny?"

She looked up from her book. "You have to keep your expectations low with Sallie," Dani reminded her.

Sunny nodded. Dani had told her of Sallie's belief that she had murdered Angelina by leaving her sick and alone at the Mayo Clinic. And how, during the two years before the police came knocking on her door, that belief had worn away at her tenuous hold on reality. Sunny could understand. She would go crazy if she were faced with that Hobson's choice for Rachel. Thankfully, with Rachel's father being a doctor, that would never happen.

Sunny had been told that Sallie had made strides at the halfway house. George visited her regularly, but it remained uncertain whether they'd reunite as husband and wife. She hoped they did. She wanted them to salvage some happiness after the misery they'd endured. If becoming part of their lives helped that to come about, she would do it even though they were strangers to her. It would be a minuscule sacrifice on her part.

Traffic moved at a snail's pace as they made their way in the rental car from Pittsburgh International Airport to Sharpsburg. The overhead signs warned them of construction two miles ahead. Sunny had barely spoken a word on the flight, and she was no more talkative now. Dani fiddled with the radio dial, found a classic rock station and settled in for the ride.

They were a half hour late by the time they arrived at George's home. A small woman leaning on a cane, her gray hair falling softly to her chin, greeted them at the door. The smell of freshly baked pie wafted from the kitchen.

"I'm Margaret," the woman said, "George's mother." She took Sunny's hands in her own and squeezed them. "They're in the living room, dear," she said as she pointed to the right. "They've been so nervous waiting for you." She looked Sunny up and down. "My, my, you've become such a beautiful woman. I never thought I'd see this day. Go, go ahead inside."

Sunny's eyes were glued to the ground. She felt a wave of fear. She remained rooted in place, and Dani took her hand and brought her into the living room. It was a small space that looked as if it hadn't been redecorated in forty years, yet it had a hominess that reminded Sunny of her childhood home in Byron. Even with her eyes fixed on the floor, she could see two pairs of feet, George's and Sallie's, side by side.

"Hello, Sunny," Sallie said.

At the sound of her voice, Sunny looked up. Sallie, a wide smile on her face, wore a summery frock. Her hair looked freshly washed and her cheeks were pink. With Sunny's first glimpse of the man and woman standing across the room, a spark of recognition flashed before her. They looked different, older, more worn, but snippets of images returned to her. She saw her mother combing Sunny's long, blond hair, telling her how pretty she was. More pictures. Of her and her mother planting marigolds in the garden, Sunny covered with dirt. Of her father sneaking her a cookie and warning her to not tell her mother. And then she remembered sitting on the bench in the strange hospital, too terrified to cry, hearing her parents tell her how much they loved her, how much they would always love her, begging her forgiveness and then walking away. Sunny strode to her parents and embraced them.

"Thank you, thank you, thank you," she said. "Please, let's sit down. There's so much I want to ask you. I know you must want to learn about me too."

"Just let us look at you first," George said, his voice choked. "We have plenty of time for talking. We didn't think we would, but now we have all the time in the world."

Sunny sat between George and Sallie on the couch and held hands with both of them. She wasn't an orphan anymore. She had a mother and father.

—The End—

ACKNOWLEDGEMENTS

My thanks must begin with my husband, Lenny; my sons, Jason and Andy; and my daughters-in-law, Jackie and Amanda, whose love and support mean so much to me.

I have benefitted enormously from the guidance of editors Caroline Tolley and Doug Wagner. I am also grateful for those readers who willingly gave their time and constructive advice to early drafts: MaryLouise Wilson, Frank Ridge, Erika Callahan, Alice and Henri Gaudette, Dave Barnes, and last, but certainly not least, my sister, Judith Greenfield. In addition, members of the Creative Writing Group of the Villages gave me continuous feedback as the story took shape, for which I'm very appreciative. Julian Schreibman helped me avoid some legal mistakes, and those that remain are solely my doing. Thanks also to Derek Murphy for his fantastic cover design. Finally, I wish to thank the people at The Editorial Department who helped make the publication of this book a reality: Morgana Gallaway, Beth Jusino, Chris Fisher, and Jane Ryder.

About the Author

Marti Green's detail-rich fiction is filled with authority stemming from her professional background in law and psychology. A passionate traveler who has visited six continents, Marti Green now lives in central Florida with her husband, Lenny, and cat, Howie. She has two adult sons and four grandchildren.

Made in the USA
Charleston, SC
16 April 2014